BODY PARTS

BODY PARTS

STORIES BY JERE HOAR

UNIVERSITY PRESS OF MISSISSIPPI
JACKSON

Fic
Hoar

Grateful acknowledgment is made to the following journals in which ten stories in this collection were first published. Some stories appeared in slightly different form or under a different title.

The Crescent Review, "Skin" and "A Brave Damn-Near Perfect Thing"; *The Denver Quarterly*, "Half Ass"; *Double Dealer Redux*, "The Snopes Who Saved Huckaby"; *Four Quarters*, "Tell Me It Hasn't Come to This"; "*The Greensboro Review*, "The Incredible Little Louisiana Chicken Killer" and "The Last Feminine Woman in the World"; *The Kansas Quarterly*, "Dark Heart"; *The Southern Review*, "How Wevel Went"; *The Texas Review*, "My Father's Voice, Lifting."

"The Incredible Little Louisiana Chicken Killer" was reprinted in *Editor's Choice III: Fiction, Poetry & Art from the U.S. Small Press*. New York: The Spirit That Moves Us Press, 1991.

"How Wevel Went" was reprinted in *Reb Fiction '90*. Oxford, Miss.: Southern Reader Books, 1990.

∞ 99 98 97 4 3 2 1

The paper in this book meets the guidelines for permanence and durability of the Committee on Production Guidelines for Book Longevity of the Council on Library Resources.

Library of Congress Cataloging-in-Publication Data

Hoar, Jere R.
    Body parts/Jere Hoar.
        p. cm.
    Contents: Tell me it hasn't come to this—A brave damn-near perfect thing—Skin—My father's voice, lifting—Body parts—The Snopes who saved Huckaby—Half ass—Dark heart—The last feminine woman in the world—The incredible little Louisiana chicken killer—How Wevel went.
    ISBN 1-57806-019-2 (alk. paper)
    1. Southern States—Social life and customs—Fiction.   I. Title.
PS3558.O33565B63   1997
813'.54—dc21   97-2625
                                                      CIP
British Library Cataloging-in-Publication data available

For Evans Harrington, encourager and gentle critic

CONTENTS

ONE

TELL ME IT HASN'T COME TO THIS

When it came, the knock at her door was a surprise. He only tapped the facing. The knock didn't sound like Polly's banging the screen, her bold announcement.

Lydia Calicutt walked fast, untying her apron, putting on a company smile. Vanilla and the scent of pastry floated from the kitchen. The visitor had come at a good time. She didn't pause to wonder how someone might have driven into her driveway without notice.

On the other side of the screen stood a rumpled black suit. She couldn't see the man inside it until she was close. He stood away from the opening, staring to one side, giving her an opportunity to observe him. That was the custom, a politeness. He was a stranger.

She squinted up and down the shimmering road, putting her greenish eyes into a net of wrinkles. The hot yard and rock driveway stood empty except for her automobile. Sunlight beat shining lines down the fenders of the old Monte Carlo and touched its chrome with fire. Heat lay like a weight on living things. The mimosa tree dangled curled palms. In the pecan tree not a jay or a crow called, though they were tough as Job's turkeys.

"Ma'am?" The man lifted a small, circular smile. She could look down on his bald spot. "Are you Miz Calicutt?"

Blue eyes flicked in his sweaty face. They steadied, fixed on her nose, and bored away relentlessly. The points of his shirt collar curled. A black tie twisted down between them like the end of an over-long dog collar. A few strands of dull yellow hair wisped across his skull. They weren't dense enough to shade it. The poor man needed a hat. Skin peeled on his lips, and he licked them. His teeth were too small for his mouth and spotty with stains.

"I'm the widow Calicutt." She planted her hands on her hips and spoke at high cry. "Who are you, and what can I do for you? Are you lost?"

"I think I am. Ain't we all until Jesus rules? Ain't we all sinners?" His voice was a churchly flutter. It sounded like the turning pages of a hundred hymnals. She was Presbyterian and didn't take pleasure in Jehovah's Witness questions.

He widened his eyes and took in all of her without redirecting his gaze. She flushed but didn't feel danger, the inevitable other half of the approach of a stranger.

Mrs. Calicutt's house sat in a hairpin curve. Each day strange men hurtled automobiles toward her—toward the window where she sat. A fringe of grass, a shell of wood, and a gauze curtain were all that separated her from fiery merger. Her heart beat terribly in such moments.

Polly warned her. "You're too trusting, Lydia Calicutt!

You can't invite in everybody who bangs your door, like it was old times."

Mrs. Calicutt lived as if it *were* old times, except that she lived alone. Her garden spread over an acre, too large for one person. Plastic milk jugs with the bottoms cut out protected the lettuce from rabbits. The milk jugs sat like helmets over fat, green faces. Zinnias and strawflowers edged the garden in bright rectangles. No one became sick in Abbeville without receiving a visit and a sack of vegetables. Mrs. Calicutt sat with the sick and the old and held their hands. "Their skins get hungry," she said, "the same as their insides." She nodded and smiled the way an adult does in coaxing an answer from a child. "And—?" she seemed to ask.

Twice a week she drove to Ruth and Jimmy's Store to buy supplies and blurt the talk she'd stored. Sometimes talk just exploded from her over anyone handy. She remembered when she could say a thing the moment she felt it, and not save it to share. It made her wistful to remember that.

Now the men she encountered were heart patients who thanked her for vegetables and visits, or strangers who yelled curses and twisted wheels as their automobiles attempted brutal entrance into her house. Hardly a whole man was to be seen at Ruth and Jimmy's when Mrs. Calicutt visited to shop and talk.

When she sat down at the lunch counter, that was the signal. Polly lit a Salem and sat down, too. She made the air dense with particles. After a few puffs only her brown eyes and piled hair were visible, like mountain peaks.

"Lord," she said, fanning a path for nervous words, "I don't see how you stand living by yourself. If it wasn't for my Billy, every little noise would jump me out of my skin."

She means she is still a wife, Mrs. Calicutt always thought. What she said was, "Men are nothing but babies. Never again."

"Huh!" Polly said. "I couldn't get along without my Billy." She rubbed her bare arms and smiled toward the door.

Mrs. Calicutt couldn't see much in Billy. His words burbled like swamp gas working out of muck. All black people listened closely to Mr. Billy's little words. His eyes zipped strangers, head to toe, head to toe. Any woman alone, who felt in danger, had only to leave her porch light off at night or turn it on in daylight. Every local knew to call constable Billy.

"—Not that anything bad is going to happen," Polly assured Mrs. Calicutt, "but if it does—" Polly slapped the counter. Her mouth constricted to a grim line and her nostrils blared at the fate of evildoers facing Billy's pistol.

Billy will never die, Mrs. Calicutt thought. *A good man's heart bursts like a papershell pecan. It bursts at nothing, nothing at all. Then you're alone.*

Talking to Polly was a pleasure. Chopping weeds passed time. Visiting the sick gave her a warm, useful feeling. But much of each weekday Mrs. Calicutt watched and listened to cars.

In rainy weather mud-grip tires buzzed like combs blown through tissue paper. Cotton wagons, shackled to tractors or trucks, chattered as they jerked their way to the gin.

Big cars, hurtling too fast into the curve, shrieked brakes and threw showers of gravel. Semitrucks, taking this byway to avoid the weigh station on Interstate 55, purred stealthily.

Mrs. Calicutt gathered news from how people drove. If Bettie Garner sped off toward Oxford in her red Torino at 8:20, she was late for work at the hospital. If she sped back toward the farm, hunched over the wheel, eyes just brown dots in her white face, she had forgotten something and was going to be even more late.

If a tractor chugged slowly the driver was a hired hand. Owners knew the cost of diesel and labor.

She studied faces she recognized, and those she didn't. Strangers were just white or dark ovals topped by different colored hair patches. Mrs. Calicutt always waved. The faces in cars with Mississippi or Alabama licenses often waved back. If she was especially lonely she imagined an automobile stopping and the driver getting out to ask directions. She imagined offering a glass of tea, and how she would tell the girls at Ruth and Jimmy's about a delightful visit with a passing stranger.

The stranger in the black suit on her porch lifted his gaze. Heat of the stove had flushed her skin and deepened the green of her eyes. She'd made the yellow plaid dress in two evenings, with her sewing machine zipping along. A white collar spread around the big tendons of her neck. Inside their fork a pulse began to throb. She wiped loose hair with the back of one hand.

"I come to see you on a matter of business." The man stared to his left down the blacktop. He shook his head and laughed at something foolish. "My car's around the bend. It's got a flat." He laughed as if the joke was on him. "It's too hot to change it." He laughed louder. "I walked all the way here."

She looked at the Pepsi Cola thermometer nailed to a post across from the door. A red line seared up the neck to ninety-four degrees. "I'll say it's hot!" Mrs. Calicutt said. She couldn't imagine a man not changing a tire unless he was at death's door, but she put on a joking manner. The screen stood hooked between them. Harold Dean's pistol was in the drawer five steps away, though it wasn't loaded. She wasn't afraid. "You're not a bill collector, are you, or the tax man? I don't have any truck with either of them."

"Ma'am, my name is Del Penne. I've bought the Hicks place five miles yonder." He nodded and laughed and shook his head as if that were funny. She wondered if he knew what a forsaken old wreck the farm was. Maybe he'd heard. He must have, the way he laughed.

He chuckled and nodded and cut his eyes as if he knew. His dusty black shoes curled on the hot concrete. Iron porch chairs beside them baked in the sun. An apologetic smile flickered on his lips. He pinched his chin. "Could we sit down, Miz Calicutt? Could I trouble you for a glass of water, please ma'am?"

Mrs. Calicutt jumped like a bird shot in the foot. That's an expression her mother would have used, *like a bird shot in the foot.* "Oh my, yes. Sit down, won't you? Sit down right there, won't you? I'll get something nice to drink." If there was one thing Mrs. Calicutt was, it was polite. "Tea? Would you like tea? Lemonade? It's no trouble."

The sun burned on the rectangle of concrete. The man braced on the arms of a green metal chair and eased his behind onto the seat. His belly moved out to perch in his lap. He lifted one haunch and then the other as if passing gas. His wan smile said that wasn't happening.

"I'll be right back," Mrs. Calicutt called.

Mrs. Calicutt's face was pensive as she stood in the kitchen, stirring sugar into canned lemon juice and water. Harold Dean, her husband, had loved lemonade. In the middle of an episode of *Hill Street Blues,* Harold Dean had set his glass on the floor, cupped one hand over his heart as if pledging allegiance, and commenced hissing. The hissing sounded like butane gas escaping a space heater. No louder than that, but just as compelling. They'd had a little quarrel, nothing at all. She couldn't remember what about. "Harold Dean," she'd yelled, "please don't go." But he went anyway, and without a tender word.

It was a terrible desertion. In a village like this she had

no chance for another man even if she wanted one. She saw herself as a pile of white ash in a dead hearth, and called herself the widow Calicutt. As she thinned and fined, her skin glowed with the translucence of a wax candle. Her nose sharpened the center of her face, and her eyes gobbled what was left. She looked otherworldly, like European Jews she saw on television, coming together in their frequent reunions of horror.

On the porch, the man scraped a chair across concrete. She hurried out carrying the pitcher and two glasses on a tray. The man took a glass and a paper napkin. He wiped his face with the napkin. It disintegrated on his cheeks and stuck to invisible stubble. Patches of paper in his whiskers made him look pathetic. "Here!" Mrs. Calicutt said. "Let me get you a wet cloth. That napkin is worthless!"

"Nome." The man held up a hand like a school crossing guard with minimal authority. He smiled a weary smile. "Just let me get some wet in me. As the Good Book says, whomsoever giveth a traveler a cup of water, verily, verily, they have their reward." He lifted his head and turned up the glass. Wrinkles opened on his vulnerable neck, making white lines in the brown skin.

Mrs. Calicutt sat down in a chair across from the stranger. Metal seared through her slip and dress. That poor man! She could barely sit still. She wiped back hair from her brow and shaded her squinting eyes. "The Hicks place? I didn't hear it had sold." She didn't say that it was a bad-luck farm that nobody had ever made a success of. "Are you from around here?"

"Nome, nome, not from here." He tilted the glass, sucked ice, and cracked a mouthful between his teeth. He glanced at the pitcher. She poured more lemonade.

"Where are you from, just to be nosy?"

"Memphis...born and raised in Memphis. Yes ma'am, Memphis, Tennessee. I was a tire builder till the Yankees closed Goodyear."

Mrs. Calicutt nodded as if something important were settled.

"When I was a girl I just begged my daddy to take me to the Peabody Hotel every time he went to Memphis. I loved that Peabody! Just to look into the lobby was a treat. That lobby was a fairyland."

"They've done it back. It's just like it used to be. Even better. They've got those ducks that ride from the roof down the elevator and waddle over to that pool in the lobby, you know? The bellhop that drives them down on the elevator carries a switch. I've seen that. He sure does. Those ducks watch that switch. They turn their beaks this way and that, but those little pea-eyes watch that switch. They know about that switch."

"Is that so?"

The man leaned forward, conspiratorially. "Ma'am, that reminds me of a saying of my daddy."

"Yes?"

He chuckled and scraped his chair close. She could smell him. It was almost the warm odor of Harold Dean when he had worked in the garden. She drew a deep breath. Something flopped in her chest.

"—Daddy said that when you've got a man by the balls you've got his full attention." Del Penne beamed, then flicked a glance at her expression and rushed on. "That might not seem a story to tell a lady, but you'll appreciate it applies to ducks."

Mrs. Calicutt gazed down the road a long minute. She'd started paying him no mind as soon as he said, "If you've got a man by the—" She knew what was coming and just excluded Del Penne from her world. That's what her mother would have done when a man spoke out of turn, and her mother before her, on through generations. You pretend not to hear men. You let their words fly past. If they forgot themselves or had no manners, you abolished them.

After the correct interval Mrs. Calicutt softened her lips and lowered her chin. Del Penne leaned forward in the green chair, his face overly wrinkled. She thought, *Maybe he didn't mean to offend.* She said, "About this matter of business—"

"Mrs. Calicutt, my ox is in the ditch. A mote is in my eye. My wine is turned to water." The man lifted his legs on the hot metal seat to ease them. "Somebody said you might, somebody who'd know." He looked at her accusingly. "They said you would."

"Who's that? They said I'd what?"

"Just somebody who'd know. They might not care to be named." He looked at her mysteriously and hitched his chair nearer. "You'd be as safe in my house as in First Baptist. I'm a widower, very respectable, churchgoer, and born-again, like yourself. I come down here to Mississippi to try to make me a living." He hitched his chair until their knees brushed. "It's this way." He looked left and right. "I need me a housekeeper one day a week."

She stared at the man a long time. Her gaze chilled at the insult. What in the world was he thinking? "Me? You can't mean me."

"I didn't say *maid!*" His hand jiggled in front of her face, flagging her down. "I said housekeeper. This other lady said if you will do it, you're the best. She said it would be all right to ast you."

Mrs. Calicutt shook her head three times.

"She says a man could eat his supper off your floor." He glanced into the dark living room. "She said I wouldn't have to worry about a *thing* if you was to do it. She said you would do it up right. She said you was fair and square to ever'body."

"I've never hired out. I was a wife." Mrs. Calicutt was surprised to hear a cat mewl in her voice.

"Nome, I don't speck you have. I don't speck you have." He looked directly at her for the first time. Something in his eyes said he understood.

Mrs. Calicutt jumped to her feet, reaching behind to

loosen her dress where it had stuck. She was in a dither. She didn't know whether to come or go. "Let's talk inside, Mr. Del, where it's cool. It's too hot out here to think."

Mr. Penne's trousers came unstuck from the chair with a subdued purr. "Yes ma'am, it is. The name is Penne."

Overlarge furniture and a 27-inch TV screen crowded the room. A fan wickered overhead. Pink wall-to-wall carpet swirled in cat licks from vacuuming. Brown twill covered the platform rocker by the window. Over the twill stretched a vinyl cover. Original cellophane wrapped the lamp shades in diagonal ripples. Antimacassars protected the sofa against soiling by greasy heads. Three windows stood open, draped by material as thin as hospital gauze.

Penne walked around the room, picking up photographs framed in shiny metal.

"Harold Dean," she whispered, "my husband." She must cling to Harold Dean.

"Was that your man's name? Are you lonely, too?" Del Penne's voice whined like a country singer's. "Lord, woman!" He bent to pat the vinyl seat of a chair. "Sit down right here. We got a lot in common! I feel so singular in this world among perverts that have abandoned the Lord and his natural ways my insides about turn to water. They near about do." His fluttery eyes fixed on hers.

She sat on the far side of the room, staring at him.

"Miz Calicutt, I'm gonna be straight with you, 'cause

that's the way folks say you are—straight." He nodded and she nodded.

"I'd reckoned on several hours."

Mrs. Calicutt nodded that she'd heard. That's all it meant. Her gaze lingered on the glass-topped coffee table. She compelled her brown, capable hands to lie folded and ladylike.

"There would just be housework for me and the washing and ironing. The pay would be whatcha call it, national wage. This person can pick the day she wants. She can do that." He nodded, convincing himself.

"Now, like I say, I'm gonna be straight with you. I been in Parchman Prison. Yes ma'am. Served twelve months time for a crime of burglary I never done. This nigger done it. He told me so his own self. Laughed at me about it, how I served his time." Mr. Penne sighed. "The first night I hid under a cot. Homos and perverts dragged me out. I screamed and hollered, but no guard came to my aid. I hollered to God in his holy mountain, but he never came either." He looked left and right. "A man is not made for it. You understand, ma'am? I'm telling you this in Christian love."

Mrs. Calicutt crossed her feet. She gazed into the yard to avoid his naked eyes. "My, my," she said.

"I just knowed you'd understand." The man slid out his short legs. "We'll get along fine." He adjusted his crotch. "Folks told me you are a widow lady."

That doesn't mean anything, she thought. *Men don't always remember where they are or who they're with.* But it was time for him to go. She scooted to the edge of the sofa and patted her knees. "Let me think about it, Mr. Penne. I will do that. I know where you live, and I'll give you a call if I decide to—"

He shook his head. "I won't have no telephone for a day or two." He didn't move. "Is that a sweet roll I smell?" He sniffed mightily. "A *sweet roll?* What would you charge me for a piece?"

She looked at the screen door and the sunlight beyond, patterning arabesques on the porch floor through the pecan tree leaves. A crow called. It seemed very far away.

He canted his head and smiled. "I'll bet you like a piece, too, now and then, don't you? Don't you like a sweet roll?"

His words were like intimate brushes by the hands of someone helping with a coat. She couldn't believe it was happening. She patted her knees and tucked her feet together in their black, sensible shoes. "I'm baking it for the church."

"I haven't had me a piece in a long time."

Mrs. Calicutt stood abruptly.

Penne remained seated. "The Good Book says take your joy among women, ma'am. It says, don't cast your seed on the ground. It says better the belly of a whore than that a man cast his seed on the ground. Man and woman was meant to be. In Parchman Prison, they forgot every bit of holy word."

"You'll have to go," she said.

He studied her with his head tilted to the side. She didn't know whether he was laughing at her or taking her words to heart. He stood and backed a step in the direction of the door. Her hands itched to slam it behind him.

"You don't think ill of me trying to buy a piece of sweet roll off you, do you?" Del Penne's clipped eyebrows lifted. His papery voice fluttered. "I never meant any harm. A man gets lonely for home cooking. I can't boil water, myself." His pudgy hand lingered on the screen door. "Could you give me a lift to my car? I hate to ast but it's mighty hot." He watched her face. "Don't trouble yourself." He opened the door part way. "Would you have a can of gasoline to get me started? I'll bring it back soon's I get to a pump. It won't cost you a dime to he'p me out."

Her face was stone. "There is nothing here for you, nothing at all. I'm a widow and a respectable lady."

He went outside and faced her through the blur of tiny wire rectangles. His fingers worked circles, as if turning an invisible hat. "Lord, Miz Calicutt! Have I said you wasn't? All I done was to offer you a job of work. All I done was to speak a plain truth."

Her expression softened ten degrees. "I can't help you about the job. I'll give you—the confection. I can bake another one for the church." She gave him a look, now

Tell Me It Hasn't Come to This

that she had control, that would anchor him where he stood. "Wait here."

He whined after her, "Do you have a Mason jar you could put some ice water in, ma'am? That blame old car may not kick off."

She shook her head and reached for the pitcher of lemonade. Ice clicked uncontrollably in the pitcher. It took both hands to steady it.

She handed him the wrapped pastry and jar of lemonade through the doorway. He sat them on a chair seat. "You look kindly pale."

"I'm fine."

He shook a Winston out of a box and hung the cigarette in the corner of his red mouth. From a two-penny box of matches he extracted one, lifted his hip, and scraped the match head into flame. He spoke through coiled smoke, the cigarette bobbing, a sardonic twist on his lips. "I don't reckon you mind if I stand out here on the public road and hitch me a ride. That won't trouble you none, will it?"

She shook her head.

Wrinkles puckered between Penne's brows. Little rolls of paper remained trapped in his whiskers. He picked up the moisture-beaded jar. "Well, I 'preciate it. Sorry we can't do no business."

Mrs. Calicutt watched him go. Heat shimmered above the surface of the road. The black trousers wrinkled behind his knees and bagged in front of them. He pulled his shoulders back excessively and hung his arms like plumb bobs.

The next day when the telephone rang Mrs. Calicutt rushed to it, but the caller hung up. It was so annoying, so disappointing, when she missed a call. She had told Polly, "Let my telephone ring ten times. I might be outside weeding the garden and get to the door just as you hang up. Lordy! I never go anywhere." But Polly puffed clouds of smoke and darted her eyes after only ten seconds of frustration. Mrs. Calicutt suspected she slammed down telephones.

Mrs. Calicutt called the store, but, no, Polly had not telephoned.

"I got to go, hon," Polly said. Her words ran so fast they stepped on each other's heels. "Every seat at the counter's full and Billy can't work the register. Bob Wheeler called about a trespasser, and two old women left their porch lights off last night."

Mrs. Calicutt visualized Polly's lips thin, her head shake, her eyes stitch across a showcase of hunting gear and shelves of canned goods, to waiting customers.

"Well, all right." Mrs. Calicutt faltered. "I just wondered if it was you."

She didn't stray far from the telephone that day or the next. When the instrument rang again she watched it *b-ri-rrring!* once, then snatched it up like a pan of milk about to scald. Penne's voice—no, his breath—fluttered through the receiver, connecting them intimately. She removed the black plastic from her skin and the private coils of her ear. His breath sounded like the beating wings of a trapped insect.

"Hello? Who's there?"

"We ain't all jailbirds," he blurted. "I got a niece is making herself a lawyer over at Ole Miss."

"What? I don't understand."

"I paid my debt and confessed to Jesus. I've turned over all new leaves."

"Mr. Penne, I told you plainly—" Had she been unjust, maybe unChristian, Mrs. Calicutt wondered? She dulled the edge in her voice.

"I know you did, ma'am. I know you did, but it ain't fair. It ain't fair to either one of us." He sounded whiny and indignant.

"Excuse me, Mr. Penne, I don't understand. I don't understand what you mean. Something is on the stove. I have to go." She replaced the telephone and drew a deep breath.

In her rocker, watching people drive by on their separate journeys, she felt more alone than before. Gazes bounced against her window. She waved to strangers but the gesture made no connection.

So this is how it would be. One day she would be too old to drive, or keep the Monte Carlo repaired, or afford insurance. Maybe she would become disabled. There would only be the road to watch.

She thought of Penne's unsteady eyes and papery voice

and tried to compromise her vision. *Has it come to this?* The telephone lay inert in its cradle. She lifted the instrument and put it down. Blood beat terribly in her throat. Her voice was undependable. *Maybe later, maybe later.*

Nausea hung heavy in her stomach. Tingles ran through her fingers and palms. She paced the floor, rubbing bare arms. *There is always television. I can watch television. People used not to have that.*

She went to the front door and looked out at an empty planet. Not a bird sang or a dog stirred. Not a motor rumbled or a tree leaf moved. She leaned her forehead against the door frame. A ball of sorrow and pity and terror swelled in her throat. She fumbled for the light switch with a blind hand. The cry of twenty-five watts went into sunlight. Emergency, it said. Emergency.

A BRAVE DAMN-NEAR
PERFECT THING

People are already acting crazy from it. Two kids painted the water tower "TROY HIGH, CLASS OF '46." The letters stood straight and identical. Then, they painted the words up and down, across and slantways—with lettering more and more bizarre, until the last rendering looked like a ransom note.

Truly hot weather isn't supposed to fall upon Alabama until July. Then the air shimmers. Macadam roads melt and stick to your shoes. Grass and trees, even people, lose their juicy essences.

This June, for twenty-one days, thermometers have streaked to 100°. A heat wave such as this has not baked Alabama since 1933, a year lost to my memory because I was four.

Women wear wide-brimmed straw hats to protect their complexions. I like the mystery of their faces in the dappled shade of brims. They carry bottles of cologne to daub wrists and necks. The air reeks of hot women. You can cross the street and hit the spoor of one thirty yards ahead, and then another that has rounded a corner, and then another. This alone can drive a boy crazy. He will do things he would not ordinarily do. He will, in the words of Mr. Joseph Conrad, discover his heart of darkness.

The way young people cope with the heat is to gather at the pool in city park to splash warm water. Girls sun themselves on the tower where they aren't supposed to, propped on their elbows. The tops of their suits hang loose, but they hold the straps or lie on the pneumatics when a boy comes up. A boy who climbs the tower to jump only gets to step over pretty brown legs, drip water, and watch girls wiggle. That's it.

My best friend, Clarke Boatright, and I don't even get that pleasure because we are gutless about heights. We were the only boys in town beneath suspicion, by reason of cowardice, when the water tower was desecrated.

On most summer days I work at the newspaper or cut grass. The town library, where I am sent three afternoons a week to study for scholarships, is quieter, even, than the town cemetery. At night in the cemetery petticoats rustle and occasionally a guy in the next car moans, trying to make you think he is getting it. By day, you hear the scrape of grave diggers' shovels. Because of the heat old people are toppling over dead, right out of their porch rockers. *Ker-thunk!* Our newspaper can always count on an obituary to fill part of page one.

The only sounds heard in the library are the hum of

ceiling fans and the scratch of a turning page. Mrs. Goforth, the beautiful young guardian of tomes, for whom I have lust, floats around in white shoes. She smiles and turns her face away in order to avoid catching me reading adult best-sellers such as *The Postman Always Rings Twice*. This book falls open to a passage in which a woman is lying on her back with her legs open. She says, "Rip me! Rip me!" to the bum who has killed her husband. He gets the sound of a roaring train in his ears and does. I imagine Mrs. Goforth as this woman.

The Pepsi-Cola scholarship I study for, when I am not fantasying about screwing Mrs. Goforth, is my only chance to escape a life of involuntary servitude in Alabama. I have consulted sweatily with the principal in his office during two appointments. He says there are no scholarships for which I qualify except Sons of Confederate Veterans. I ask about Harvard. He rares back and says he doesn't know a thing about northern schools. No one from *here* goes there. I ask my father. He says ask your principal. I say to my father, "Will you send me to Harvard without a scholarship?" My father is a substantial man, and his belly substance shakes as he laughs. His look says, *Are you kidding?* His voice says, "My father gave me twenty dollars for college. It was all he had. I lived in an attic without heat and ate ice cream and cheese from the school's dairy two meals a day. I'd have thought I was rich if I'd had five dollars."

This is one of those hopeless circles I maze around in.

We get along fine when we work together. When we talk our words buzz past each other without significant guidance, like Hitler's missiles.

The Pepsi-Cola company has invited the best 442 white, high school minds in the state to sit for exams covering vocabulary, mathematical ability, and abstract thinking. Our principal has praised winners of the Pepsi as the best brains in the state. These brains, accompanied by their bodies, will attend the college of their choice. Pepsi-Cola will pay tuition and $1,000 a year. Get that, a *thousand* dollars—with another depression coming on, communists everywhere, a Russian atomic attack looming. God bless Pepsi-Cola! I will pray for them in the cool vault of the First Methodist Church, where my mind is usually serenely empty.

On Monday, Wednesday, and Friday I compile word lists at the library. Some days I drudge through mathematical problems. Abstract thinking is beyond me. I am unaware of consequence in more than an elementary sense. Study and you get good grades. Go too far and the girl gets pregnant. That sort of thing. I never dream that if you pick up a single thread it may take the rest of your life to reel it in.

On this particular Friday, while I sweat over a problem involving two automobiles approaching each other at forty and sixty miles an hour, the front door squeaks. Mrs. Goforth manipulates yellow library cards with her soft white hands. I believe that if she ever wanted to signal a man that she wished to be screwed, she would indicate it with a meaningful shuffle.

Cobwebs flutter on the ceiling as the door opens. It is not every day a stranger enters this quiet place. I raise my gaze from *The Hamlet*. I have just read a terrible description: "The bright, blatant daisies of flamboyant Spring's spendthrift beginning ..." Can William Faulkner have committed this?

Clarke says I am a genius at picking bad sentences. He said this after I hooted at Shakespeare's "Yellow leaves, or few, or none" hanging upon those boughs "where late the sweet birds sang." Get real! *Yellow* leaves, or *few*, or *none*?

Clarke says if I become able to recognize good sentences, I will be in fine shape. I say to Clarke, get screwed.

Anyway, in saunters Clarke. Mrs. Goforth smiles. Clarke glances around and sees me behind an ostentatious stack of books. I want every Rotarian in town to know that the poor drudge staggering his way home under them is I. Rotarians award the Rotary International Fellowship. That is a fallback position if the Pepsi-Cola company screws me out of my entire future.

But what is Clarke doing inside a library?

Clarke and I compete in a friendly way. It is not serious. He addresses Life with such sentences as "It don't matter." He accompanies this expression with a shrug. The shrug gives the appearance of having been launched by a slovenly mind.

I have warned him that there are only two chances for him and me, the Pepsi-Cola scholarship and the Rotary International. Otherwise, we will live the doomed lives of our parents. Our minds won't get beyond green lawns and bomb shelters.

He smiles and shrugs. "It don't matter, Josie." He pronounces José as if it is a girl's name. All young males are Josie to Clarke. It is a way he prevents teasing about a mistake he made in Spanish class.

Clarke walks as if his feet hurt, but he is our team dash man, the fastest creature on bunions. He hobbles to where I sit, slaps the back of my head, and whispers. "Why ain't you at the pool, Josie? Cookie's there in her one-piece suit, and this sweet life is passing you by."

Mark well what I predict. When Clarke attempts the most important sentence of his life, maybe before a Spanish firing squad, illiterate sounds will adhere to his lips.

He whispers to me that other guys are checking Cookie out.

"Who?" I demand, and look threateningly at empty corners of the room.

He wags his head like one of those plastic saints drivers mount on their dashboards and grins idiotically. "Can't say that. I promised. But it looks like these other guys ain't going to wait forever."

"Tell me everything you see," I instruct Clarke. As my best friend, he knows my passion. There will never be another girl in the world for me, but I have not yet told Cookie so inti-mate a fact. I want to keep her intellectual respect.

Cookie is a sweet, sweet woman. She looks into my eyes and listens to my large words. She browns in the sun like Egypt. Henna scent drifts about her. I dream about Cookie in a split Egyptian dress reclining against a pyra-mid. She is waiting until I grow up.

Any white person can splash in city pool for fifteen cents. I allow myself two dips a week because I am a seri-ous person cutting grass, working at the newspaper, and preparing for college. Also, my heart and hong run wild when my eyes see Cookie's thighs and bosom banded at the suit edges by white skin.

The city park is a place of thin shade. Old oaks with sere leaves droop over the badminton courts. Yellow grass sprouts in the tennis court. Its limed boundaries are barely discernible.

The log canteen on the concrete apron beside the pool is an artifact from CCC days. Bleached shingles hide its decaying logs. A thin-boarded porch leans upon its front. A trellis covered with trumpet vine stands at one corner of the porch and a slender oak at the other.

No lifeguard sits on duty. Irene Smathers, a married woman who returned to town to live with her parents, is custodian. Maybe she is supposed to lifeguard, but she never does.

Irene wears a slack bathing suit. You have no desperation to look down her meager chest. It hangs depleted, like old Africans' bosoms. A burning Chesterfield droops from her lips. She sits all day in the canteen, squinting through clouds of smoke, flipping pages of *Liberty, Blue Book,* and *Saturday Evening Post.* An oscillating fan drifts tropical air against her face.

Lines around her eyes deepen and her lips thin when she must sell a Coke for a nickel, or rent swim trunks to a man so desperate to escape the heat he will risk catching jock itch and creeping crud. She hears nothing that happens outside the canteen door.

Once, while Irene was deep in a fictional dream involving stampeding cattle, a child fell into the water, gurgled to the surface, and sank again. Clarke offered him a boat hook and pulled him to safety. Irene never looked up from the Ernest Haycox western she was reading.

A walkway eight feet wide runs between the pool lip and the canteen in which Irene sits, hating us because of our youth and unmarred lives. It takes a nervy cannonballer like Fergus, who will go for the pool edge, to boom down from the high tower and cascade a splash on girls on the porch, on the rag.

"—Fergus, don't do that! Don't you dare! *Fergus!*" they cry.

Squealing makes him wild. He plunges with an idiot grin on his face, knees tucked, fat arms flailing. Fergus would dive from the white cliffs of Dover to hear one woman squeak his name.

Other than the cannonball from the high tower, one other daring leap is possible. This is a dive from the canteen roof. It would be an act of insanity or summer-desperation to commit it. To succeed, a diver would have to launch nine feet out, flip his feet up, and turn down sharply. The dive would require the ninety-degree angle of a carpenter's square.

Fergus is full of nerve and wears a reckless grin but gets no credit because he is hideous. He drinks Tabasco sauce for a dollar. He chews glass. During our junior trip to Washington, he paid a bellboy to send up a Chinese whore. He meant to sell us tickets to watch him screw. He would demonstrate that her vulva ran crossways. The bellboy could not find a Chinese whore; we hooted in relief.

On the twenty-first day of the heat wave Fergus scratched himself under the left tit, put on his reckless grin, and said, "Watch this." He climbed the trellis to the canteen roof, walked the ridge pole to the point nearest the pool, and fell forward over concrete. When nearly parallel, he pushed straight out. His body bowed, his shins and feet flipped, and the entry was Olympic.

Simple and clean. Stunning. There followed a big, hollow silence. The dive was nothing because Fergus is without fear. He surfaced, blew bubbles, and said, "Honk, Honk"—a tug ushering a liner into harbor.

Girls could have thought he was exceptionally brave.

You cannot tell about girls. "Stupid bastard," we boys muttered, looking darkly at each other.

On July 29, 1946, Clarke persuades me to leave the library and go to the pool. Once there, I stop paying attention to him. The reason is that I see Cookie sprawled on a towel with arms and legs apart for secret places on her to brown.

She is a long symphony of muscularity and softness, flatness and roundness. While my mind creates poetry, my hong revolts and seizes control of my body. It is like a kamikaze Jap climbing against the sun for his suicidal run. I have to sit down.

If I could dive into ice water, everything would be okay. But I cannot. I wonder at what hour after dark I can slink home. Are stronger jock straps to be had? Where, oh where? When will the clothing manufacturers of America wake up!

She tugs up her suit top and waves her fingertips. I wave back in a careless, manly way, still seated. She stands on shapely legs, adjusts her suit, and dives a little girl, flop-dive into the water. Clarke mutters that he thinks I am stupid to act "cool and de-boner" around Cookie. I say, that's funny, Clarke, real funny.

He and I sit with our feet dangling in water at the shallow end. This is where I am compelled to sit. Clarke squats like a jug. Though his outside is not much different from anyone else's, he has a contained center. Most people see only his surface, but I am clever at sizing up competition.

Clarke doesn't seem to notice that I win all the academic competitions. If he decides on chemistry, I take it, too. If he announces for the position of business manager of the school newspaper, I discover a consuming desire to be editor.

Sometimes we act more thirteen than sixteen. The day after *Cyrano de Bergerac* played at the Ritz, Clarke appeared at school with a doeskin glove hanging in his hand. He'd liberated it from his sister. He wasn't queer or anything, it had a purpose. He slapped me across the jaw, shouting, "You cad, sir, take that! And that!"

Hair erected on my neck. I thought wildly that he meant to challenge me for leadership in English.

He struck a fencing pose and poked me in the chest with a pencil, chanting, "And, as I end the refrain—thrust home!" Then he let the glove hang. "You okay?"

"Fine, asshole. Do you want to fight?" I said.

"Hell, no."

"How'd you like it if old Cyrano had slapped your chops?"

"I wouldn't like it, Christian. How do you like it?"

That's the way Clarke is. Ve-ry strange.

Fergus kicks a big splash on me. The jerk has swum underwater to the shallow end without my notice. I dodge and cuss him. He swims away, snorkeling for girls' hairpins.

Further out, Cookie backstrokes. The wires of her bra fin water. Her legs refract crookedly, but that is an optical lie. They are the most elegant, shapely, nut-cracking tongs ever seen. Now get this. She also has a brain. In our high school she ranks about tenth in Plato's order.

Abruptly, Clarke stands up. He smiles at nothing in particular. The sun goes behind a cloud. The effect on me is déjà vu. "Don't do it!" I say, without fully understanding what Clarke is not to do.

He looks down with the sweet, dreamy expression of a bulldog hanging on forever. "Why not?"

"Sit down and cool it."

He hot-foots it around the cement, leaving evaporating tracks. I hot-foot after him. At the side of the canteen, he shakes the trellis. I reach past his back and rattle it hard. This same trellis supported two hundred pounds of fat Fergus.

He plants his toes. The boards are an inch wide, and his big and second toe are inadequate splayers.

"Are you out of your mind?" I say.

He climbs another step.

"After Fergus did it, this will be copycat. It's not worth doing."

He climbs past me.

"You're just going to make an ass of yourself, that's all. That's all you're doing."

A wilted crew cut and a bump-spotted back move past my gaze.

I say desperately to his back, "The probabilities are that

you will spill your brains, break both legs, or climb down. You'll be known as Captain Queeg, or Old Yellow Stain."

Mavis Harrison pokes her nose and face through the quivering trumpet vines covering the trellis. She stands on the porch, looking through from the other side. She's drinking a Coke with peanuts in it. I watch through the vines as her tongue curls into the bottleneck. I think, *Oh, my Go-d!* She walks to the porch edge, leans over, and squeegees wet hair. "He's not going to do it, is he?"

"I don't know." I try not to take advantage of cleavage as she bends over the rail because I lust mainly for Cookie.

Pale parentheses of hair frame Mavis's face. Her pale legs stretch on and on, and she mashes her box against you when you dance. You can forgive her a lot because of these fine qualities, even though she tattletales.

"Miss Irene! Miss Irene! Clarke's going to jump!" Mavis screams. I look at her molars and hold my ears. Because she yells into my face, I'm entitled to look into her cleavage. Probably I would have anyway.

Irene doesn't raise her head from the stampede in Clarence Budington Kelland's novelette. The siren yell gets everyone else's attention. Heads pop up. Girls step off of the porch and curl hands over their eyes, forgetting that Fergus may splash them and do God-knows-what damage to their menstruation.

Sun-bleached heads and brown faces and arms poke over the tower edge. Women in the pool with their kids put their hands on their hips, and rock back on pastel pelvises.

Clarke crouches on the roof like a rope walker, hands out. Air ripples upon the green asphalt. A chicken would fry on it. My eyes squeeze shut and sweat stings them. The sun pushes the top of my head like a heavy hand.

"Hot on your feet?" I say.

"A little. If I crash, I bequeath you the Pepsi-Cola scholarship and the Rotary International."

"Bequeath, hell. You can't bequeath what you'll never have."

He looks down. "I'm going to fly, man!" Muscles in his back and thighs flex.

The six of us on the ground shade our eyes with cupped hands. Wearing sunglasses is unmanly. From across the grove in the pavilion, the homogenized voices of the Ink Spots drift from a radio. The music fits the surrealism of what's happening. One of Dalí's melting watches could fold across the roof edge, drip off, and look natural.

Clarke toe-walks the ridge of the roof. The buzz of our voices falls away, and I don't hear music any more. At the point of roof nearest the water, Clarke lifts his arms. His legs tremble violently. His head bows and his fingers point for the dive, though his posture looks like supplication.

Cookie comes out of the water, tugging her suit. Little chill bumps stand on her brown legs. "Come down this minute, Clarke Boatright," she orders.

Clarke backs away from the edge, turns, and toe-walks

to the far end of the roof. He squats there and buries his face in his sweaty arms. It is not because of Cookie he has retreated.

As Cookie stands beside me water drips from her body, spots the pavement, and instantly vanishes. She turns up her dear face. "I'm worried."

It is like being stabbed to the heart with a dull stick. I think wildly that I will climb to the roof, walk past Clarke, and dive. *To hell with everything. Goodbye.*

"Make him come down, Jeff."

"Yeah, Jeff!" Fergus squalls from the pool. "*You* dive. You're the great leader." He brays that laugh.

Oh, how I do hate Fergus May. He is a green taste in my mouth. I can feel people look at me, remembering that I am the Boy Scout who can never walk a log without falling, the dance committee member who doesn't even *offer* to decorate beams in the gym, a sixteen-year old who won't dive from low tower, a person who is gutless about heights.

And then I think this. If I can climb the trellis, walk the length of the roof, and jump, even blindly, I can face anything else in my life. *Anything.* I am so scared of this, I can face the worst life can do to me.

I'm not going to jump! I say to myself. I put my foot on the trellis and climb to the top. *I'm not going to jump.*

Before I can scramble over the edge Clarke reaches out a big hand and pushes my face. It's a hard push and his hand is dirty. I dodge and scramble, but he shoves the trellis with his foot. It sways wildly and wood cracks.

"Son of a bitch!" I screech. "You trying to *kill* me?"

He bends down to put his face level with mine. Tiny pupils look out of his red face. Sweat and dirt bead in the creases around his neck. He smells awful. His voice buzzes. "Jeff, listen, and listen good. I can whip you. You know it and I know it. Get away from this roof. You can't come up here. I'll shove you off."

"The hell you say!"

We grapple at the roof edge. I throw a foot over it and he stomps it. I get an arm up and he rasps it across gritty asphalt. I withdraw to the other side of the trellis and pant.

"If you want to do something useful, bring me a Coke," he says.

I scowl for about ten seconds. Then I back down the trellis, go to the Coke machine, and do as he asks.

For two hours Clarke squats on the roof, alone and ignoble. He is a stranded hawk afraid to fly and afraid not to. Those black eyes look down. He advances to the roof edge and retreats.

Coke drinkers drift back to the shade of the porch. Girls on the tower settle out of sight. Mothers of little children forget their responsibility to scold.

Everyone but Cookie and me stops paying attention. She stands so close sometimes her thigh brushes mine. My hong pays no attention. It is in retreat.

Irene comes out and orders Clarke down. She says she

will telephone his daddy if he doesn't do it. Irene and Cookie go to the pay phone on the porch. "Do you have a nickel?" I hear Irene ask.

I clamber up the trellis. "Okay, Clarke. There's no place to go but down."

He grins. "There's up, as in 'Up, up and *away.*'"

"Let's get this over. Walk to the edge and jump. You can do it." I go back down.

Clarke moves wearily to the point of the roof. Those old bunions must really hurt.

"Clarke's going to jump!" Mavis shrills for the fourth time. Not many people look up.

Fergus yells from the pool. "Now hear this. Clarke will *not* jump."

My throat tightens. I know he will. The words I think at that moment are—what I pray is—what I've wanted all along is—for him to miss. *Miss it! Clarke, please miss it!*

My toes curl on concrete, my fingernails cut my palms, and the bottom falls out of my stomach. Cookie clutches my left hand in both of hers and—get this—presses it to her bosom. This remarkable event is beyond all my dreams. I leave my hand against her softness, but am hardly aware.

Any perfect physical act you recognize instantly. A good basketball shooter stands in air. The ball curls off his fingertips. You foretell its trajectory and hear *swish* before it kisses the net.

Clarke pushes high. The sun flares around his silhouette. One leg hangs like a loose scissor blade. *"In!"* I yell to Clarke. *"In!"* I pray to God, pounding my fist.

You have heard the crack of a breaking stick? It surprises me that a worthwhile human body makes so ordinary a sound. I hold my ears against it, and against the silence which follows.

Bubbles gurgle in the chop of water at the pool corner. The skein of baby oil which rode the surface has vanished. Fergus dives toward the body on the green bottom. He clutches Clarke by the arm and pushes to the surface. Our many hands drag Clarke over the side, scraping his back in our eagerness. A little abrasion weeps on his left shoulder. The left leg hangs wrong. Blood and something white bulge under the skin.

We boys feel relief. After this, no one of us will be required to spill his brains on concrete, or crawl down that trellis indelible yellow.

Someone rubs Clarke's face and chest with a towel. A ridge of white surrounds his strangely smiling mouth.

Cookie grips my hand and says, "I said the minute he went up there, 'Cookie, he's going to jump.'" She always addresses herself by name. Such a girl needs a wonderful figure.

When I have watched Clarke loaded into an ambulance topped by a whirling red light and carried away, I walk home by instinct. A neighbor passes on the sidewalk. I see his face as a white blur and hear, "Jeff, are you all right?"

A Brave Damn-Near Perfect Thing

"Fine, thank you, sir," I say. This is a lie.

My life has taken a significant twist. I may not be able to tell for a long time whether the change is for the better. There are questions for which I have no answers, and I must work my way through them. What made Clarke create this challenge? Why was my strongest wish for him to fail? Why does my father want me to attend the University of Alabama and study accounting? Why is the appearance of grass of overwhelming importance? Is Plato relevant today?

Clarke lies on a military cot with his left leg hoisted by pulleys and cords and window weights. It is 7:05 P.M., and the nurses have finally let me in because I am desperate. An oscillating fan hums in the corner. Sweat stands on his brow. His eyes are terribly large. He waves to me with the deliberate movement of a diver on the bottom.

"I'm not your friend," I squeak.

His eyebrows lift.

I can't say another clear word. This horrible wheeze is all I can squeeze past my goozle. "You dumb ass! I *made* you miss. I *wanted* you to miss. Don't you know anything? I wanted you to crash and die." These words force their way out.

His left hand lies under his head. Dark, wet hair points in different directions from his flattened crew cut. His skin tone blends into the pillowcase. "How did you make me miss?"

My hands gesture wildly. My eyes dart around the room

to venetian blinds, paint-chipped walls, neon bar light, and white enameled cot. "I willed it."

Clarke hasn't the spark for more than a flickering smile.

"Don't laugh at me. Words can make things happen. I willed you to miss."

"Why?"

"Because it was too perfect. You were reaching way beyond me. It was a brave, damn-near perfect thing."

His teeth show, a little grayer than the sheets. He shakes his head "It was stupid, Josie. And, no way. It don't matter what you thought. There's no way you made me miss."

"But, I wanted you to."

He looks at the wall, considering. "Okay, I believe you. In that case, I'm going to win the Pepsi-Cola scholarship off of you. I was going to let you win that or the Rotary International, but now I'm going to win them both." He rolls his head. It makes a dent in the hard pillow. "You're pitiful. You're really pi-ti-ful, Josie. You're the most ignorant guy I ever saw."

I humbly drop my gaze. But if I wasn't guilty of mental murder, I'd have said he couldn't win at tiddley-winks.

He stares with that big-eyed, opium look. "Don't you know that every man thinks the worst thing in the world? We're all Hitlers and bullies and sex fiends for about a minute every week." He smiles. "We've got these hearts of darkness, you see."

"You bastard!" Oh, I'm mad! He'd said he'd never read

Conrad. Now I remember Mrs. Goforth's smile of recognition when he walked into the library.

Clarke talks in the wispy, patient voice of a grandparent. "Don't you know anything about this screwing world? What it's going to do to you, kid, is just—sorrowful."

A knock patters on the door. Cookie sticks her head in. Her skin holds the sheen of baby oil and iodine. Her hair hangs straight from many wettings. The sclera of her eyes shines pure white, and the irises look as blue as three-hundred-yard depths of the Aegean Sea, seen only by Greek fishermen and *National Geographic* photographers. I want to dive into her unobstructed depths. I shove back my chair and stand in reverent lust.

She steps inside the room wearing a sundress, wooly white socks, and penny loafers that toe a little inward. Her right forefinger coils split ends of hair. Uncertainty is adorable upon her.

"My turn, guys. The nurse said one visitor at a time. Jeff, you have to come out, please."

I mumble "Okay," but linger in the door making desperate conversation. They pay no attention. It is dumb, dumb, dumb to leave them alone. Clarke's stories about a stranger wanting her, watching her, come back to me ... *Et tu, Brute?*

My obligatory twice-a-week visits to the hospital are hard on all of us. Books stack in the corners of his room.

Our competition is in the open. Cookie comes to visit carrying more books. She watches Clarke study, wearing a doty expression.

He opens a page and Z's his finger down it in two seconds. In addition to being a speed-reader, he has a photographic memory or is bluffing. Miss Zurcher at the society desk on our newspaper, who wears a green eyeshade, pokes multiple pencils into her raddled gray hair, and finds occasion to come around her desk to pat pretty brides, has one. I know they exist.

For the scholarship competition in September four of us will assemble in Miss Garner's homeroom. Even though Clarke has the memory of a spirit-duplicator I will defeat him with plodding, turtley competence. But, I won't *die* if I don't win the Pepsi or the Rotary.

There are revelations that have come with the one Clarke gave me in the hospital that I am not the King of Bastards, but only an ordinary one.

I have wasted eleven years of my life by being a grind. That pissant Fergus will graduate without honors but be ready to whip the world. Clarke has met and conquered his greatest fear, while I stagger under a load of old, smelly ones. People who attend the University of Alabama are *not* dying of shriveled brains. And, I am ready for a new girl with less sweetness, longer legs, and a hundred stories I've never heard.

My senior year will be better than endurable. I'll be editor of the newspaper, third trumpet in the band, and chairman of the junior-senior dance. Its theme will be "Stardust." This is what I've planned.

The gym will be adorned with blue streamers originating at a large illuminated star located directly above its center and terminating low on the walls. Small stars hanging from these streamers will glitter in multicolored light. Backboards will be covered in blue construction paper. In the center of one will hang a paper moon.

Before the final dance, junior girls wearing silver tinseled costumes will present seniors with novelty paper hats and noisemakers. After several minutes of joyous uproar, a Biederbecke-like trumpet in the band will unfold the mellow notes that cry *Some-times I won-der why—*.

And then, in a darkened, transformed fairyland that was once a gym, a sentimental smile will play across my lips. I'll be dressed in my only suit, which happens to be pinstriped, double-breasted, and sophisticated. I'll take old Mavis in my arms. She'll toss the silver parentheses of her hair and flick that tongue she squeezes into Coke bottles. Mavis won't complain if I bruise her gardenia corsage while holding her close. The song will be "Stardust," the last dance of our best-ever high school year.

SKIN

"I'll bet ten dollars my Big Yazoo cuts grass faster than your whatzit," Rollo says. He pokes Lloyd in the chest with a finger the size of a fat sausage. "—and I don't even know what brand you got!"

Rollo's downy hair points up like he is a Curly chicken. He sprawls half across the porch and scratches his belly. Not much bothers Rollo except women.

Will Ab hugs his narrow self to keep from shaking to death, as he does of a Monday. Vitalis slicks his hair, and a pitiful skull shows through the black strands. "Twenty!" Will Ab snaps, like a man popping three aces on a table. "A hundred!"

"Will Ab, you don't even have a mower," Edmond says. Edmond is about the size of a fice. He has a keen but worried look from keeping order among large men.

"I'll get one."

"You're on," Rollo squeaks in his fat-man voice.

"I want some of that!" Lloyd jingles the change-maker he wears because his jeans are too tight for pocket entry. Sunlight glints on a bare chest with ten yellow hairs in its center. No passing girl is going to miss his pecs and other braggable stuff. In the baritone of an announcer on a classical radio station, which Lloyd is not, he says, "I'm the one with a fast mower."

Fast mower, hell! Lloyd has the world by the shorts. No beer belly he's got to pat and cherish. A Chevrolet Silverado four-wheel drive with chrome bumpers, bed liners, splash guards and California break-aways. Twenty-six years old. And *Ruby*. Everybody just looks at him and sort of hates him.

Above their heads stubbed limbs stick up on the porch's whitewashed cedar posts. A fan hums in a window. A circle of nap clots pores in a rusty window screen in front of the fan. N E H I   O R A N G E is impressed in faded colors on the front door.

The men sit on drink crates with a checkerboard on their knees because Gator thinks it is picturesque. He has hid their chessmen and cane chairs. He is unlike all storekeeps in the history of Troy, Alabama. The fool wants to attract strangers. He *likes* them. He tells the checker players to turn and grin at the road when cars pass by. His new expression for all occasions is slick and smiley. He plans to make this a tourist mecca.

He has already turned it into the United Nations of Alabama, Edmond grumbles. "Who else has put a Vietnam man behind a counter?" Gator is as bad as a chamber of commerce, he says.

Lloyd is about to lose his third checker game when he announces he has mowed his yard of grass in forty minutes. Rollo is playing him blindfolded. Lloyd does not have time for strategy because every two minutes he must toss his hair like a salad.

Drink crates creak. Somebody groans.

Lloyd gazes into the distance with half-closed eyes and chin insufferably cocked. He stretches his legs. This shows his privates in outline. "I got the fastest mower in the county. Bar none," he says.

"Who gives a shit!" Edmond snaps. Edmond will fight any of them in a heartbeat. He has been to college several semesters and despises as trash every thought Lloyd and Rollo have. They don't worry about federal judges, civil wrong lawyers, niggers, or other current events. They have greased and slid back into the Union.

Rollo lifts a happy face. He utters the same glad cry he used to utter at age five when he found baby rabbits he could love and squeeze to death. "How much you bet?"

Lloyd stops clicking the busman's change-maker, stops feeling his pecs with the other hand, and gets electric. Bones fluoroscope through the skin of his face. "'Fore God! 'Fore God! Ruby timed me!" It is like leaning your ear against the horn of the *Delta Queen* to hear him baritone at full cry.

"That's a sweet voiced woman, Ruby is," Edmond says. Then he mimicks her, "*S-u-p-p-e-r ' s on!* Does Ruby always time you, Lloyd?"

Skin

Will Ab whirls his pointed face and mutters very dirty language. He aims the words at the floor so nobody has to take them personal. Folks weary of fighting him during his Ruby fits.

Ruby is beauty. She has a wet, red mouth, snapping black eyes, a wobbly way of walking, and two memorable, bouncing, elastic gazongas. A merciful God gave them to her for survival. The girl's mind makes such a buzz as you hear in a seashell or from a starter connected to a dying battery.

Ruby looks as if she'd topple off her clear plastic spikes at a nudge. The natural position of her legs looks accepting. This is wrong. She won't except for Lloyd. She is gone on Lloyd. Will Ab is just sick about it.

Right then Rollo's wife, Maria, comes switching out of the store, banging the screen door behind. "Don't talk to me about this," she screeches.

"I never did, honey," Rollo says. "I never said a word to you, honey."

Oh, oh! Two honeys in two sentences, and in public. Everybody commences scattering. Will Ab slaps his pockets and discovers he's out of cigs. Lloyd eases down the steps toward the Silverado. Edmond wanders inside the store to the candy case, where he stares at Mounds and makes spit run in his mouth.

Maria peers into Rollo's face. "What is this you are doin'? You are gamblin'?" She don't like the odds in gambling.

Colombian women are built low to the ground. This is

handy for picking cocoa leaf and coffee beans, although her family has been in another line of work practically since powered flight.

Rollo met Maria in a Miami airport. She and her family steal luggage as a profession. The are the Flying Wallendas of their craft, highly respected. It makes Maria wild to think of the celebrity she gave up to marry Rollo.

She tells him how lonely she is, and how she has to be among her *peoples* because she is *lonely*. She wants them all to move to Alabama.

Rollo nods and nods. His face puffs and his mouth sucks. His eyes roll in half circles, horizon to horizon, above Maria's gaze. "Get home, woman. Go tend your garden," he grunts.

This garden is planted to the sunny side of their Jim Walter two-story. She's got endive, basil, parsley, mint, and marijuana, 'cause cocoa don't grow here. The marijuana is of Colombian descent. Rollo pulls up every plant she puts in the ground more than two. He don't want low-flying airplanes to spot them, or deputies to take special notice because she is foreign.

Growing two marijuana plants in Pike County, Alabama, don't put Maria down with Juan Valdez, but it is a social descent. She says, "Good shit, man, good shit!" but there are tears in her smile.

Will Ab and Edmond watch through the screen door as Maria carries on about how she cries in her sleep to see mama. She is pleading to a deaf man. Rollo is prim about money. Don't worry about counting your change if he hands it over, or about him paying you back if he borrows. He complains about Maria's family. "They're proud folks. Proud of *thieving!* Don't see a thing wrong with it. No sir bob."

Rollo married Maria on the rebound from unfulfilled desire for Ruby. Maria was the marriage equivalent of joining the French Foreign Legion. Now, he rocks on his heels, looking down at her. "I can just *see* your mama in Gator's store." His voice is as windy as a puff adder's you've poked with a stick. "She would steal him out of business in a week. She'd be worse about thieving than two pickup baseball teams."

Will Ab squints through the screen and reaches inside his shirt to a cross that hangs on a silver chain. He'll reach in and rub it when he makes a bet or stares at a woman he wishes to have relations with. He thinks the cross is God-magic. You look over and there is Will Ab, eyes gone shiny, his hand pumping inside his shirt among hair and titties. He leans forward to do it. The hunch is not good to see.

Inside the store it is dark, narrow, and familiar as a pocket. Scents of cheese, coffee, fried onions, and dust mingle. Gator clicks salt and pepper containers together. There is no reason to move them; he just does it. Quang polishes the counter with an old diaper. He is always wiping something. Edmond says he would love to have Quang attached to his car as a giant windshield wiper.

Outside, a hot breeze stirs. Jesse, the black handyman, shoves Gator's push mower over daisies and Johnson grass that sprout through gravel. Jesse bruises weeds all the time with that thing, but never gets dominion over them. His work is like Muzak. Gator hasn't given Jesse a file in four years. If the blade is sharp there will be less work for him to do.

Rollo squeaks in his tiny voice, "Maria, I'm about to slap the pee out'a you."

She yells, "Do it, then!"

"Git to the house, Maria!" Rollo is as serious as a man talking to a dog chewing his pet cat. "Go see to your garden."

Maria howls, "Talk, talk, talk. This is all you do, talk." She plants her hands on her hips and spreads her stubby legs. She jiggles every move she makes, which is why Will Ab is wild to get at her. "You promise my peoples come. When?"

Pow! Rollo smacks her face.

Will Ab jumps to his feet and jerks up his khakis. He flashes Edmond a hard look. "Stay offen my back, homo."

Will Ab can look hard. He's got stony eyes, pock-marked skin, and this roached face like a Wilson Allen stud. He looks like a man who'd take every advantage in a fight, but he won't. Edmond is the one who will.

What Will Ab intends is to act-out. He means to try to rescue Maria. This will cost him an ass-whipping. Then, he will slip over to their Jim Walter when Rollo is away.

Skin

There is nothing as sweet in life to Will Ab as another man's woman.

Edmond trails Will Ab to the door, looking right and left for ax handles. His mama named him after an English sissy in a Harlequin novel, but Edmond is one mean mother. He will jump in the middle of your back, lock on, and beat among your head and ears. He will lay up in a dark corner and smite you from behind. He can fit in small shadows. Watch out. The first lick he hits is to the back of the neck with something hard and edgy. Don't meddle with Edmond.

He is ferreting into barrels and behind the door, but Gator has moved the ax handles.

Maria stands with her mouth open as Rollo's big-fingered handprint develops on her cheek. Black hair falls like a beaded curtain over her face. Through it her eyes blaze.

Rollo is indignant, as a man will be when wrong. He cocks his hand like a pistol hammer. There is a silence.

In the yard Jesse purses his lips and locks his hands behind his back.

Lloyd sits low in the Silverado, watching.

Inside the store, Gator and Quang press close behind Edmond, peeping over his shoulder.

Will Ab pumps the cross in his shirt front. He pushes through the door and bangs the screen. "You, sir! That's no way to treat a woman." He's trembling all over.

Rollo squeals like a caught pig 'cause his lips are so stiff they won't form words.

Will Ab commences prancing with his back straight, chin tucked, and fists cocked in a style he adopted from Gentleman Jim Corbett's picture on a boxing calendar. A loose board goes *thumpty-thump, thumpty-thump* under his feet. Will Ab is strange. He reads things and listens to the radio and takes it for real. He believes the President, the Governor of Alabama, and Baptist preachers. He's a redneck romantic—a kind of human fodder, ready to be eaten up by good-sounding words. If he'd lived during the War he'd have enlisted and died, owning not a slave.

The prancing is interrupted by this. Will Ab has no ass or hips. His khakis slide down and he must wrist them up.

Edmond hates it when Will Ab prances. He explodes through the door and lands astride Will Ab's back, flailing away.

"Get this homo offen me!" Will Ab yells.

Edmond tears at Will Ab's ears. He locks his legs around Will Ab's skinny belly. He can't get any purchase in the greasy hair, but he slides two fingers inside Will Ab's cheek and commences ripping.

Gator totters out of the store, drying his fingertips on a sparkling apron. He is about eighty-two and very weak. A weak or scared person don't mess with noblesse. They will kill you.

Edmond clings to Will Ab like a squirrel which has scampered to the last limb. Gator fans a hickory ax handle with a blue seal upon it. He looks like a housewife aiming a fly swatter.

Skin

"Here now," he says, "you'll be the ruination of Will Ab's face." Gator speaks in the sweet voice of a boy. The voice is something time has overlooked to take from him.

Will Ab gurgles and stretches back his thumbs to gouge Edmond's eyes.

Rollo quits laughing. He waddles across the porch and slaps Edmond's head. This is moments before Gator would have manslaughtered Edmond. Rollo weighs 290 pounds and drives tacks with the heel of his hand. Edmond bounces off the clapboard, not ripping off Will Ab's cheek because of likely reprisal.

Then Will Ab long-steps around the porch, wristing up his britches, cussing homos and morphodites. They are the cause of the troubles in America, in Alabama, and on this very porch. There is a homo and morphodite conspiracy.

Gator drops the ax handle and it clatters on the steps. Quang picks it up. Edmond, whose head hurts too bad for him to fight Rollo or even Will Ab, mutters that if he had a Vietnam man in a duck blind on opening day he could finish him as a retriever in record time. Taking a line, marking, and all.

Rollo swills orange pop. He is thirsty from action. Edmond is eye level with Rollo's knee, thinking about hamstringing.

Quang touches Gator's arm. "Please, sir." That don't mean he is addressing Gator. He says to Gator what he wants everybody to hear.

Gator turns his whole body, rocking side to side, *totter, totter*, because he is fused. "What?"

"I would like ..." Quang giggles. This means it is serious. "I would like to race."

"What?" Gator asks.

Unease, as would follow an old lady's step-ins dropping off, or a fart escaping a preacher, keeps everyone quiet.

Edmond bounces to his feet. "Wait a damn minute!"

Lloyd beams and says, "Sounds good to me." Maria clasps her hands. Rollo chuckles. Will Ab never loses step in his pacing; he is indifferent to such as Vietnamese. On Gator's face there is the shine of a mountain as the rising sun touches it. This man is a visionary. "An international competition?"

"Hell no!" Edmond points a trembling finger at Quang. "They did it at Pearl Harbor, and Korea, and Vietnam, and now they are doing it in Pike County on Gator's porch. This is an American race. No outsiders. The entry fee is *one hundred* dollars."

Gator says in a wondering voice, like a prophet's, "We can post signs in Opelika. Tourists will come from far and wide. The race will be called the Alabama Lawn Mower Derby. It will be notorious."

"Famous, you mean," Edmond says, but he is astonished. Gator is some hell. He should have lived in a city ... been a Yankee.

"How come I got to pay a hundred dollars?" Rollo

squeaks. "'Cause you say so?" He looms over Edmond, who is busy pointing a shaking finger at the Yellow Peril.

Quang grins. "I have hundred dollar."

"*Je*-sus," Edmond says. "Don't you know when you're not wanted?"

You can only say such things in Alabama if you are drunk or mean to fight. Rollo scowls. "Back off, Edmond."

Lloyd tucks his chin for better voice. "Yeah, Edmond, back off."

Gator's eyes wander around the floor, searching for the ax handle Quang picked up.

"Why you say he no enter, homo?" Maria screeches. "His money green like yours. Let him race!"

The Vietnam man bows to Jesse. "I have hundred dollar. *He* is American."

Jesse stands eighteen feet away, lips pursed, hands in overall pockets, not regarding anyone. The expanse of gravel and the porch height make the distance seem farther, as if they're looking the wrong way through a telescope. But Quang and Maria cross the distance in a flash. Maria yells, "We can beat them! Help us!"

Quang waits silently. He reminds Edmond of a house dog watching a man eat, ready to grab what drops.

Jesse's liquid eyes touch Edmond's. His grandaddy belonged to Edmond's grandaddy like a horse or a dog. Jesse's mama was Edmond's nurse. Now he calls, "Mr. Edmond?"

"What?"

"I am going to do this, but it ain't against you. It is my right."

"Whee!" Maria yells.

His lifelong Negro friend a backstabber? A Vietnam refugee and a Colombian cocoa-leaf picker challenging the white race?

Edmond clutches the porch rail to steady himself. Twenty-eight folks are left in town: five true whites, a Colombian, a Vietnam man, and twenty-one blacks. Loomis Beardsley, stationed in Korea, has married a Korean. Loomis will sponsor about eighteen of her peasant relatives to live here before they drift away to cities. Loomis thinks she married him for love. *Love!* Edmond will tell you what kind of man Loomis Beardsley is. "If he was at public stud, he is too poor a specimen to turn in with a herd of cull women."

Edmond thinks he is the only entire man left among them. When he cusses federal judges, Rollo replies, "Damn right!" sprawls his legs, and belches. When he yells the Voting Rights Act just applies to Southerners, Rollo's expression remains at beer glaze.

Color rises to Will Ab's roached face when he hears Edmond carry on. He moves out of the circle of flying spit like an old dog removing himself from a lawn sprinkler.

Once Edmond asked, "Isn't that right, Will Ab?"

Will Ab said, "How many disadvantaged have you left your fire of a night to help? How many clothes have you give to poor folks that ain't worn out? How many times have you affirmatively-actioned? None, I'll warrant."

Regardless of larger differences, Rollo, Lloyd, Will Ab, and Edmond are unified by their wish for a Derby victory.

Rollo and Lloyd rework gear boxes and install new pistons in Lloyd's riding mower. Rollo helps Lloyd, rather than enter his own mower, because his bed is cold without Maria and she don't like him to gamble.

Edmond is attaching a clipper under a sulky. Propulsion is to come from Miss Peter Axworthy, an eighteen-year-old Standardbred mare on pension in his pasture. "There's not an engine in the world that can match the heart of a race mare," Edmond declares.

But when the gasoline motor that runs the clipper pops, Miss Peter rolls her eyes, kicks, and goes wild. Jesse declares she is old as Methuselum, and it is an imposition to make her work. That's all she knows, Edmond says. She is not making a crop, she is pacing. Pacing is her business, as a bird's business is flying.

Without the clipper engaged she settles into a CLAT-TER-*clatter*, CLATTER-*clatter* gait. Her neck stretches and her mane and tail flow in the air. Spume flies. Behind in the sulky, Edmond is enveloped in a sweet, hot cloud of sweat. His goggled eyes peer around her flanks toward a vision of Ruby cracking a bottle of champagne over his mower, and her lipsticky kiss. *"Come on, Miss Peter!"* he howls.

Jesse follows Edmond about. He wants to be friends

after conspiring with the enemy. "De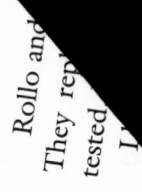
retainers," Edmond says over his
thing civil-wrong lawyers ever did
Not having to go bail. Not having
cold and rain to see if somebody's
ing to listen to somebody's lies I k
to make me shout *Free at last!*"

Miss Peter's chrome-finished race harness
rot. A new set costs six hundred dollars. Edmond splices
and repairs the leather with a Handy Stitcher. In an hour
he repairs six inches. With blisters on his fingers he yells
to Jesse, "Get your ass out of here. Go associate with
them that use your name. You're under foot." This is a lie
and a physical impossibility. Jesse is twice as big as
Edmond.

Jesse reaches for the harness, wearing a patient expression that has passed through his family for a hundred and
fifty years. Edmond flings the harness on the grass. "Leave
it alone. It can't be fixed."

The next morning when Edmond takes the leather
from its hook he sees that Jesse took him at his word. If
he cannot count on Jesse, what has Alabama come to?
Edmond staggers around the barn lot dragging fifteen feet
of leather like a gored horse dragging guts. Treachery is in
the air. Edmond feels like Miss Peter Axworthy on a
wooden bridge—hollow noise underfoot, empty shaking
all around, and horror in the heart. He wants to bolt, roll
his eyes, and kick.

Skin

Lloyd fine-tune a Briggs and Stratton motor.
...ace clutch and gear box. High octane fuel is
...Rollo grins and peeps, "Looks good!"
...loyd swirls their machine around anyone's grass that
...eds cutting, pluming white smoke and crying, "Testing,
testing." Edmond clocks him at twenty miles an hour.

Will Ab buys a tinny, promo mower and studies a
greasy mechanics' book. Pot metal parts surround him,
and chromey socket wrenches, and fumes of anger. Edmond says Will Ab's wrenches got drop forged by being
dropped from a tall Korean building. Will Ab's speed is
twelve miles an hour.

Quang and Jesse scavenge the neighborhood for parts.
Quang welds iron pipe and an old tractor seat to form a
skeleton frame. The axles come from a child's wagon.
Gator's mower hangs under the belly, raised and lowered
by a lever from a horse-drawn hay rake. A washing machine motor propels the thing at fearsome speed. Rollo
sniggers at it, but Edmond does not laugh at oriental ma-
chinery with neat welds and a purring engine.

Jesse steals glances at Edmond. His lips pook in sorrow.
He is in love with the Vietnam man's mower, but full of
guilt. He tries to time the mower's speed with an old railroad watch which has a broken second hand.

Edmond times it from behind an oak tree as it zooms
the road, enveloped in a red dust cloud. When it stops,
Quang catapults through the top like Andretti at the
Indianapolis. "What time?" he cries. Jesse stares at the

watch and scratches his head. "About a minute and a half," he says.

It is doing twenty-two miles an hour.

Will Ab assembles his mower and chugs it in small circles behind his trailer. This is a secret test. It makes six circles and blows a gasket.

Miss Peter paces a mile in four minutes with the engine under the sulky off. When it is over veins stand like cords upon her, acrid sweat drips from her body, and her head hangs. Edmond yearns to pit her true old heart against a machine, but that time is past. He withdraws from the race and offers to help any white man.

Will Ab snarls, "Fuck off." Lloyd strokes his pecs and radio-announces with eyes half closed, "Thanks, ol' buddy, but no thanks."

Being accepted does not matter. Edmond frets about the speed of the opposition's machine. It will defeat Will Ab, maybe Lloyd. There is nothing he can do to make their mowers faster. Does he have another responsibility?

He will not cheat. If four whites cannot win fair and square from one Negro and one Oriental, they deserve to lose. Pride is everything to a man who has nothing else.

After the home-boys time Quang's speed, Lloyd stops clicking the change-maker. Will Ab throws all his chrome wrenches at trees. Rollo drinks an extra six-pack and glazes his face.

Edmond is sure they want something of him. Is victory worth more than honor? The question makes him sweat.

One night he puts on his white sneakers, walks to Jesse's house, bangs the porch floor with the heel of his hand, and yells. Jesse comes through the door hitching up his overall straps. He is old and gray, with a dropsical belly that shapes him like a pear.

Edmond puts on his good-old-boy grin. His tongue is sweet and greased with vernacular. "Jesse, this thing has got out of hand. Gator wouldn't of started it when he was in his right mind. You know that. It's upset the whole community. Think what will happen if y'all win and Rollo and Will Ab get their feelings hurt. What if you don't never get a kind word or an easy dollar from them again? This ain't your race, Jesse. That Vietnam man don't mean a thing to you."

Jesse scuffs the toe of one cracked, patent-leather shoe and stares into the distance. "I can't hardly pull out on the man. I can't hardly go back on my word."

"All right." Edmond's voice is hard and ringing. "You have made your bed, you Trojan horse."

The next morning Edmond demands that Gator fire the Vietnam man for the theft of four lengths of galvanized pipe and two sets of used ball bearings. Because a man stacks things in disordered piles about his acreage does not mean they are abandoned. A man never knows when he will need stuff. "I am willing to swear out a warrant. Quang is a thief. They both are, but there is no sense in jailing Jesse because I will have to bail him out."

Gator rubs his bald spot and says in a penetrating voice, "How much you reckon them things is worth?"

"Four or five dollars. Every bit."

"Quang," Gator calls. Vietnam man is behind the counter, wiping something. "Open the register and ..."

That is all he gets to say. Edmond jumps off the stool and walks out before the Vietnam man can hand him five dollars.

This thing must run its course.

A few days before the race Ruby drives to the pumps, gets out of the Silverado, and toddles up the steps in a little red skirt and a black satin jacket. "How y'all like my cheerleader costume?" she cries. She wobbles to Lloyd and plants a crimson kiss on him.

"Fine," the men chorus. "You look *fine*, Ruby. Real good."

Lloyd smiles, sleepy-eyed.

Edmond *hates* him for possessing this unearned treasure, a woman with legs like Kentucky wonder beans, frisky eyes, long red nails, sharp-edged lips, little nubby white teeth, and the largest bosoms in Alabama on a white woman.

She beams on Edmond a glance such as a lady must have used to inspire her champion to skewer a knight. She puffs her hair with little pats from the bottom. "Lloyd's gonna win ain't he, Edmond?" Her voice is not the prettiest thing about her.

"He sure is, you pretty thing," Edmond says. "Ol' Lloyd's got the fastest mower in the county."

While the contestants give full attention to final Derby trials, there is intensified correspondence between Maria and Miami, Florida. Thick manila envelopes arrive. Three roped-together boxes of household goods are delivered by bus. Edmond sees all. He warns that once the goods are here the mama, the papa, the brothers, and the distant cousins will not be far behind.

"Ha," Rollo snorts. "Ha." It is a sound without humor because Maria is rooting for Vietnam man and Jesse.

The night before the race is nearly moonless. Wind whips gray clouds through the sky. Undischarged electricity tingles in the air. Edmond's polyester pajamas stick to his chest and legs. He cannot sleep so he dresses. Then he walks to the store. Behind it is Gator's garage.

"This is only a walk," Edmond tells himself, but in his pocket nestles a package of white powder wrapped in folded paper. "I won't do this," he tells himself. But he moves from shadow to shadow, short of breath, his heart kicking.

The shed windows are open to the wind. Inside, Edmond sees a body sprawled on a mattress and the angular shape of the gook's mower. That is the way Edmond thinks of Quang now, as the gook. He remembers Pearl Harbor, the rape of Nanking, and the Bataan Death March. He visualizes the bodies of good men dead along the Yalu.

Jesse is the worst of guards. His breath whistles. He is arranged with folded arms on a pale mattress, sound asleep. A nightgown hikes on his right thigh, and his lips gleam with spittle.

Edmond tiptoes into the room, reaches across Jesse, and twists the mower's gas cap. He spills confectioner's sugar from a V'd paper container into the gas tank.

It is done.

Jesse turns. His arm flops and strikes Edmond's leg. Edmond jerks back, and Jesse's hand bounces to the oily floor. The breath catches in Jesse's throat. Then wheezing resumes.

Edmond's steps drag on the walk home. And yet there is satisfaction. How long can an engine run before sugar destroys it? Edmond crawls into his bed, wondering this, and sleeps well.

A banner in Gator's pasture, the only unsheared grass in three miles, proclaims, HOME OF THE ALABAMA LAWN MOWER DERBY. Gator makes ready for the race behind a concession stand of two drink boxes. He wears a blue shirt and tie, black trousers, high-topped shoes, and cotton apron. White hair plasters his skull. His dentures reek of Polident.

An older Buick with a hanging fender pulls off the road a hundred yards away. Dark faces poke through every window. Gator waves welcome, but no hand flashes in reply. Everyone in the pasture waits, and the people in the car wait.

Quang squats beside his mower and twists a spark plug while mumbling in a foreign tongue. A war-surplus flying suit bags upon him. Celluloid flying goggles dangle around his neck. On his head clamps a tight leather helmet that makes him look kamikaze.

Edmond watches him. The loss of honor is only a little stretching, a minor inward tear. If he does not think about it, it does not hurt.

Ruby waves a bottle of California champagne she plans to crack and pour on Lloyd's head when he wins. It is an idea she got from a photograph in *People*.

Not a dust cloud hovers in either direction on the road. Gator flips the cover of his pocket watch.

Rollo and Lloyd rev the Briggs and Stratton motor: *udden, udden, UDDEN! Pow! Pow!*

Will Ab, dressed like black death or Johnny Cash, turns the key of his Sears Roebuck mower. *Pop, pop, pop,* it goes, one-lunged and maybe morphodite. He eyes the circle of faces with a hard twist of his head, but catches nobody making fun.

Quang and Jesse stand apart from other racers. Quang twitches with excitement. Jesse is quiet and serious. Their mower does not require testing. It clocked twenty-six miles an hour.

Fifteen or more cars drift down the road as silently as vultures. Big cars with purring engines, holding hungry kids and indulgent parents. People jump out of them and hurry across the field, smiling with hard brightness, demanding to be entertained.

"Gentlemen, start your engines!" Gator yells through a funnel of cardboard.

Ruby stands behind Lloyd, chewing her thin lip, clasping her hands, and bumping her knees together.

Gator's arm chops down and Lloyd boils out in a cloud of white smoke. His neck is rigid with pride. Quang shears past him, spewing five-inch Johnson grass in a rusty green arc. Will Ab putter-putters behind, hunched over his wheel and ferreting mean looks to the side.

They are at the first turn! A man in the crowd adjusts the focusing knob of binoculars. Ruby and Maria scream and jump up and down, their skirts whipping. Gator cries, "Egg salad sandwiches! Root beer!" The explosive shouts of children pop like firecrackers through the din of mowers.

They are in the far stretch! Across the waving grass, Quang's Tinkertoy vehicle whirs four lengths ahead. Goggles shine. His helmet strap dangles. His feet pound and touch pedals, making the strong corrections of a pilot holding a World War II fighter plane on a runway. Lloyd juts his head and leans over the wheel of his smooth-cutting red mower. Will Ab chugs behind, wrapping his legs and arms around his machine like a spider taking its life.

Edmond wonders if the refugee racer needed more

sugar, and regrets that he is so ignorant of sabotage. "Come on, Will Ab!" he yells.

They roar past. Quang skids at corners, making mothers cry out and grab for children. A haze rolls along the ground, under the burning sky. Stemmy Johnson grass dries in windrows. The odors of cut grass, exhaust fumes, and yellow mustard mix in the air.

Two jolting backfires punctuate the roar of engines. At the far end of the track Quang's mower drifts fumes, and hacks the cough of a three-pack-a-day smoker. Lloyd gains two lengths on the curve. Will Ab makes his move, pounding the side of his mower with a whip hand. The crowd screams. Gator's youthful voice penetrates the din: "Peanuts! Boiled peanuts! Hot dogs!"

Quang's engine dies. He pulls the starter rope three times, jumps from the seat, and pushes. Edmond imagines him as a rickshaw boy, and doesn't feel any pity. Quang pushes hard for the finish line forty yards away. Lloyd roars past him and the checkered flag flutters. Quang strains to be second, head down, legs digging. The crowd howls. And here comes Will Ab! Elbows whipping air, crouched above the tractor seat, yelling a Rebel yell, he putters into the lead by a cowling. Oh, it is grand!

Jesse pouts as he and Quang trundle their mower to the shed. He thinks everybody conspires against him. The world is a big spiderweb to Jesse. Everybody does *not* conspire against him. Just, sometimes, Edmond does.

Ruby gives Lloyd a wet kiss that makes the other men

shudder, they want it so. Maria coos to Rollo and looks up from under her lashes. She is a woman of hard, foreign roundness. Edmond roams his desperate eyes among the fresher colored girls, who grin and yell and slap their hands in extravagant gestures.

Will Ab strides to the shed, grinning without malice. "Y'all ran a good race. You had us beat till the last hill."

Quang shrugs. "Motor quit. No power." He takes off the gas cap and looks inside with a flashlight. "Ahh! Bad gas."

"What!" Edmond says.

"Here, now," Will Ab fishes in the tank with a folded piece of paper, sniffs it, and licks as delicately as a dog does a hot grill. Will Ab does not want to believe his taste buds. He licks again. "Boy, you been cheated."

Edmond looks left and right for suspects.

At first Quang's face shows nothing. He has learned that Americans believe Orientals are stoical. Then his expression crumples. He pulls his hair, stamps the oily dirt, and says "Shit!"—except it sounds like "Sheet!" Tears stand in his eyes.

The men glance at each other. Jesse puts his hands in overall pockets and walks off. Will Ab fans his hands like a football referee signaling *no touchdown*. "I ain't having any part of this. All bets are off."

Quang fiddles with the choke and pulls the starter rope. Everyone wishes he wouldn't. The engine makes a *puck, puck, puck* sound, such as is made by hens.

Will Ab snatches off his granger cap, flings it to the

ground, and grinds it with his boot. Vitalis-greased hair stands upon him like hackles on a pitted cock. He is ready to fight any of them, or preferably all.

Rollo squeaks in his high voice, "Boys, why don't we give the pot to Quang and Jesse?"

The others nod. Edmond feels like *sheet*. His friendship with Will Ab may never recover. Will Ab draws deadlines of acceptable behavior that others cross at their peril.

As soon as he is given the prize money, Quang tells Gator, "I go now. I leave. Thank you."

Gator says, "I'm sorry. I truly am. But I don't blame you one bit."

With the gook gone there will only be Jesse to remind Edmond of dishonor. He will set Jesse to cutting grass by the roadway, like Uriah the Hittite, and an 18-wheeler will come along and pop him. He fantasizes this in the dark of his mind.

At bus time Quang walks to the road carrying a carpet-bag.

"Hey. Where you going to, Quang?" Lloyd yells from the porch.

Gator stands with his hands under his apron. "Racine. Quang is going to Racine."

"He must've asked somebody who's never heard of any city but Racine, South Bend, and Cairo," Edmond grumbles. "Not one white man lives in Racine."

Everybody turns and looks at Edmond with the same expression. "I didn't do a thing!" he yells. "'Fore God!

Why are you looking at me? *Je*-sus *Christ*." Edmond's Coke crate bangs down and his boots scuff across the porch. He has to face Quang, in public, or Quang will board the Trailways and Edmond will be left with an oriental albatross forever.

Edmond stands beside Quang with his hands in his pockets, looking down the road. "All's fair in war," he says. "You had to lose."

"OK, Jack." Quang bobs his head. He seems happy.

"You don't want to go to Racine, though. Go somewhere else. Go to the coast where Vietnam people are doing well, taking away the fishing and shrimping from fifth-generation Americans."

"OK, Jack."

"Edmond."

"OK, Edmon'." Quang hisses a laugh. His hand flips strangely. "Excuse please. All American look same to me."

From behind them comes the whisper of Jesse's swing blade. It hangs weightless above Jesse's shoulder before falling to harass weeds. *Swish, swish.*

Vietnam man walks to Jesse and bows. Jesse lays the blade on the porch. They give each other race grips. Jesse's eyes squint. "Go for me, too, Brother," he says. "Go for me."

The Trailways bus speeds into sight under a cloud of red dust. It whooshes to a stop and the driver reaches across and pulls the door lever. His hat brim is back and he looks weary.

Skin

71

Quang picks up the carpetbag Gator has given him. He stares at the lovely green hills, bare of commerce. Those dark eyes of his are a strange terrain.

From the porch the men call advice and good-byes. They prop their feet on the rail and look around their boots. Gator waves his apron. Rollo says, "Take care in the big city." Lloyd advises, "Don't take no wooden spices."

Quang gets aboard on the other side. The interior looks like the inside of a frosted beer bottle. People stare out with distorted eyes and misshapen faces, here a warped nose, there a smudged mouth.

The men on the porch do not see Quang again. He sits on the opposite side of the bus. Maybe he does not mind going to Racine, which Edmond says is the armpit of America.

The bus rolls away, gathering quiet momentum.

Rollo smiles. He draws a deep breath. "PHEW!" he shouts.

Everybody but Gator and Jesse and Edmond howls. Lloyd falls to the floor clutching his belly, tears upon his face. Will Ab grins evilly, showing narrow, stained teeth. Edmond, who should be rejoicing, remembers the stare of the Vietnam man. He pulls at the foot of an incomplete thought, trying to birth it.

"Wait! When that guy comes back, he'll own this whole countryside. Call me Oral Roberts, but I see this as in a vision." He swings his arm in a circle. "Dummies! He'll own every foot. I wouldn't be surprised if he doesn't put up some damn factory. How would you like that?"

Will Ab sneers. Rollo and Lloyd exchange weary glances.

"Mark my words. You and yours will work for him and his. For yellow men carrying carpetbags. I tell you, boys, America is changing."

They smile. Edmond's mouth is too full of spit for him to say more. Also, he does not wish them to see him trembling, so he goes inside. When his eyes adjust to the gloom he sees Jesse behind the counter tying the strings of a white apron. "Jesus," he says. "What next?"

A fourteen-and-a-half ounce can of Crest Top tomatoes thuds from Jesse's hand.

"What are you doing back there?"

Jesse's wrinkles deepen.

Gator's old eyes are blue as bird eggs. "You want something to eat or don't you? And if you got anything to say, say it to me, not to my help."

"Hell, no, I ain't eating here. Not ever again!" However, Edmond is thinking this: Gator does not blow his nose in winter. He picks his nostrils because blowing causes colds. Gator only dips his fingertips when washing because he does not like the feel of water. Jesse is as clean as wood smoke. His palms are white from scrubbing.

An unmistakable roar fills the room. It is the Trailways bus making an unprecedented return. It pulls to the side of the gas pumps, whooshing air.

The driver steps down in polished black boots. He is a jolly fat man of legend, always a joke, and sunny eyes. Today his smile quivers near collapse. "Yes'm," he says. "Yes'm. This is the place." The voice stretches under tight control. He snaps, "Rollo Pickins! Rollo Pickins!"

A woman about four and a half feet tall engineers herself around the chromey bus front. Unkempt hair dangles across her angry features. She throws ill-sounding words over her shoulder in a foreign tongue. This woman's spine bows backward and her palms turn the wrong way. A magnificent leather bag hangs from each hand.

Maria appears from nowhere, shouting, "Mama! My peoples come!"

The baggage thief drops someone's luggage and hugs Maria with moans of joy.

Edmond snatches off his billed cap, but it is only out of habit. *They are throwing women into the line. This one is somebody's mother.* He wears the dazed and ragged look of a defeated army. *OK. Stack arms. Let chaos reign, you liberal fuckers. You deserve what you get, America. Bring on the Sterling wide-mouth beer and its glaze. Bring on Vanna White.*

The checkerboard slides from Rollo's knees. Bottle caps rattle on the floor as he stands. His hands paddle like a drowning dog's paws. Horror puckers his face, and his short happy life flashes before him. "Mama," he says, "where'd you git them bags?"

MY FATHER'S VOICE, LIFTING

The dog's tail raps the porch floor, then Papa's footfall sounds. The screen door swishes on the spring Papa made and bams shut. He forgets to ease things.

Mother says "Whist," and closes her eyes. She digs into flour and salt in the basin. The blue dress creases between her shoulder blades. Tendons stand on her arms.

Papa says to me, "Hi there, Gal. Why ain't you in school?" His voice—baritone when he talks, bass when he sings—can pop chilly bumps on your neck.

"—Aren't," Mother says over her shoulder. Mother was a schoolteacher until the Depression. She lost her place because she is a married woman. The school board was nice about it.

"—Aren't," Papa says. He puts on a comical look and walks to the calendar tacked beside the back door. A yellow pencil tied to string hangs beside it. Phases of the moon printed in red guide planting: quarter moons, half moons, full moons. All moons wear cheerful faces. All but the full moon rest on lazy, curved backs. The June moon winks a thick eyelid. Under some days rain drills in slant marks.... That it rains on those days is a *story*. It has not rained since July, and then a sprinkle.

Papa's scrawl records "drenched team," "planted corn," "sold sow—$10." I know that calendar by heart. It troubles my sleep.

Under September, 1932, a date is marked and labeled "school starts." The other important day, after crops are gathered, is unmarked but looms large. That's the day Papa tells the landowner, Mr. Russell, if he wants to hold over, and Mr. Russell says yes or no. If both are yeses we can live in this house another year, and Mr. Russell will furnish necessities from the commissary until the crop is gathered.

It makes my stomach hurt to think about it.

Papa backs away from the calendar, squinting. His khakis hike in back when he bends. The thin heels of his lowcuts wedge toward center. I tuck my shoes under my skirt.

"Good as I can see," Papa says, turning to me, "this is a school day."

"Sir?"

"Why are you home?"

"Leave her alone," Mother says.

"We're going to keep you in school."

The baking powder can that was in Mother's hand suddenly bounces from the floor. She dumps flour and salt from the granite bowl in a frenzy; dust flies.

"Rachel?" Papa says.

Trembling from the heels, she faces us. Floury hands wrap tight in her apron. The new baby swells the reset buttons of her dress. "Mr. Lindsey, we must speak in private."

"Rachel, you're all right." Papa's voice eases along, the way it does among spooky cattle. He walks to Mother. She jerks away.

My, my. How many times in the past I've cherished those words when I hurt, or when something frightened me. You're all right is all I ever needed. I held those words close in the dark and they warmed me. Now, they don't seem enough.

Mother tells me good words won't buy bread, clothes, or shoe leather. I think she means words don't make up for what's lost and gone.

Every woman must learn the hard way about men and their dreams, she says. Their dreams are not the same as ours. They live in the future, and we in the past, in a proper world.

Now Mother's words pop like penny firecrackers. "There's no baking powder. I don't have a dime. I can't make proper bread. And there is all that money lying there."

She is a cornered animal behind the table. Papa squats beside the mess on the floor and scrapes it onto a torn piece of cardboard. His hand brushes the planking.

My Father's Voice, Lifting

"Mush is fine," he says. "I like mush. We've got sorghum. It'll be a feed."

"Don't talk like a bumpkin," Mother snaps. She has attended Blue Mountain College and does not tolerate poor usage. "What are you doing in my kitchen? This is my place."

"I don't mind cleaning it," Papa says. "It's for Dog. She's got to have a bite to eat."

The dog has been trouble since we moved onto this plantation. Mr. Russell, the owner, right away looked Papa in the eye, hitched his suspenders, and said: "I won't have a man farming for me has a hound or a bird dog. This ain't a year for sport."

They squared off in the road in front of this very house. Mr. Russell had just swung down from his horse and stood with reins over his arm. The horse puffed and shook itself.

I stood beside the wagon wheel, looking up. The sweetish odor of horse sweat was stronger than the Oxydol and woodsmoke scent from Papa. My bonnet hung in my hand and the sun burned a hot circle above my braids.

Mother sat on the wagon seat straight as a nail, wearing her schoolteacher dress. Mother never sweats. She laughed a glittery laugh, looking at the house. She said, "I'm sure, Mr. Russell—" and then broke off, knowing that even for her it was the wrong time to speak.

The dog sashayed around in the way. "Get! Get!" I

whispered in a mean voice, but she wouldn't slink off as she will when caught watching chickens.

Hunkering in the dust between the men, fanning it with her tail, she loved us with yellow eyes.

Behind Daddy's head spread the limbs of a fruitful pecan tree. I looked up from under his arm. He seemed as tall as that tree. The brim of an old felt hat shielded his eyes, and those eyes didn't flicker.

Mr. Russell's puckered mouth hung open and dark. Something brown stained the corners of his lips. Sweat beaded between his jowl folds. It was interesting to think about—how men are—because I knew he wanted to be clean.

Mr. Russell's laundress told that she irons him three white shirts a day. He owns fifteen, she said. My papa has one white shirt, with collar and cuffs turned. Men can't help being messy, Mother says.

Mr. Russell lifted a foot and parked it on a wagon spoke. Hightopped shoes poked out of wrinkled seersucker pants. "—'Evening, Miz Lindsey." He twirled a Panama hat in one hand and squinted through glasses that wouldn't stand any kind of a lick. I'd never before seen rimless glasses worn by any man but a postal clerk. I'd never before seen a grown-up with such little-bitty hands. Papa nudged me with his knee to mind manners.

Mother said from the wagon seat, as if to herself, "My, my, a new tin *roof* and fresh *screens*…"

Mr. Russell said, "And there is a new cookstove, Miz Lindsey. It's got nickel trim and two ovens. This is the best house on the place. It's an overseer's house."

Mother said, "Just think."

Papa shifted a little to one side like a dog that had rather not fight, but would. I turned clear around.

"There are a hundred men in twenty miles who'll take this place," Mr. Russell said. He was too polite to say some of them had families of "account," a wife and children to work the fields.

"—I picked you, Lee, because you're a good farmer who's had bad luck. And frankly, I'm unhappy about the school board letting Miz Lindsey go. She was a good teacher to my Ruth."

Mother nodded.

The shake in Papa's voice when he answered scared me. Mr. Russell could have thought he was afraid. "The dog and gun will help feed us after crops are in, Mr. Russell. The bitch keeps off varmits, and don't bother—doesn't bother stock."

"Well, Lee, generally dog men are not good farmers. As a rule they're kind of trifling." Mr. Russell chuckled. "I know better of you."

"Yessir."

"Tell you what. I'll take a chance. In the War I commanded Mississippi boys like you . . . narrow in the chest, and between the eyes. They'd *go*. You were too young for France, I reckon."

"Yessir."

"That figures. Otherwise you'd probably be—. I never knew a man named Lee to be a coward." He pulled the roan around, hopped on one foot, and swung up. "I hope you will be happy here, Miz Lindsey." He lifted the Panama to Mother and smiled down at me. I warmed from my toes up. We had a home again, and a good owner.

Mother's lips curved. Mr. Russell's courtesy said that even as a straw boss's wife, she still had standing. We were poor but nice.

"—Lee, you draw at the commissary until you make a crop. We'll get together after gathering. My business manager's name is Prudhomme. You'll know him. He's a thick-necked fellow. Wears a fuzzy vest. Real tight with my money, except he's a fool about Louisiana sugar mules. He'll probably put a big-footed team on you twice the weight you want. Thank God, he don't talk Cajun!"

With a wave of the hand, Mr. Russell cantered away across the flat land. The roan gelding kicked dust. Jaunty red suspenders bisected Mr. Russell's shirt. Land that he owned stretched flat, rich, and furrowed to the river. To me, he looked as grand as the statue in Memphis of Nathan Bedford Forrest on his war horse. Only Papa is grander than that. Pride filled me. He stood up to Mr. Russell and saved our bird dog. He would take care of Mother and me, no matter what.

The first thing Papa did after carrying Mother across the threshold, with her kicking and twisting her neck to see if anybody watched, and me giggling behind, was to see to the mules, feed the dog, and clean the shotgun.

Carefully he unwrapped the L. C. Smith from folds of quilts. A nail tied to a string dropped through the barrels, made a little *ching*. Papa pulled a cloth dipped in oil behind on the string. A gun, he explained, is like a man. It carries any dishonor all of its existence. "This gun was gave to me pure by my daddy," he said, stroking the receiver. "It never went Klanning. It never shot mating animals or baby things. It never shot animals not fit to eat, or game that flies when on the ground."

"...was *given* to me," I thought, as Mother would have thought. My eyes just glaze when anyone makes grammatical errors.

I am twelve and becoming a lady. It is easy. A lady doesn't sit with her dress up. She doesn't be loud in public. Inside she can be screaming. In her mind she can be standing on her head, buck-naked. Being a lady is practical. Men tip hats and open doors and give you candy. All they and other ladies want is for you to look shy and act modest and go to church. Being a lady doesn't have to affect your insides.

Men are different, even plain men. They have notions. They talk about honor and such as if words live and breathe and sit down to dinner.

Goodness, me! Any lady in Mississippi would trade all

the honor in the state for a good meal, a warm house, and her family gathered safe.

It was two used-up calendars ago that we first came to live on Fairhope Plantation. Then, with eighty acres to farm, good prospects, and sixty-five dollars in cash in the plantation safe, Papa sang in the evening and was happy. Mother bustled about making curtains to fit the long windows. I loved their wavy, bubbly panes and kept them scrubbed with newspaper and vinegar. Mother taught me to make a rag rug, and we snipped and threaded rags onto the frame to make one for the sleeping loft.

The next year nature let just enough rain fall to fool cotton into sprouting so the sun could burn it away. The harder men worked the land, the more it dried up and blew away.

Women held prayer meetings for rain. Men muttered about blowing the levy and diverting the river. They hired rainmakers. Nothing helped. The *Commercial Appeal* reported, and Papa read at arms' length at supper, that in a single day in April, 1932, one-quarter of the land in Mississippi sold under a sheriff's hammer for a few cents an acre in taxes. "You don't mean it?" Mother said, and bit a thread on the shirt she was repairing.

But she cried when her own garden browned before harvest, and when the big-footed sugar mules, Jeff and Andy, broke corn stalks.

Kitchen shelves, lined with glinting Mason jars and

stacks of pewter-colored rims, waited to be filled with food.

"What will we do? What will we do?" Mother cried in the garden. Her skirt dragged in the dust. Tortoise-shell combs dangled, and her bronze hair looped from its bun.

"Don't you worry," Papa said. "I will take care of you. There's sixty-five dollars in Mr. Russell's safe that guarantees it."

And sure enough, we held over and kept right on drawing at the commissary without paying cash. I guess Papa is the hardest working man on this plantation.

Already many have left. Young field hands slip away at night to hop a freight, leaving debt behind. A sad procession of adults departs often. Mr. Russell lends a team to move their goods, and gives each family three dollars in money. Some leave for the three dollars.

Mr. Prudhomme said to Papa that this cuts the draw on the commissary. But hard times are not easy on Mr. Russell. He sickened to the heart one day watching a column leaving Fairhope, going down the dusty road. Mother and I held each other's hands and tried not to cry. Mr. Russell toppled right off the roan. Now, his chest hurts on hot days or when he rides. The doctor drives out weekly. Some field hands slip to Papa black beads for Mr. Russell to string around his neck. Mother fluffs her skirts, scandalized, and orders all unholy charms out of her house. Papa pockets the beads and chuckles as a man will at the notions of those more ignorant than himself, when he has little else to laugh about.

Because Mr. Russell leaves his house only on important occasions—to speak the eulogy for a hand who worked for him, or to meet on settling-up day—ordinary business is conducted with Mr. Prudhomme. Papa looks grim on Saturdays when we draw supplies. He refuses to spend the sixty-five dollars in the commissary safe.

Things are worse on other plantations, and for colored people. There is a song they sing, or kind of moan, in Rosedale and Helena. It comes from alleys or their cafes, in the dark, from behind torn screens. When we are late in town on Saturdays getting Mother's medicine and I hear it, my teeth chatter. I want to hold my ears.

Well, I went to the boss at the commissary store
Folks all starvin', please don't close your door
We want more food and a little time to pay
Boss man laughed and walked away.

Now your landlord comes around when your rent it is due
And if you ain't got his money he'll take your home from you
He'll take your mule and horse, even take the cow
Get off my land, you're no good no how.

The whish of Papa's hand wiping across the floor is interspersed with the tapping of Mother's foot. She wants him out of the kitchen.

I watch Papa dump turnip tops and potato peelings into the flour and salt he's scraped from the floor. Grease pours into the bucket. He says to Mother, "You want to cook this for the dog?" She snatches the scrap bucket and turns to the wood burner. He says to me in a voice that holds a don't-fool-with-me tone, "Now answer me. Why aren't you in school? Isn't that all you've got to do?"

...*all you* have *to do,* I think. Tucking my shoes tight under my dress, I say, "Yessir. I want to go to school."

"I wouldn't let her," Mother cuts in. "Her shoes don't match. One is brown and one is black, and they have cardboard in the soles. We can't spend money on shoes. This year I'll teach her at home. It will be better that way. You'll see, Mr. Lindsey."

"—I don't mind the shoes, Papa."

A white line rims his lips and there is stillness, stillness, as when you wait for dynamite planted under a stump to explode and splinter it. He almost whispers: "I've got sixty-five dollars in the safe. At a tax sale, that would buy a hundred, a hundred twenty, acres. It's a fortune. Now, get yourself to the commissary tomorrow and order that girl the best shoes in the drummer's catalog."

Mother turns from the stove. "We can't, Mr. Lindsey. I need a layette. It is essential."

Heat crackles on the tin roof. The scrap pot simmers behind her.

"My momma never had a layette. I never knew what a

layette was. We'll have to pay something on account if we're to hold over. You have to make do." Papa takes a folded receipt out of the Bible and hands it to Mother. "The commissary can't touch the money without this. See you get a new one."

In silence he picks up the bird gun and a handful of yellow shells.

"—Will you be back for dinner?"

"I'm not hungry," he says out of his pinched face. I am both sorry and glad to hear it. Sorry, because he must be fooling us, and I love him. Glad because there will be more potatoes and turnips for Mother and me.

When shadows lengthen in the afternoon, Papa strides in carrying a gallon bucket of dressed birds. He pokes the shotgun into the corner and drops onto a chair. "This country is about hunted out. The field hands have tapsticked every rabbit. Anybody with a shotgun has skillet-shot the partridges. Lordy, Lordy, I'm tired. Dog and me hunted to the river."

I peek into the bucket. The skinned, long-breasted birds piled inside are not quail or doves. My guess is robins. Papa once told me that you can eat any bird that runs. Quail run. Robins both run and hop. They are between trash and game, depending on the time of the year. Hot Septembers are bad months for eating wild game. I am intently watching when Papa opens his eyes. I say, "Are these—?" Slowly, slowly he lifts a finger to his lips.

I feel like yelling "Robins!" but I am hungry.

"Rachel," Papa says, "pan fry these birds for supper, please ma'am, with gravy. Missy and me can eat a dozen."

Mother says, reaching for the flour tin, "Quail are *such* a delicacy."

During supper I giggle and eat until I choke. Mother jerks up my arm and beats my back. "Missy, don't laugh while you swallow."

Afterward, as she braids her hair and Papa fetches his nightgown, my chin rests on the sleeping room ledge so I can look down and remind everyone of things to do before the lantern flickers out for the night. This involves timing. I must not sound bossy ... Papa's face glows as he bends to the wick, and I yell fast: "You forgot to clean your shotgun." He turns down the oil and puffs. In the dark I say, "You forgot to clean Daddy Lindsey's shotgun!"

He doesn't answer, or do it. Papa makes me real mad. There is no reason to let fingerprints set in rust.

When Papa is near, Mother wears a brave face. Most of the time when he works the fields she gnaws her lip and looks old.

Then one day this significant event occurs. Mother takes a folded sheet of paper out of the *Fannie Farmer Cookbook,* sits nervously at the table, and reads a letter to me. There is about her a glow, as when she has baked a beautiful cake, or the house is sparkling clean and satisfactory. Her skin has the downy texture of a gardenia.

"Dear Mrs. Roosevelt," she reads.

"—Mrs. Roosevelt!" I scream. "You're writing Mrs. Roosevelt?" In my entire life I have never known anyone to think beyond Knowlton or Helena or Rosedale. It is incredibly daring, almost unimaginable, for Mother to send words to a newsreel person in Washington, District of Columbia.

Mother nods and reads:

About a month ago I wrote to you about our situation. Several weeks ago I received a reply to apply to the Welfare Association so that I might receive the aid I need. This I am unable to do.

Please, Mrs. Roosevelt, I do not want charity, only to be trusted until our situation improves. As proof of my sincerity, I send to you in this envelope my dearest possessions to keep as security, a ring my husband gave me when we were married, and my mother's wedding band. Perhaps the value is not high, but they are of worth to me. If you will consider buying the baby clothes, please keep the rings until I send you the money you spent. It is very hard to face bearing a baby we cannot afford to have, and the fact that it is due to arrive soon, and still there is no money for doctor or clothing, does not make it any easier. I have lost my job as school teacher because the school board fired all teachers who are not natives of the state, and all with husbands. I am insisting that my little girl, now thirteen, keep up her schooling and not hire out. As a mother yourself, you will understand this. We must manage—but without charity.

I am a woman of pedigree as good as your own. If you still feel that you do not trust me, it is all right. You do not know me or the family I come from. But if you decide that my word is enough with this security, here is a list of what I will need.

2 shirts, silk and wool, size 4	3 pr. stockings, silk and wool
1 wool bonnet	2 slips—outing flannel
2 pr. wool booties	2 muslin dresses
2 doz. diapers 30 × 30, or 27 × 27	1 sweater
3 straight flannel bands	3 outing flannel nightgowns
1 large blanket (baby), 45" or 50"	

If you will get these things for me, I would rather no one know about it. I promise to repay the cost of the layette as soon as possible. We will all be very grateful to you, and I will be more than happy.

Sincerely yours,
Rachel Lindsey (Mrs.)
Fairhope Plantation
Russell's Landing, Miss.

Mother smooths the paper and lifts her face. "There! Don't you think that should do it? Mrs. Roosevelt will understand. She is the mother of our country."

"—but, Mother." I squirm on the chair. "You can't send your rings."

"I must humble myself. This fate has come upon me and my family because I have been proud. God has punished me by putting us in a situation."

Inside of me there is turmoil. Papa says Mr. Hoover

caused the Depression. Mother says God visited it upon us. Mr. Russell says it's the "little men in spats, who are now raining out of tall buildings." I do not not know what to believe.

"Papa is not going to know about this," Mother says. "I took the rings off weeks ago because my hands swelled. That's the truth." Mother cracks the table drawer. "Here they are. I'm taking them out of the drawer now. Where I send them is my business." She wraps the rings in a square of newspaper and licks a long envelope and a two-cent stamp. "You're not to breathe a word. I've trusted you with my most important secret."

"No ma'am. I never will, ever."

This is a solemn event, a bonding to Mother and to all women as by conjure. If Mother's most important secret is the letter, there are others. If she goes behind her husband's back, it is not wrong. As I become a woman I will manipulate men, too. Papa will be squeezed to a rim of my life occupied by males I care for and manage. My stomach hurts with grief and loss.

Mother sends me daily to the commissary for the mail. The store is a long tunnel, dark with old smoke. A hooped pickle barrel squats to the right of the door, and galvanized tubs of potatoes and onions gleam at the left. Greasy cheese cut geometrically wedges under smudgy glass; broad cutters stand with lifted blades crusted with old rolls of it. Odors of vinegar, cheese, cornmeal, and bed-ticking tickle my nose as I walk past barrels, stacks, bolts of cloth, and twine-tied paper sacks, sniffing mightily.

My eyes light on toothache remedies, Bayer Aspirin, Standback powder, Black Drought, White Wonder salve, and Lydia E. Pinkham compound for ladies. There are lump sulfur, asefetida, epsom salts, camphorated oil, and caster oil. Mops and brooms hang from the ceilings. Tools rank in corners. Canned goods crowd shelves with blue and red labels. Plows, chains, hames, and collars are glimpsed in the warehouse room beyond the back door.

At the end of one counter a paper cutter stands bolted under a brown roll of wrapping paper. On the opposite counter a cash register operated by a crank *dings!* in soprano.

But the most important things in the store are a red ledger with pencil entries under the name of every plantation family, and the squat iron safe. In it Papa's sixty-five dollars lives, reaching its protection over our lives.

The U.S. Post Office occupies the only part of the store barred above counter high. Wanted posters with hopeless faces slew crookedly around a grill. A hungry slot opens its mouth for letters. Tacks pucker to the wall a yellowed picture of an American flag, rippling in perfect regularity, and a new profile of President Roosevelt, who looks cheerful in spite of polio.

Each day when I call out, "Anything for us, Mr. Wilson?" the store clerk sets a green visor over his eyes, unties his apron, and walks into the post office to glance into slots. "Not today, Missy," he says, as he takes off the visor and straps on the apron. He wears a yellow pencil behind the right ear, which is permanently bent outward, and he is keen about bookkeeping. I hope not to see Mr. Prudhomme, whose smile is fuzzy as a caterpillar, and who doubles his body in units until he is *upon* you before you know it.

Going to the store gives me the chance to windowshop in jars of peppermint patties, puffy orange candies shaped like peanuts, and all-day suckers, big-faced as saucers. On this plantation, children are doled a handful of candy on settling day and at Christmas. These are times to anticipate. Wishing-for is longer fun than eating is.

There are no letters for us, but this not bad news to me. When Mother's letter arrives I must spend more time on geometry. Guilt about my joy in Mr. Wilson's calling, "No letter, today, Missy!" only strikes when I see Mother's face. My steps falter. The new shoes drag in the road.

"—Anything?" she calls eagerly from the porch. And again, "Anything?"

We are UDC, DAR, and Presbyterian by way of South Carolina, Mother tells me as if it is nothing. These words are initiation, like the words of Masonry men are secret about.

My initiation comes with glasses of tea and with molasses cookies. Mother's voice floats between us. She says, "Isn't that funny?" or, "Isn't that darling?" I am let know that Mother could *never* have married Papa if her mother had been alive. "Goodness! She would have been scandalized. She'd have gone to pieces." I am let know that Papa is one of the "finest, kindest, most-dear men in the world," and there would have been no justifiable reason for objection. And I am let know Papa is not one of us. "Girls are different," she says. She means more.

Papa is sweet and earnest. I see him through her eyes. They are the wrong ends of spyglasses that make things small and clear. For too long I have been looking at him with magnifying eyes. He starts the load and plows straight down the furrow. Mother hovers and darts into this and that, exploring, testing—aflight!

But this baby is hard on her, and I know that Papa is to blame. She resets the buttons on her largest dress, and scolds Papa for asking her to go out with him in public. She rests in bed. Her face bloats and her legs swell. Two dark eyes sit in her puffing face. She frets that a snake she took fright at will mark the baby. Dust settles over everything.

At night I watch Papa from the sleeping loft. My head is in shadow among books and a trunk. I hide my eyes behind half-closed lashes. He slumps in the bright cone of light made by the lamp. One hand falls open. With the other he pinches the skin of his brow. This is a secret act.

When things are at their worst, and Mother and I have given up hope, the layette from Mrs. Roosevelt arrives.

Everything Mother asked for! I can hardly believe it. Mrs. Roosevelt is truly the mother of our country. The miracle happens while Papa and I have gone to Rosedale for medicine for Mother's swelling. When we return, she is sitting in her rocking chair with things piled around her, cuddling pink booties and a bonnet.

"What in the world, Rachel?" Papa says.

"I wanted to be here! I wanted to be here!" I yell, jumping up and down until my skirt fills with air and mother flashes me a *remember yourself* look.

"Mrs. Roosevelt ..." Mother whispers.

Papa scratches his head. Water-slicked hair layers on it. His face is brown below the gray eyes and pale above them.

"It's Mrs. Roosevelt!" I scream. "She sent the layette Mother asked for! Mother wrote a letter to her!" I fling diapers this way and that, counting. My nose whitens when I overstimulate. Skin of my face stretches tight enough for the bridge to pop right through. "Everything's here! Everything's here!" I yell.

"Well," Papa says. "Well, well. How did this—? You feel better now, Rachel?"

Mother nods, her face chalky. Shadows circle her eyes. She peeps at us from distances within, clever as a pet racoon, and as ungovernable.

Papa shifts his weight. "I'm trying to understand this thing. You asked for charity?"

I pull his hand. "No, Papa. Mother wouldn't do that.

You don't know her at all. She sent Mrs. Roosevelt her rings. She borrowed the money!"

A sick feeling hollows my stomach. Mother's words of initiation weeks ago flash into my mind. She said, *my most important secret.*

Daddy's hand rasps the length of mine, palm to fingertip, as I withdraw from him. My glance holds guilt and defiance.

"Oh, that's how it was. You sent her your rings." Papa doesn't understand, but tight lines in his face relax. No charity has been taken.

"You were never to breathe that, young lady," Mother says tartly, but her expression is relief, as if she ... as if she *wanted* me to tattletell.

This makes no sense. An ache begins in my head. Things are being said other than in words. I want to lie down in the cool and have Mother lay wet rags on my brow. She says I am delicate. This may be the time to go to pieces. I run to the upstairs ladder, sniffling and sobbing. The line between going-to-pieces and carrying-on is narrow. One will get you petted and the other fussed at. I don't always get it right, but this time I escape upstairs to the ragged books that take me to better places. I hold my hopscotch piece, a green, flat plug of glass from the bottom of a Coca-Cola bottle. Sniffles and sobs escape me. They are real. I don't know why. We are all nervous from the heat.

A male's deep voice drifts from below. "Near as I can figure, we didn't make but forty pounds of lint to the acre. The drought just took it. But we'll be all right.

We're better off than most." Papa chuckles. "At least, we're not eating snakes. Now that you have this layette, every worry is off my mind. I just hate you put up your rings. It don't sound real motherly of Miz Roosevelt to take them."

I peep over the side. Mother holds up a bonnet. "She sent pink."

"—I wonder what she does with folks's valuables."

"Mr. Russell's coming! Mr. Russell's coming!" I yell. Way off—so far it appears as an ant on a road as wide as darning thread—the Ford phaeton Mr. Russell now rides in wends its way across the plantation.

Taffeta rustles as Mother switches to the window. It is Sunday, and she wears her only black dress with a new white collar. One finger pokes between the pages of the Bible in her hand.

Papa's stockinged feet hit the floor. It is his only day of rest. Sunday is also the only afternoon during crop-gathering a man can talk business without interfering with work.

Of course, on Sunday he cannot finalize a transaction unless he is an infidel.

"What time is it?" Papa says. He inspects Daddy Lindsey's railroad watch on the bedside table. "—two-thirty?" He treads the floor softly, and leans behind mother. "I don't see anything."

"There's nothing to see," Mother declares.

Chug ... chug ... chug. The distant motor speaks like a

tiny frog in a cow-track puddle. Only my ears are new enough to hear it. "Yessir, this is the day!" I sing out. "Mr. Russell's coming."

All week we have waited. No, a week and a half, each day eyeing the calendar with the picture of Jesus riding a cloud and the invitation to trust your loved ones to Henry Mortuary. Cotton is picked and packed into field sheds. Nubbins pile low in the crib. Papa has said to me, "Quit your fretting. It will rain when it will rain. And Mr. Russell will come when he will come."

Papa wanders away from the window and sits on the bed. He picks up the *Commercial Appeal* and puts it down. He falls back on the stiff cornshuck mattress mother needs for her back, and stretches.

"Missy," Mother says, "I won't have you crying wolf. No more of it."

"Yes ma'am. The car is close enough so that you can see it now." I say this sweet as sugar, and without pause.

"Mr. Lindsey, put on your shoes." Mother is the only woman on the plantation to call her husband "Mr." to his face unless Mrs. Russell does. We are not acquainted with her.

Papa reaches for hightops, pulls down his shirt, and adjusts his suspenders. Mother tries to wet-comb his bobbing head as he laces the shoes. "Be still. Be still, sir!" she fusses.

Chug, chug, chug. The rapid-fire noise is audible now to grown-ups. Papa lifts his head. "Listen to that motor," he says.

Mr. Russell usually has the phaeton started by a dash of gasoline in the carburetor, and a turn of the crank in front. His driver does that, then rushes behind to pour five-cent kerosene into the tank. Combustion with kerosene is slow. The car lurches, belching plumes of white smoke. But this day an oily contentment sounds from the motor.

"Look!" I yell.

"Quit smudging that window, Missy, unless you want to scrub it."

My mouth falls open in an exaggerated way to show surprise. My nose turns white. "It's Mr. Prudhomme."

"What?"

"—It's Mr. Prudhomme. Mr. Russell didn't come."

"Hell." Papa jerks his suspenders. "What does *he* want."

"Mr. Lind-sey!" Mother exclaims. "Remember yourself."

Heavy footfalls echo as Papa stalks to the door. He turns. "Rachel, I don't have time for such as that … just don't have time for it. Here's this jake-leg business manager instead of Mr. Russell."

Bang goes the screen door and I jump, though I see it falling. We are all nervous from the heat.

Mother stands still. I ease to the front window where I can peek between curtains. Broad'us is driving, reared back in the front seat on the black leather. Sleeves roll to the elbows on his fat arms, and a felt hat with four matches stuck in the band cocks on his head. He's looking proud because he doesn't have to jump back and forth between the crank and kerosene can to keep the phaeton rolling.

"Turn that motor off," Mr. Prudhomme orders. A

striped shirt under a fuzzy vest and loud-spotted tie say he does not work in the fields. The shirt collar cuts into his puffy neck. Hair prickles on the sides of his head and skin shines through, like on a hog. The white line shaved around his ears projects them into gristly prominence Big hands, red from scrubbing old grime under the skin, are folded on a ledger. At the commissary he calls for a basin of hot water and a towel at noon and at 4:30. I do not know what the washing is for because he never gets dirty.

The motor dies. Prudhomme says from the back of the car, "Good afternoon, Lindsey." He has weighed the distance between Lee and Lindsey, you can tell.

Broad'us leans on the wheel, nods, and says, " 'Mist Lee ..."

"Hey. How're y'all," Papa says.

Broad'us pulls down the greasy hat. His eyes flutter in a sleepy way, and soon his broad chin rests on the blue shirt.

I like colored people's manners, and their eyes—large and soft, and most of the time, kind. My eyes squinch to blue beads when I am angry. They burn through the curtain now because Mr. Prudhomme sits like a school principal, talking to Papa.

Mother brushes past me, goes onto the porch, and leans against the door. If she is concerned about Mr. Pruhomme seeing her pregnant, it does not show.

"How do', Miz Lindsey." Prudhomme flicks a glance, nods, but does not lift the hat. Broad'us says nothing; he is not here.

"What can I do for you?" Papa's tone pops like sheets drying in March wind. Ordinarily, he would ask a Sunday visitor into the house for a glass of tea.

Heat shimmers in the yard, on the car radiator, between the men. They squint under hat brims.

"—Would you like something refreshing to drink, Mr. Prudhomme?" Mother's voice floats, a chunk of ice in a sunny pond.

"Nome, nome." The business manager removes his hat, twirls it by the brim, and wipes his brow with a sleeve. "I'm just here on a matter of business."

Mother does not excuse herself. Silence grows.

"I don't mean to be short." Papa smiles. "—but all of my arrangements are with Mr. Russell."

Prudhomme twirls the hat. He talks into it. "I'm truly sorry to tell you, but Mr. Russell is on his death bed. Yessir, he is in death's agony. He rasps for breath all through the house."

Mother's hand crawls to her throat. Papa stands very still; his mouth hangs a little open. He listens like a woodsman to the far off sound of something coming.

"The children have been called. Father Robertson is there." Mr. Prudhomme sighs. "Mrs. Russell called me up to the big house and passed the whip. That's the long and short of it."

He opens the ledger. "Because the old man took special interest in you, I've drove out to say how things stand." He licks his thumb and turns a blue-lined page. "You made five hundred pounds of lint." Papa nods. "—At five cents a pound." Papa nods. "—That's twenty-five dollars, with your share twelve-fifty. Against that you've got a draw of forty-seven-fifty down at the commissary, and—"

"—and," Papa says, "I've got sixty-five dollars in cash."

"—less eight-fifty for one pair of girl's shoes, and forty-five dollars for one layette."

"One layette?" Papa has heard something way off, and now it is upon him, without making a sound coming. It is bigger than he thought.

"Yessir-ree. Your receipt shows two deductions for those amounts signed by Mrs. Lindsey. First class goods. That right?"

"Yes, Mr. Prudhomme." Mother's voice floats from a distance.

"What?" Papa says.

"The layette, Mr. Lindsey," Mother says.

"Sure, sure." Papa looks like a throat-cut hog that doesn't yet know it's dead.

"—I'll need that receipt, signed over."

Mother sweeps into the house and brings it. Papa signs the back of the creased paper and hands it to him.

That is all. Nothing big. Just a name signed on a piece of paper, and the security Papa bragged on is gone. Neither of my parents look at each other. Something hot floods my stomach and throat. Kicking and screaming would help, but I practice smiling. My eyes are blue dots reflected in the glass, and my nose is white as fresh bone.

Prudhomme folds the ledger. "Next year we furnish potatoes, beans, salt, and fatback. Seventy-five dollar limit."

"Uh, can the balance hold over?"

"Wish we could ... wish we could. Ordinarily, that's what we'd do. Yessir, that's what we'd do. Only way to get the furnish back. Now, you got to settle up."

Papa looks bewildered.

"—There's talk of this AAA. The president wants Congress to pay not to grow crops."

"Us?"

He brays a laugh. "Not hardly ... owners. If it passes, the fewer folks, and the less land plowed the better." He looks across the burned fields. "That's the long and short of it."

Papa stiffens. "We had it in mind to move."

"Fine. If you want to leave, the sheriff can set aside bedding and other exempt stuff." Prudhomme talks to the inside of his hat. "We got to replevy all the cotton and corn. You understand? We got to distrain for tools and supplies. You understand? Miz Russell won't stop you leaving, 'cause like I say, it's a losing proposition." He wipes his face with a handkerchief. He has freckled hands. There is silence from us.

"—Whatever's left of the debt after the sale, you're bound by law for." He sighs. "I reckon we got to get back the baby clothes."

"The hell you will. No-way they were furnish! The price of them came out of my cash money."

Prudhomme glances up. The eyes in his long face are impenetrable, chocolate colored. "Right." He looks relieved. "Broad'us, start up!"

Broad'us steps out and cranks the car. It putters contentedly.

Prudhomme calls over the motor, "Business is business." The felt hat sits squarely on his young, peeled head.

I think of Mr. Russell, big as Nathan Bedford Forrest on the roan, thin shanks around the saddle skirts, black hightopped shoes poking into stirrups, and his dropsical face smiling down. I will not look at his coffin. No, I will shut my eyes when it passes. By dying he has betrayed us.

When Mr. Prudhomme is gone, Mother sweeps into the house with Papa close behind. I ease outside and draw hopscotch squares in the dirt beside the window. Hopscotch is a silent game.

"I expected money from my sister or Mrs. Roosevelt," Mother says from the kitchen. "It was to be a temporary charge. How could they do me so!"

Papa says, "It was crazy, Rachel. I'm not gonna' say too much because if you were a man, I'd beat hell out of you."

"Mr. Lindsey! Don't you dare speak to me that way!" Mother cries.

"Somebody should'of took a stick to you long ago," he declares.

But that night, below in the dark, he rumbles in that voice that cannot whisper, "You did wrong, but hard times don't make anybody better. They make everybody little." He coughs. "I even—it gets to where a biscuit on the platter seems bigger to me than anything. That's the truth. And that's all I want to say."

There is silence for maybe a minute. Mother's voice comes softly from their bed, "Not you, Lee ... not you, ever. Don't you know I've seen you work through dinner rather than eat when there is just enough for Rachel and me? I do love you, in my way. You must remember that and forgive me, always."

My head sinks behind the ledge of the sleeping loft. I burn with shame to hear her humble voice. My father is a liar. We have not all gone crazy. I examine my conscience and can find no fault. Never have I wanted his food, except when we have dessert. I cannot believe he would want mine. He has made Mother feel like a black dog. She didn't make all the commissary charges. She only charged a layette until her own money came. She only wanted one little thing to be right again.

Security is nothing if it comes from a man. I wrap my arms around my sides, and hold myself, and rock in the dark because Missy Lindsey is all I can count on in this world.

My father has fitted oak to hickory to oak, like a woman backing dress material, in making a fine cart. Oak forms the bed. Persimmon hubs cup the axles. Hickory axles connect the hubs and form the wheel spokes. Every wood on the plantation except pecan carries in its grain a special carpentry use. God blessed pecan trees to be fruitful, and made them brittle. Otherwise people would cut pecan trees for ordinary use.

From the end of the wagon-tree, shoulder straps are attached to enable my father to balance the pull. With canvas stretched on the hoops above the bed, the cart looks like a miniature covered wagon

I want to address my father as Mr. Lindsey, but do not think I may. There is cool politeness in Mr. Lindsey, and room to advance if ever I feel friendly. I call him nothing. Resentment settles into my bones. It is not fair to blame everything on him, but that doesn't matter.

Mother totters about, thick and awkward, accepting our attentions, but present only in body. She did not watch our possessions being sold. She did not attend when neighbor-women packed bedding, furniture, pots, and pans into a borrowed wagon hitched behind borrowed mules. She has retired into a little room in her mind until things take a turn for the better.

It was exciting at first to think of moving … to see the cart being built and the wagon loaded. It was wrong, but I could not help it. My eyes dilated to take in all of it. But we have no place to go. The roads, people say at church, are filled with cars and wagons and carts such as ours. Farmers without farms dream of Oregon or California. I wonder where we will sleep tonight.

Heat presses my head unrelentingly. It makes me feel like a garden stake being pushed from the top into thick mud. Boards of the wagon seat cut off the circulation in the backs of my legs. Lines to the mules' bits threaded between my fingers bulge them apart. Soft things thrust against my stomach walls. I wonder if this is what it feels like to feel pregnant.

Behind me, in a basket on the wagon bed, are the gifts of other farm families. The basket holds ten sweet potatoes, a syrup bucket of clabber milk, a small jar of butter, a pan of biscuits, and a bottle of new-cooked medicine to settle Mother's stomach.

Mother sits on the wagon seat beside me, dressed in black. Far down the plantation road stand rows of cabins occupied by field hands. More distantly, just dots across the flat distance of a mile, are the single houses of sharecroppers. People are on the porches, watching. They must be sad to see a lady like Mother brought low. Bidding them good-bye for her and driving the team are my jobs. I am not as delicate as she.

As if he has read my mind, my father calls, "Let's go, Missy. Don't sit there like a block of sugar." He loops the rope harness attached to the cart shaft over his shoulders, and leans into the load. The cart starts, making wheel trails in the dust. He does not look large, hitched to a cart

"Rattle the lines and cluck," he shouts, "and keep those mules off my heels."

Dog plods slowly, then turns to watch. Usually she races ahead, yo-yoing between wagon and adventure. Mother and I say nothing. Father makes all of the noise. He is somebody who would shout in a funeral procession, I think.

I squint down the plantation road through blinding sunlight, across a flat, unreal world. Harness creaks. Dust grinds under iron wheel rims. The sweet, thick odor of mules envelops us.

At the first row of houses people stroll out and stand in yards, or beside the road. Some grin and call shyly, "Bye Mist' Lee ... bye y'all," or, "Y'all do good!" like a prayer. Some say nothing, fear in their eyes, as if our going tells their future.

I hear father's voice drift back: "Jake ... Billy ... Betty Jo ... y'all take care, now! Keep your plow lines straight!" He must be grinning. I see him turn his head and wave, as much as the load will allow. My nod and smile are genteel, for Mother. It is good that I have practiced smiling in all kinds of moods.

And then we are clear of the cabins. Voices fall silent. Dog comes to slink beside the wagon. The road narrows ahead, and there is nothing to see but field after field of stunted cotton and in the distance huge trees, stark in death for lack of water and sustenance.

The smile trembles on my lips. "Mother," my voice quavers, "help me. I'm scared. Please talk to me." But Mother is remote, in the little room in her mind where no one can follow.

I try to think of the protections against the world packed into our wagon and cart: two mattresses, a well rope and bucket, rub board, six jars of canned berries, a side of bacon, five hens, a turning plow, ax, file, gourd dipper, cedar water bucket, wash pan, black skillet and pot, six blue granite plates, Mother's coin-silver spoons, her four settings of china, our clothes, twenty-seven books, a grinding of meal in a fertilizer sack, Daddy Lindsey's shotgun, and a rocking chair. We are not really poor. Still, gloom settles over me.

After a little distance father begins to sing "Only One Step More" in a voice that treads deep into bass. Hair prickles my neck the way it does when I read truth and beauty in poetry, hear *Stars and Stripes Forever* by Mr. Sousa, or see the American flag snap in wind. Papa sings:

> *I have known a life of sorrow, I have borne a heavy load,*
> *Hoping for a glad tomorrow, As I walk this rocky road;*
> *Soon my journey will be ended, And my cares will be o'er,*
> *Soon the hill will be ascended; It is only One Step More.*

And then he goes deeper for the refrain. "One Step More!" he rumbles. "One Step More ..."

The mules perk ears, and step up. Dog runs out from under the wagon. I shiver and shake, every hair on my head prickling. "Mother," I say, "just listen to that man sing."

She cannot hear me from that distant room, but he—ahead, leading us—he can hear. There is nothing behind us to hold on to. There is only the road ahead. I lift my faltering alto voice to join his.

My Father's Voice, Lifting

BODY PARTS—A MEMORY OF 1944

Let me tell you how I fell in love with Susie.

Mr. Sardo, our office manager, stood at the front edge of her desk the first day she came to work at Artie's Print Shop. If the desk top were the blade of a paper cutter like the one in the back shop, he would have been the right height for beheading. Bingo! Into the basket. He is a perfectly formed midget, who wears three-piece suits with a gold watch chain, crisp white shirts, built-up shoes, and his hair slicked down with Rose Oil.

That day he explained the office system and the flow of work, cocked back in shiny black Buster Brown shoes, with his thumbs in his vest pockets. He looked up at Susie from the level of her pencil jar and dictionary.

Out of the periphery, his quick eyes caught me doing nothing. "Billy, come explain how we use photography in the work," he ordered in his cheery way.

In Susie's expression, when she looked at me over the top of his head, there was no mirth. She did not disparage in her mind a little man who could have gotten a job yelling, "CALL FOR PHILIP MORRIS!" or have traveled with Ringling Brothers Circus as Tom Thumb. There is natural sweetness in her.

I scooched my chair close and talked in my low register about emulsions, ASC numbers, and lenses. Her eyes shined resiny as heart pine. She watched me for ten minutes with absolute attention. I felt as if I were taking Holy Communion with her. Then she laughed at herself. "Billy, this is all beyond my register. Science is like a silent dog whistle to me. You are tootling a message I am not getting. You must help me another day." She touched my shoulder and then excused herself.

Susie walks in a maddening way. She cannot control the rampant femaleness of her hips and thighs. My shoulder and heart burned where she touched them. And my hong, which seems wired to my heart.

Perhaps she spoke in that original simile by accident, I told myself. I loomed around her desk, smiling spasmodically, whenever I was free of work. I smile spasmodically when terribly nervous, not otherwise.

"Go away!" she hissed, shooing me like a chicken. "I have to work, Billy, or I will lose my job."

I lust for your talk, I said inside myself. *I want to possess your verbs and body.*

Susie and Gladys, a payroll clerk, are the only two girls in the office. Susie's job is to examine for spelling and punctuation errors the flotsam and jetsam of manuscripts which Artie's Print Shop of Montgomery, Alabama, turns into vanity books, pamphlets, catalogs, mailing pieces, trade magazines, and a monthly newspaper, the *Southern Farmer*. She majored in English at Montevallo College, and has the superiority about her of English majors who have read books that you have not. They possess this superiority even if they are starving while teaching in high schools.

I thought it was self-sacrificing of Susie to work at Artie's. She was meant to be an indulged woman whose only duties would be to charm her husband with words and wreak sex upon his body—or have a career in book publishing in far-off, wondrous New York City. She favored us with her presence.

This was not everyone's opinion. Harold, our master printer, said she earned no more than his apprentice, a lout named Bewick Coulter, and was not worth that. He said she was full of highfalutin crap.

Harold happened to be in the office to complain about the calendering of the last shipment of paper the day that Susie did not come to work because of a cold. A tight printer's cap made of a folded newspaper clung to Harold's head. His belly jounced in a skimpy T-shirt. "Hubba! Hubba!" he yelled. "Susie's at home alone? I'll go! Send me, coach!" He flopped his thick arms and hopped in a way he thought amusing. God knows, I hated Harold Ray … his blue, inky claws … his arms jiggling in ropes of fat and muscle … his eyes rolling crazily. He was altogether loathsome in his soul.

Mr. Sardo said in his high, midget voice, while staring

commandingly at Harold's belt buckle, "I'm sending Billy." He walked away snappily, as if that were that.

Susie wore a housecoat to the door. It swept the floor, a purple, passionate thing with two rows of buttons. Maybe under the buttons it zipped. Maybe under it she didn't have anything on.

I handed the manuscripts around the door and mumbled, "I've got to get back to work. Hope you feel better."

"No! Don't go, Billy. I feel absolutely deserted." She tugged my sleeve.

After I hobbled inside she fixed two cups of cocoa and chattered away. I sat on the edge of her couch holding a book in my lap. She sat down beside me and showed me pictures of her parents and brother in a picture album. It was wine colored with a gold rope framing the cover, and a gold B-24 embossed upon it. That was a popular cover wherever Army Air Force bases were located. We were at war with Japan.

Susie and I sat together and held the album upon our laps. I was busy thinking of icebergs and polar bears and snow in order not to visualize naked legs, so I didn't hear much she said. Making polite conversation is just making the right sounds, anyway. It doesn't require that your brain be functioning. And then Susie said something about photographers, and I stopped grinning. It even took my mind off her body.

"You can tell a lot about photographers by the photographs they take," she said. She pointed to a picture of a family group. "Unimaginative photographers always pose people facing the camera. Mean photographers catch a girl off guard with her hair in rollers or both eyes shut. Insecure photographers want smiles. 'Please smile,' they beg. 'Say cheese.'"

I stared at her. "Say that again, please."

She blushed. "This terrible cold—"

"No! It's not your cold. You're talking fine. I can hardly tell you have a stuffed nose. Honest. It's just—"

"What, Billy?"

"—that I'm a photographer and I never heard that, never thought of it, even. It's true. I know it's true because it vibrates inside my chest like a bell."

She smiled. "You're a funny boy."

And that is how I knew Susie was the girl for me. What if she was six years older? You do not hear the truth every day. You do not hear it every week or every month. When you hear it you must mark that as an exceptional moment, and the person who speaks it as exceptional. Even a little truth is a great gift.

Our science teacher showed a film one day. It was of salmon returning to the streams where they were hatched. They jumped rocks and banged their pink and green scales away. Their jaws hooked and grew too crooked for them to feed. Eventually, all of them died. It didn't matter. The image of salmon leaping and wiggling high in the air, fighting their way upstream is engraved on my mind. It is the truest thing I ever witnessed. The desire to drive up a channel, and poetry, are the strongest forces in the world.

Lately, I have begun to notice Gladys. She eats Goo-Goo Clusters delicately and chews ice from a Coke cup without being offensive. The hard plumpness of her bosom and bottom drives my hong wild. Her lips slide back when she sees me to display sharp teeth the nearly transparent gray of raw rice. I want her to nip me. She is plumper than Susie and heavier in the thighs. I know because her stockings rub together. I have acute hearing for womanly sounds.

Gladys wears perfume that makes me dizzy. She tells me with eyes chocolate as Goo-Goo Clusters that she can deny me nothing. Already, she has surrendered. She turned aside her face and became very still while I lifted her hand from the ledger and saw that Susie earns a dollar fifteen an hour. That was an abandonment of responsibility, and Gladys is a good person. It grieved her.

I stop often by Gladys's desk when Susie is in the ladies' room or Mr. Sardo's office. Her bosoms point sharp as equilateral triangles. All girls get themselves rigged like shark fins, but *Gladys*—Gladys has horizontal mountains. She touches my arm as we talk. I don't touch her in return because my hong would leap into an erection disloyal to Susie. It has no conscience at all. I do not understand how it can want other women when my heart loves only Susie. Except for a small piece of my mind, I

Body Parts—A Memory of 1944

am as out of control as that male lion in the zoo on Vandiver Street that paces, wheels, paces, and roars, paces, wheels, paces, and roars. Over and over, all day. The keepers poke raw meat to it with a stick. It slaps food away, but it would die to screw.

I have no hope of taking Susie to the office picnic, but Gladys is only three years older than I am, not six. I am a little afraid of her because if I get her alone, I do not know if I can count on her to stop me. I may not know everything a man is supposed to.

Sex is not just following your hong. I learned that from Dr. Lucian Oates's book, mailed to me in a plain brown wrapper. Once I thought sex was natural. I thought men did it the way bulls do, except on beds and car seats. That is not so. That is low-class sex. The man must think, think, all the time. There are buttons to hit on women. There is a special way to do every act. Women get bored and smoke a cigarette on you, or go frigid if you do not do everything right and in correct order. Screwing is a terrible responsibility.

What a cold and callous bastard I am! What I have not mentioned is that there is a war going on. My very own father is overseas fighting Japs, while I yap on about an office picnic.

When the Japs attacked Pearl Harbor I was sitting in a swing shooting wasps with a Daisy BB gun. My father put on his uniform and rushed to Maxwell Field to volunteer for overseas duty. My mother cried and threatened to shoot him in the leg. He talked her out of that. She telephoned her two sisters to come live with us.

A *National Geographic* map on my bedroom wall shows the islands of the Pacific. Red pins mark the territory we hold, and yellow the Japs'. The heaviness of the war hangs over us every day. We save tin cans, and roll tinfoil, and have victory chickens in the backyard. I will enlist in the Marines when I am seventeen. And yet there is a different world, which is real, too. It is made up of a midget, a broken-backed mail room foreman, a fat printer with high blood pressure, two women, an old man, two callow boys, and various misfits and war rejects who work part-time at Artie's Print Shop in the summer of 1944.

If there is a man I admire in my everyday world it is Raymond, foreman of the mail room. I sense that he is going to show me how to become a man. God knows, they are in short supply. If it were not for Sir Walter Scott and Robert E. Lee and Captain Colin Kelly and Lou Gehrig, I would not have any idea.

I live with three women, my mother and her two sisters. They are not decrepit but they are in their thirties, getting on. They did not have a brother, and only my mother got married. They do not know anything about being a man—I mean *anything*.

My aunts seem to work a minute or two every day. When they are not at work they are at home directing me. Three women with nothing to do but stick their heads out of the windows, spy on you, and yell, will pretty well yell the initiative and manhood out of you. *Billy-what-are-you-doing* is what I think my name is.

My brother doesn't take up any of their attention. He is five and wears an angelic expression even while smashing frogs between bricks. He calls this making flat frogs. It is his work for the summer. But I am the one they whisper about, the one in the dangerous age.

I have fallen into blackness among these women. I have lost my greed for peach cobbler, banana pudding, and books. I am too dispirited to complain about cutting an acre of grass with a push mower after five and a half days' work at Artie's. My mother says I must have mono.

I am sad to think that Susie must someday join the ranks of these inflicters of wretchedness. But she must. It is in her hormones. Women get more-so with age.

I hope to God my dad comes home to rescue me. Mother needs rescue, too. She is befuddled by the harpies. Like Ulysses's old dog, I will lift my grizzled head to greet him. I hope he comes in swinging a samurai sword and breaks some glasses. I hope he scuffs the triple waxed floors with his boots, cleats mud onto the rugs, and fingerprints the door facings. When he sees the spiritless thing they have made of me, I hope he drives the harpies from the castle.

When the *Southern Farmer* has been printed I work in the mail room as a wrapper. Raymond is foreman there. He arrives at work at 7:50 A.M., walking into the editorial offices with languid grace. He favors white Arrow shirts with long pointed collars and folded cuffs with gold-plated links. The trousers of his gray or navy tropical worsted suits are pleated and cuffed in spite of the wartime style of no cuffs. The jackets fit loosely. His black shoes shine brightly, and his socks hook to garters so that you never see any white meat. He changes from suit to clean khakis before work, but he never steps outside the building—even for a cup of coffee—without putting on the suit.

He is slender and long-faced like Fred Astaire, except that Raymond's jaw and back were broken when he was run over as a kid. His dark blond hair sticks tight to his skull. One eye is smaller than the other. None of this matters unless you study him feature by feature. The impression he gives is grace and worldly knowledge and command.

It is hot and humid under the tin roof where we work. Our work space is thirty by fifteen, lined with shiny metal tables on each long side. At the far end of the room glimmer two tall, finger-smudged windows, one with the sash raised, and the other blocked by a jointed sliding board which extends over State Street. Down the sliding board each month, and into the open doored mail trucks, goes the end product of our work: one million tabloid newspapers, yellow-labeled, wrapped in brown bundles, packed in dirty gray sacks.

At 7:55 Raymond limps to his work station and slips bicycle clips around the sleeves of his white shirt. He rubs glycerine into the fingertips of his left hand, stretches a black rubber guard over his right thumb, checks the paste reservoir of his clipper, and bumps the blade to clear it.

Each of us responds in our own way. Mr. Caudle's hands shake as he shuffles a stack of newspapers. In my position, far down the shining counter, I repeatedly crack my knuckles. It is a habit I have given up except in extreme emergencies such as waiting for Raymond to begin work. Melvin, another operator, gushes smoke from his nostrils, grinds a Lucky under his heel, and lounges to his position. The operators lift their clippers. We wrappers lean forward expectantly.

I have never seen a faster operator than Raymond, and I hope never to wrap behind one. In a swoop, he gathers two feet of newspapers from a waist-high stack, ruffles them in one bump for easier feeding, and plops them onto the counter. His left hand feeds single newspapers. His right hand strokes the clipper roller and bumps the blade, all of this simultaneously and with such speed that his thumb would blister within an hour except for the rubber guard.

Raymond's labels never paste over text or photographs in the sloppy way Melvin's do. His attention to detail, lavish expenditure of energy, and determination to be the best operator in the city affect us all. We would follow Raymond anywhere, even in an assault upon Japan.

Having an office picnic is not Raymond's idea but

Harold's. I have no respect for Harold. He blows cigarette smoke on me, carries a sneak pistol about his person, and talks about screwing prostitutes. No one of character would screw a prostitute unless he was berserk for it or suffering life-threatening aloneness. I have looked into the faces of hookers on State Street. Because thousands of Army Air Corps men are stationed at Maxwell Field, Montgomery attracts girls from everywhere. They seem to live at a distance from their bodies. You could do it with one of the fresher ones, but your mind would hate it. The younger they are, they more business they get. Men are lining up fifty deep around some houses. Screwing one of those girls would be like honging a sewer.

I may do that. I may actually do that. I will give up hoping for love when I am about forty and hong a sewer. My Boy Scout senior patrol leader, who is high minded as well as practical, advised us never to do it with a girl we'd mind marrying. "Why?" I asked. Every boy's face turned toward me, smiling. "She might get PG," the patrol leader explained patiently, "and you would have to get married."

Ha! I would do it with any nice girl who was catatonic for thirty seconds. I would do it with Mary Belle Henshaw, who is acne pits and blushes from earlobe to earlobe. I would do it with gargantuan Laverne Dowdy Piggot, who when reading a part at school in *The Merchant of Venice,* was dumb enough to say, "Stick me, sperm me," instead of "Stick me, spurn me."

I do not know why I say such things. I love only Susie but I get the fetid crazies. In the mail room there are two hundred fifty-three clippings on the walls showing naked women, or women in bathing suits so tight the elastic cuts into their thighs and bosoms. None of the real women who work downstairs in editorial will come up here. I don't blame them. Some sex-crazed fiend, who was once an innocent boy, might lurch from behind the mail sacks and hong them before he knew it.

Every week Melvin brings a newly scissored stack of pin-ups. He has already papered all the walls. Only the best of the new girls can be displayed in a few remaining bare spots. Raymond is the judge.

He hitches to the stack of mail sacks, dragging his bad leg, and sits to consider the clippings. Melvin rubs his hands. He leers and croons. "Look at them boobs, Raymond. How'd you like a little of that, Raymond?"

Raymond says in a soft voice, without looking up, "I think I did, two years ago in Nashville."

This is a high moment. Raymond seldom says anything about women I can hear, although I have damaged fine ears by straining them. My ignorant laughter rings louder than anyone's.

Raymond studies the pictures with his different sized eyes. He cocks an eyebrow. "This one. She's got class."

Melvin jumps to the pot of white glue, smears a gob of it on the wall, and presses the image to it.

Melvin doesn't have a girl. I can't understand that. My

mother and the harpies say that Harold and Melvin are white trash, not poor-but-nice like us. I thought white trash girls did it all the time. I thought they did it with their brothers and daddies, and in dirty carnivals with ponies. Melvin surely must know some white-trash girls.

All the girls are wild about Raymond. Every Monday he limps into the office smiling that certain smile. He's pale and worn out. He's used up. My mother says Raymond looks dissipated.

Melvin listens at the top of the stairs that lead to the mail room for the *thunk* of Raymond's bad foot on the steps. When he enters the door Melvin yells, "Boy-oh-boy. You done it again. Tell me … tell me."

Before the day is over they are in a corner. Raymond whispers to Melvin while Mr. Caudle jabbers in my ear about fishing. Raymond glances over Melvin's shoulder to keep me located. There is a conspiracy to keep me in ignorance. The reason is either that my dad is editor-in-chief, although away fighting Japanese, or Raymond and Melvin have correctly judged the wrath of the harpies.

The harpies want to keep me a boy. They kept me from shaving until fuzz hung heavy upon me. I looked like a golden gorilla. My mother bought me knickers until I was the last boy in America wearing them. When war came the manufacturers of America said, "No. We will not manufacture knickers for one boy in Alabama. It is too great a strain upon us. Everyone must wear pleatless, cuffless trousers and save tin cans to win the war."

I am six-feet-two at fifteen and a half. My body is bony, with stringy muscles upon it. The harpies say I have *pl-enty* of time to grow up, that I am only a boy. In two years I will enlist in the Marines. Thirty-five hundred Americans died on Saipan. This is on my mind.

I am eager to do my part in any manly undertaking. Sometimes I load newspaper sacks onto the slide. The sacks weigh between thirty-five and ninety pounds, depending on how tightly they are packed. As the trucks are loaded, the men play a game of surprise burn-out. A feeder stands on the filled mail sacks, and throws them to the slide man. Unexpectedly, he will throw a hard one. The slide man must catch each sack and feed it onto the slide before the next arrives.

My hands are fast. If a rattlesnake fell out of my medicine cabinet like a toothpaste tube, I would catch that sucker in a grip of iron before my mind could say "Take heed." But my muscles are not strong enough to carry out commands when the sacks are heavy.

While I lift a ninety-pounder onto the slide, Melvin throws a forty-pounder, hard, from the top of the stack. I do not cry out, but I am knocked through the window. They drag me inside by my feet.

The next day I mow the grass at home with one shoulder hanging low. It is useless to complain to women supervisors that your collarbone is broken when they cannot wait for you to finish mowing, so they can outfit you with sewing scissors for trimming sidewalk edges.

Body Parts—A Memory of 1944

The collarbone grows back crooked, but I learn that too late to get any good out of it by moaning among the harpies. In every jacket and shirt I buy, the right hand hangs low. That sucker nearly touches my knee.

A print shop whittles you down. Bewick Coulter is missing two fingertips a paper folder ate. Both of the deaf and dumb Linotype operators have parchment-looking burn scars crackling upon their arms from squirts of molten metal. The big Hoe press has crushed the top muscle of Harold's forearm, where the tattooed dancing girl's thing is. He cannot make her wiggle by gripping his fist, and it is a grief to him. The journeyman printer hobbles on account of the slippage of a newsprint roll he was peaveying into position. Acrid gasses from melting antimony and tin and lead in the unvented composition room will give you a throbbing headache. Some people who do this work act crazy.

In the mail room I work until sweat drips from my chin, my fingers stiffen with dried paste, and my starched work shirts wilt. Only then will Raymond shake a Lucky from his pack, turn up the radio, and sit for five minutes beside the airless window. His smoke drifts into the room, constricting my lungs while I rest.

He has the timing of an actor. With his angular grace and long-faced good looks, he reminds me of the second lead in a musical comedy. He is not crazy like the men who work with molten metal. A lively intelligence brightens his eyes. He regards me with amusement. A thin hand cradles his crooked jaw. He looks away, shakes his head, and murmurs to someone in the wings, my shadow, maybe, "You'll never make it, son. You'd better bunt."

At this praise I grin like a fool.

Boy Scouting and the *Boy Scout Handbook* have had a great influence upon me. Except for a fuzzy warning against nameless unmanly practices which deplete a fellow's strength and wreck his moral character, the handbook is filled with useful information. It is all very specific.

My favorite part is how you can pick up a dead dog off the roadside, skin that sucker, cure his hide, and make a dandy drum head. There is a picture of a laced drum with feathers dangling, which you get off of a turkey. You use another feather to paint a vermilion, jagged line for decoration.

The handbook says a boy surviving in the wilderness must kill and eat frogs, song birds, snakes, mice, and stray cats or dogs. One day after reading this, I went out of the house in a dream involving starvation and shot a mockingbird with a BB gun. I brought him home in a rusty tomato can to cook.

One of the harpies looked into the can and commenced wailing. My mother cried. By the time they got through with me, I nearly bawled, too. Shooting a mockingbird is the next thing to shooting a person, they said.

Well, I shot that sucker in the gray throat right in midsong. He nose-dived into a thorn bush the way a Zero would plunge into the Pacific. I didn't feel a thing at the time but awe and power. I had convinced myself that I was starving, and that I was going to eat that bird. Get this. I had convinced myself that *my mother* was going to cook it.

I am not so much evil as thoughtless. My imagination gets loose and wild in the vacuum created by thoughtlessness and lack of information. Take condoms.

I wish the *Boy Scout Handbook* gave instructions about how to use rubbers. I would like to be prepared. The closer this picnic gets the more nervous I become.

Am I really expected to walk into a gleamy drug store among women, who always seem to be standing around the pharmacist, and say in this voice I can't control, "I want to buy a pack of Trojans, please."

Then, this little bald-headed fellow will look up while I rain sweat on his glasses and say, "How old are you, sonny?"

For sure, I am not going to buy condoms from a dispenser in a men's room in a filling station! Right under pictures of women in their panties, leaning back with their mouths wide and their legs open, going crazy for French Ticklers, are printed these words: "Not for the prevention of pregnancy."

Does that mean the condoms are of low quality, maybe full of little holes, or that it is against the law in Alabama to prevent pregnancy? I don't know.

There is another problem. Say I borrow a condom. How do I keep it on? There may be a harness nobody has bothered to mention, like the elastic garters with snaps in front an officer wears when he's got on socks. You understand?—a thing that would go around my hips and have this snap in front? Who am I going to ask? One of the guys at school?

Are you kidding?

Let's advance this scene. Susie and I are together. The time has come. Do I say, "Just a minute. Excuse me, Susie." And then I whip out this device and apply it? While all romantic activity ceases? While she *watches*?

I wonder if I should practice. I wonder what her reaction will be. I think I know. As sure as I produce a condom, she's going to think *he doesn't respect me*. If I'm prepared for sex, I don't think she's a nice girl overcome by alcohol, or who has lost her head. She'll come to her senses and say, "Take me home."

Before the condom problem is solved I get transferred to the pressroom. Bewick Coulter, the apprentice, has snagged a fingernail in the folder. The dummy has already lost two digits.

Harold is now my boss. I show him what fast hands can do. I snatch jammed newspapers from a running folder with never a miss.

Harold yells, "Watch it! Don't do that. I mean it." But I can tell he's glad I am working the folder rather than Bewick Coulter. If you have to shut down the folder every time a newspaper jams, you will never get the run completed.

Harold has folded me a printer's cap from a newspaper. He went into a corner to do it. It is a mystery known only to old printers. You can unfold a cap with the creases still in it, but you cannot refold it and make it hold. It will unravel on your head, and you will walk around unaware, looking sillly.

Because I have fast hands that can snatch newspapers from a running folder without losing digits, I have Harold's approval. I am not sure I want it. A boy is known by his enemies, someone wrote.

Harold wears a T-shirt without an overshirt. Only veterans are entitled to this style. It is an identification for them. Harold's T-shirt is dirty and tight. A cigarette pack and a folder of matches are rolled in one sleeve. Out of his armpits come black hair and a Limburger smell. He says women like it.

His fat arms flex tattoos, and make them hump in sexual movements. The skin on him that is not purple is patchy with hair and the color of a dog hide I soaked two weeks in lye water to make a drum. I think Harold has printed upon his skin an advertisement of what he is. He has made himself into a poster and an advertisement. He does not understand purity or decency. He seduced his niece on a porch swing though she is my age. His talk coats my thoughts with slime. I have to read hard, ringing poetry to clear my head.

Yet, I like the printer's hat and the fast, dangerous work. When I stroll into the editorial office the hat squeezes enough to slant my eyes. It covers my wavy hair. The girls say, "Oh, Billy," in a swoony way. Their mouths go round and they put red nailed hands to their lips. Mr. Sardo glances up and shakes his head.

Susie parades to the watercooler. I follow, watching the switch of her hips, and sneak glances at Gladys. Gladys bends close to her ledger.

Every grown man in the shop has asked Susie to the picnic, except old Mr. Caudle. She has said she and Gladys are going together. The men will not accept that. No, she is going with one of them and share goodies from her basket. They are circling.

I am nervous and sweaty. I say, "Susie, would you, uh—What are your plans about—"

"Would I go to the picnic with you? I'd love to, Billy. I'm *so* glad you asked me."

I reach to adjust my glasses but they don't need it. The glasses frames are pressed into my skull by the hat. I smile down out of slanted, chink eyes. My heart bulges. I love Susie as I love "Horseman in the Sky," "The Man Who Would Be King," and "My Last Duchess." I love her as I do the plays *Hamlet* and *Macbeth,* and that is very purely.

I stride back to the print shop. Harold sneers. "What did she say, kid?"

" 'Yes.' She said, 'Yes.' "

Harold's lips flop into a loose circle. The cords in his neck swell. "It was the only safe thing she could do." He jams his thumb onto the press switch. The switch is the eye of the Fate that denies him Susie. The press spews newspapers, faster and faster, clanking and groaning. Harold strolls to a corner of the room and lights a cigarette. He yells to Bewick, "Mind the press."

Bewick backs away. His face pales. His thyroidal eyes look like plums in a saucer of milk.

I am delirious, thinking about Susie. I can do anything.

A paper flops in the big rollers above the folder. It slaps around and around. I reach chest high and snatch it free. Delicately, perfectly. Another newspaper flaps. We are on the verge of a big jam.

Part of the jammed paper rips. Clever as a pickpocket, I dip for the remainder. Rollers nip my fingers, then draw them in. "Hey!" I yell. This is wrong! It can't be happening.

The rollers grind with the sound our washing machine makes in squeezing a bedspread.

"Shit," Harold yells. He jumps for the switch, the cigarette tumbling from his lips.

Bones in my hand and forearm pop. Thick stuff drips from the rollers and forms a red lake on the inky floor. Blood stands high on the greasy ink. The pool of it widens, bulges at one side, and spills into a crooked stream.

Something screeches. It is not the press. Everyone moves fast. I do not screech for nothing.

I get my sound stopped and quit tugging. It is very quiet in that room except for my panting. No one comes in from editorial because Mr. Sardo waves them back.

Raymond grips my belt from behind, helping me to

stand. Mr. Caudle faces me. "Look at me, Billy," he says. His eyes are pale blue and circled with gray cataracts. He recites, "The Lord is my shepherd; I shall not want."

My gaze strays to the blood. Mr. Caudle says, "Look here, Billy. Pay attention to me." Pits deep as rice grains spill across his nose. Wispy hair fans his skull. I mumble his words. This old man is strong.

Later, they told me this.

When Mr. Sardo telephoned the Montgomery *Advertiser* and Paragon Press for help, the union pressmen closed those shops. Printers ran through the streets the four blocks from the *Advertiser* to Artie's Print Shop. Our press is two stories high. They disassembled it to release the rollers that gripped me. They swarmed over the black monster and reduced it to a jumble of metal parts.

Except for the jing of metal on concrete and grunt of effort, the work advanced in silence. Harold was in command—pointing, snapping his fingers for attention.

I came to myself on the way to the hospital. The injection opened my mind. I babbled. "I am grateful to Mr. A. E. Housman, who taught me I am mortal. I am grateful to Lorbid Butler, who broke my nose in fifth grade when I asked, 'Why don't you pick on someone your size?' I am grateful to my dad, who told me the world is not fair and only a fool thinks it is. And to Casper, our yard man of yore—"

"—of yore?" the doctor in the wrinkled jacket inquired.

"—of yore, who taught me a certain low cunning. And

to Sugar Mason, our maid, for the millions of favors she has done me. And to—"

The doctor touched my bare foot. "If you are praying, boy, remember this weary drudge. Britten is the name. Prayers for yourself are premature."

Maxwell Army Air Force Base Hospital changes my life.

My mother is very attentive. When she thinks I am asleep, she hums, "Where have you been, Billy Boy, Billy Boy?" My aunts read Yeats and Rossetti and Housman aloud. They don't like it, but they do it.

There is time to consider my future in the military. I have seen an Air Force captain at Maxwell Field who has barely enough parts left to get about. A British flying officer on detached duty has a peg and a patch and a little thin mustache. He stumps along with a crutch under his arm like Blind Pew about to pass the Black Spot. Apparently, the British will take any remnant of you and strap it into a Spitfire. I have nothing against Spitfires.

About this nub. It is about a foot long, hairy, with a red, slick head. It's totally outrageous looking and has its own weird desires. It says, *Scratch me! Scratch me!* I do, but I can't find the place. It wants to pick up a glass or turn a page. It thinks it can. It thinks it has fingers. It *feels* them.

Betsy Crenshaw is a brown-eyed nurse's aid so plump her breasts round in happy half-circles above the starch and white of her uniform. Everything about Betsy bounces—

her turned up curls, the sound of her steps, the most female parts of her body.

She is not tall, and must lean over me to take my temperature. She dresses the hong—I mean the nub. There is a tenderness about her as she does this. It stands erect from my elbow. I have tried from modesty to offer it horizontally. She gently erects it and applies unguents with her fingertips. She talks to it. "There! You're looking better today." She strokes the hard forearm under it. Her mouth curls at the corners. This is a literal-minded, sweet girl. She does not know she is being affectionate with a giant hong.

The doctors put on display in my room a sergeant shot down over Germany who does things with a clever pair of meat hooks. He opens a door, turns a page, and lights a cigarette. He finishes every movement with a flourish. He is as proud as a man with a trick dog.

But the revelation Betsy offers vibrates with truth. I stop insisting that the nub be bandaged, and hiding it under a sheet. I am the only boy in Montgomery, Alabama, licensed to walk the streets carrying upon my visible person a giant, symbolic prick. I will sail under my true flag for the first time in my life. The potentialities are awesome.

Most of the time before I get back to the office I lie in bed and fantasize.

I visualize five men coming from the shadows to menace Susie. They discount me because I am tall, thin and one-armed. They do not know I have read Charles Martell's book on judo. They want to hold and violate Susie. I want to do the same, but it is different with me. They are evil.

I kick one in the glottis. Another has a serrated knife. I bend his wrist inward until the hand unfolds and the wrist snaps. One is down on his back. I leap into the air, tuck knees, and pile-drive my number 12-A Stacy Adamses to the center of the earth. His chest is between my heels and the earth. All of his ribs splinter and break into his heart and lungs with a good sound. Upon the last attacker I clamp the Japanese Strangle Hold. The Charles Martell book says never practice this hold. Use it only upon a Jap in combat. This is an emergency. He dies with a horrible gargle.

Those who can crawl drag themselves away. Susie clings to me. Unthinkingly, she rubs her thighs and little breasts upon me. Her red hair blows against my face. I stare fiercely in the direction of the vanquished.

This vision is unsatisfactory. I substitute Gladys for Susie. Most of Gladys's clothes have been ripped away by the assailants. I wrap her in my cloak. She looks up at me with submissive Goo-Goo eyes. She sinks to the ground in the shadows, drawing me with her. I leap with joy to my reward, dominating her totally.

It is late summer by the time I return to Artie's. Leaves are browning on the oaks. The one pair of ginkgo trees I know are yellow shimmering things. In a single day they will flutter down all their heart-shaped leaves.

Body Parts—A Memory of 1944

"Bil-ly!" Susie cries when she sees me, and runs to hug. Sex fiend that I am, I think only about her breasts mashing against me. Here is a person giving me a warm friendly hug, and all I think of is her personal attachments. It is sickening. I am unworthy of such a girl.

Mr. Sardo shakes hands, offering his left very naturally. He says, "My boy, it is fine to have you back." Mr. Sardo's hand is just large enough to grip three of my fingers, but the grip is manly.

Gladys hovers in the background, eyes shining, wringing her hands.

Harold rolls in from the print shop, grinning like a bulldog and jetting smoke from his nostrils.

Raymond strolls into the editorial office without first having changed to his suit.

Such is my homecoming.

I have missed the office picnic, but I soon find out that something else has been planned by the men. It is to be called a fishing trip. I mean to go. I will make Raymond feel sorry for me, if I have to. I will get that low.

When I'm around Susie I wear the sleeves of my shirt half rolled. She shifts in her chair. She crosses her legs and jiggles her foot. These are sure signs of sexual readiness, Raymond advised Melvin. She giggles and whispers to Gladys when she thinks I am not looking. Gladys blushes.

Upstairs, Melvin chain-smokes. He fills his glue reservoir indifferently. Sometimes it falls off the clipper while he is working. This is a professional disgrace.

Raymond is to provide him with a date for the fishing trip. The girl's name is Iris. He says to Raymond, "You think she'll do it?"

Raymond smoothes his slicked-down hair, takes a deep drag on a Lucky, and shrugs.

"But you said—"

"Yeah. I said she's been known to. You can't tell."

They stand at an open window overlooking the street. I lean in another, pretending not to listen. The radio at the end of the counter rattles "Boogie Woogie Bugle Boy of Company B." It's the Andrews Sisters. Down below a blonde drives by in a cream Chevy convertible, her dress pulled above her dark stocking tops. The room falls silent except for the radio. Melvin doesn't whoop and whistle, or yell "Nooky!" He just stares, and turns to Raymond, and sweat stands on his lip.

"Hell, Raymond." A naked whine sounds in his voice. "You promised."

They are talking openly. It is as if in doing a dumb thing like sticking my hand into a running press I have been through an initiation and am now a man.

Raymond says to Melvin, "I'll think of something."

Over and over that day Melvin asks Raymond what he is going to tell the girls to persuade them to come. Mr. Caudle talks to me in a loud voice, his mouth pinched, but I can hear Raymond anyway.

"I'll tell 'um we're going to fish and have a few beers, just for the afternoon. What happens after that—"

Body Parts—A Memory of 1944

"Who-eee!" Melvin shouts. Then he snarls, "You want to walk home, baby? Do you?"

About this time the single most memorable event of my life occurs. My father returns from the war. He arrives by train wearing eagles upon his shoulders, a big smile, and carrying a briefcase chained to his wrist. He is a courier. We all join in one big hug at the steps of the train car: my mother, my little brother, my dad, me, and the briefcase.

I am taller than he is. He puts his hand high over my head and laughs. He gives the nub a frank look, but does not pay it any mournful attention. We have already talked about it by V-mail.

There are unsettling events, however.

He does not throw the harpies out of the house. He *thanks* them for coming to live with us, and for helping to keep the family together.

He lets my mother boss him just the way she always did. Oh, she flutters around wanting to please, but if she wants the garbage out, she wants it *now*. I am amazed to see him obey in good humor. The tyranny of women is terrible. He will soon be reduced to trimming sidewalks on his knees with scissors, for God's sake, once she gets used to having him home.

More unsettling is this. After he has been to the office to see the crew he mentions Raymond. His voice has exactly the tone Raymond's has when Raymond talks about me.

My dad tells a joke. "Do you know who the best jungle

fighters are, son?" He answers it himself. "The Japanese. The Aussies are next best.

"What about Americans?" I ask.

"They don't qualify. They move the jungle and then fight."

"Ha, ha," I say, but I am getting uneasy about him.

One great thing he has done is to outfit our Ford with a knob on the steering wheel, and covert the emergency brake to operate with a pedal.

As long as we fish, build tomato flats, or repair the house for our victory chickens, everything is fine. When we talk, we don't seem to understand each other.

For instance, I ask him to put on his flight jacket. It is fudge-colored leather with printed, silver eagles upon leather epaulets, and a patch with a big 5 in a shower of shooting stars on the shoulder. That's the Fifth Air Force emblem. He tugs on the jacket, and places the hat without a grommet on his head, and takes them right off.

"Where are all your ribbons?" I say.

"They aren't worn on flight jackets," he says.

I brood about the Purple Heart he wouldn't take. "I want you to have the Purple Heart. You earned it."

He looks at me with an inscrutable expression. He's a plump man in rimless glasses with a middle thicker than his chest. "It wouldn't have been the right thing. I was only hit by shrapnel. It was a scratch."

Here I have this hero figure I have counted on, and he won't be a hero. Not one damn bit. He stands in khakis with the flight jacket on his arm and the hat in his hand.

He wants to get back to carpentry, but takes time to talk. "I was an administrator in uniform, son. I helped fighting men do their jobs. Don't make something out of me I wasn't. A lot of good men died."

He won't understand what I need from a returned veteran with three years' service overseas, a case of yellow fever, and a war wound. He lets the homefolks down. But even I know better than to say this.

One day at lunch at Walgreen's I ask Raymond if I can go with him and Harold and Melvin on the fishing trip. I wink elaborately as I say "fishing trip."

He pulls his chin. "Okay, kid, just so you know the score."

When we return to the mail room, Melvin gets mad. "Damn!" he yells. "You backed out, Raymond. I knew you would. You got to keep all the good stuff for yourself."

Raymond smiles that smile. "Calm down. The kid knows the score. He'll only be with us until dark."

Melvin flashes a glance of hate my way. "He's got a girl?" He snarls, "Okay, the more the merrier." He turns to Mr. Caudle at the end of the counter. "You come too, Pops. Get your ashes hauled. Be good for you."

Mr. Caudle keeps wrapping papers.

When I invite Susie to the fishing trip she answers in a louder voice than I want her to. Women are always doing that.

"Billy! I can't believe you'd ask me to go to the lake with *those men* when they are *drinking*."

"Who said anything about drinking?" I move closer so she won't shout.

"Excuse me?"

"Who said anything about drinking?"

Red hair flies as she shakes her perm. "No, no, no."

"Why not?"

"'Cause."

"Because why?" I try to keep my voice from deep vibrato. It sinks there and shakes when I talk about a date.

"Because of what they say. They say they are going to take the girls twelve miles out of town and *leave* them if they don't—. That's why!"

I stretch my eyes wide to show shock. "That's terrible! Where did you hear such a thing?"

She jerks her thumb toward the ceiling. "Raymond and Melvin and Harold, that's who. They're a bad influence on you."

"Oh, *no!* If you think this is that kind of fishing trip, I'm sorry. I would never invite you to anything like that."

This fib does not cost me one bit of suffering. After I lie more, she agrees to come to the lake if there are other girls, and if she and I travel in our own car.

The trouble I anticipate with Dad about getting the car doesn't develop. "Sure," he says. "Have a good time." Then I ask him about the war. It looks as if I would know better. I mention "yellow-bellied Japs." He puts down his hammer.

"General Saito," he tells me, "was an old, fat Japanese general on Saipan. He lost twenty thousand men to bombardment and close fighting. We burned another twenty

Body Parts—A Memory of 1944

thousand out of the caves where they were holed up. When he had three thousand men left, no artillery, and little ammunition they broke through the 27th Infantry."

"I'll bet the Marines were mad!" I say. "The Army let the Japs through."

Dad doesn't pay any attention. He seems far away.

"This was his command. 'Whether we attack or whether we stay, there is only death. However, in death there is life. We must use this opportunity to exalt true Japanese manhood. I will advance with you to deliver still another blow to the American devils and leave my bones on Saipan. I will never suffer the disgrace of being taken alive, and will offer up my soul and calmly rejoice in having lived by eternal principles.'"

"What happened?" I say.

"He ordered his adjutant to shoot him because he was fat and clumsy and might be captured. The three thousand charged in a last hurrah—that's what *banzai* means. In all the fighting on Saipan we only captured seventeen hundred people. Most were civilians. The few soldiers we picked up were incapacitated. Whatever the Japs were, they weren't 'yellow.'"

He is telling the truth and I hate it. This is not a revealing little insight. It is a truth that turns my world. For three years I have been the man in the family, worked hard, and hated Japs. What is the point if the Japanese spoke as nobly in defeat as Romans about to fall upon their swords? What is happening to me when I prefer to believe my lie rather than hear a truth? My dad has a gift for putting me in real gloom. A positive gift!

Luckily, I have the fishing trip to distract me. Saturday arrives. Raymond lives on Jefferson Avenue, past the stockyards. Streets get narrow there. The houses are what my mother calls "Depression houses," by which she means they are stucco or wood framed, on cramped lots.

Raymond's shiny blue Chevy with fishing poles strapped to the side is parked on the street. Susie and I pull in behind it.

We get out and walk to the Chevy just as Melvin staggers out of the screen door of the house lugging two cases of Bud. He stops in his tracks. Raymond limps out dressed in khakis and wearing an orange baseball cap. His long face and different sized eyes look silly under a baseball cap.

"For Christ's sake," Melvin mutters.

Raymond doesn't say anything. He looks at Susie.

Melvin scowls. "For Christ's sake!" He walks by us and drops the beer on the back seat of the Chevy.

"I'm looking forward to this," Susie chirps. "Have either of you ever been outfished by a girl? Well, you're about to be."

Raymond's eyes squeeze even smaller under the brim of the old orange hat. He seems beyond reach.

I crack my knuckles loudly. "Let's get going, you guys."

Raymond's hands fumble in air. "Kid, something's come up. The other girls couldn't come. Melvin and me, we thought—" His voice trails off. "Maybe you'd better go on home."

Susie lifts her head, looking proud and scornful. "Let's go, Billy."

As I whip the Ford into the driveway to turn around, Raymond limps to the blue Chevy carrying two crooked cane poles. He doesn't look at me.

Susie sits on the far side of the seat. I feel as if she can see right into me. She can look into my mind and see what a jerk I am.

We get to her house. I go around and open her door. She sits there.

"We don't have to go in, Billy. We can go someplace by ourselves and have a nice afternoon. Someplace like Beavers Lake." She touches my hand. "Let's do."

I feel sick about Raymond. I don't think he ever had any girls lined up. I think it was all just talk.

We drive to Beavers Lake and walk around the edge in yellow leaves. I hold her hand when she jumps marshy places. We sit and talk under a tree. The whole shore is ours. The other couple on the far side—he wears a white shirt, she a yellow blouse—wander into the woods.

Susie wears a sailor suit and a brimmed straw hat with a swallow-tailed ribbon hanging in back. My blue shirt, she says, matches my eye color.

Our skins brush. Our hands touch. Quite naturally and easily, while we are sitting under an oak tree, I kiss her.

She returns my kiss gently. It is such a kiss as you could

give your aunt, on the cheek. Then her mouth opens. This must be French, my mind says. The feeling is wet and un-usual. I kiss her and stroke her, and she lets me. "Billy!" she protests when I unbutton her sailor blouse to let out the chickadees. "No ... no. You must not, must not." Her voice is like a water bird's. I lay her down in the leaves.

She takes hold of the nub. She is fascinated by it. I get worked up by her tugging on the nub. This goes on. I have a problem. I have to use my good hand to hold me up over Susie. I cannot unbutton with the nub. She does not help. She does not care.

I say, "Susie! Susie! Susie!" but she does not pay any at-tention. I plant my head under her chin, bow myself into the air, and grab for my belt and buttons. I rip off three buttons and commence thrusting about her person. Nothing on her is accessible. My body is blind.

Be cool, I think. Remember Dr. Lucian Oates's map of a woman's zones. I am trying to commit rape. It is impos-sible to do without help. She gets a knee in position and skillfully injures me, then sits up with one hand to her mouth.

"Billy, what happened? What happened to us? I've never done such a thing. I don't know what came over us!"

Her words do not vibrate in my chest as truth. "Nothing happened to me!" I fumble with the nub, try-ing to get into openings in her dress. She closes them with two busy hands. I try, but it is over. She tubes lipstick onto her mouth and combs her hair. I want to rip out my own hair and bang my skull against a rock.

She says, "Well, what's the matter with *you*? You didn't expect me to go all the way, did you?"

I am not sad at losing Susie. I hate her. It is getting hard to know anyone. I look at my father and think, here is a middle-aged man who has seen stuff that I have not. He cannot be wrong about everything.

Since he returned, my mind has developed a sickening habit. If you give me a coin that shows heads, plain and simple, I turn it over to look at the other side. I do this with everything people say. This cast of mind destroys the foundations of belief.

On the flip side, Raymond is a phony, Harold is a hero for saving my life, Susie is unfeeling and selfish, and I am disloyal to Susie and my mother's moral teachings.

Gladys and I are screwing. According to what I've overheard at Artie's, men are supposed to love 'um and leave 'um. But screwing makes me feel different from that. It makes me feel what boy scouting tried to teach me—to be kind, and helpful, and protective, and trusting, and loyal. Gladys and I are secretive, but do not feel guilty at all. Frankly, I don't expect that to last if my mother discovers what is going on and drags us naked before God. But I've got to get over letting her make me feel guilty. A man cannot face Life with an albatross of guilt hanging from his hong.

Summer is gone, and with it my job at Artie's. The ginkgo trees have showered all their golden leaves. The air is crisp and snappy, like a hard apple. My brother and I buy school supplies at Woolworth's. He gets a paste pot, Blue Horse tablets, fat pencils, and crayons. I buy a Parker pen with a marbled case, black ink, and a ream of unlined paper.

I am attending Consolidated for the last year. My friend, Jack Thatcher, sidles up to me on the school grounds.

"That bother you?" He nods toward the nub.

"Not much."

We talk awhile and he says that on his birthday his girl-friend let him. She's going to let him again Christmas. This is an anemic-looking blonde who will live to be ninety, and control Jack every day he lives. As in a vision I see him with his hands curled, whining for it with no shame.

We talk about courses we are taking. Jack tolls them like names of the war dead. "Chemistry … biology … algebra … history … English."

A sudden joy strikes me. I hear my bewildered voice say, "I'm really glad to be back. I am!"

Jack makes a circle in the dust with his toe. "Why? I can't stand the thought of it."

"Teachers. I mean, they know what they are talking about." I fumble for the words. "They don't have doubts."

Jack rips out a vulgar sound.

"No, wait. Maybe they're not sure after school, or in the summer, but here they're sure."

I think it through and the words come faster. "I am glad to learn the years the Industrial Revolution began. You wouldn't think a thing like that could be dated, would you, but someone has done it. I am glad to learn that sulfur burns with a yellow flame, and that pi always equals 3.1416."

"Sulfur—" Jack says. His fat face breaks into a smile. "We can make stink bombs in chemistry. We can drive everyone out of lab!"

"Sure," I say. I am wildly excited about the school year. Whatever else it will bring, it will bring certainty. I will hold onto that for the short time still that I can.

TWO

THE SNOPES WHO SAVED HUCKABY

The minute he stepped from the train in Huckaby, Mississippi, in 1932, Wevel Snopes should have frozen. He should have held his foot suspended in air the way a man does on hearing the whisper of a rattler. He should have shook the dust of that village and backed out.

Three little wonders occurred for anyone with eyes to see. A circle of light about the size of a flashlight beam shined down to brighten ordinary dust to crazy beauty. Rainbows vibrated in the air, promising pots of gold in mundane places. Out on the Mississippi River, as far as the eye could see, the hot brown surface frothed. Big catfish fluttered up from their cool depths. Fishermen stood in boats and cracked paddles on their skulls. The pops sounded like musketry. They threw out any bare hooks they had, and fish jumped for the glitter. It was a jubilee. Huckaby had never before attracted heaven's favor.

In '22 and in '27—almost indolently, almost sweetly, with a lick here and a curl there—the Mississippi had overflowed. To rivermen it was a betrayal like having a pet cat go mad and bite the baby.

And drought! Drought cursed Huckaby, too. In '31 the sky hung brazen and clouds wouldn't darken. From where cotton rows began at Huckaby's porches to where they narrowed and converged near the Tennessee line, plants held only pecky squares. After boll weevils made a subtraction the wisps left at harvest time weren't worth picking. Corn planted in deep loam by the levee produced nubbins. Pulling back a husk was like opening a crone's lips. A grain here, a grain there, hung on thin red cobs.

Five ramshackle buildings remained. They stood on pilings facing the river. After the flood of '27, storekeepers hadn't the confidence to rebuild the square. People prayed for a miracle to save Huckaby, any miracle at all.

In the flat distance of the Mississippi delta a steam engine raced away with six yellow flatcars. A horse tail of smoke floated behind it, and the stench of burning coal hung in the air.

The gaunt figure of Brother Wevel Snopes emerged from drifts of smoke. Beside him stood A. P. Gooch. Greasy curls stood upon Gooch's head. Bandit eyes shone out of his face.

"Wait a minute, Old Eye-talian," Brother Wevel said, and lifted his arms to the empty street. The cuffs that shot from his coat sleeves had been turned. His rusty suit glittered with wear, and cardboard lined the holes in his shoes. But he spread his arms and smiled as if deputations from churches had gathered in welcome.

Once signs had announced each of his appearances. On country roads they leaped from the void to scream REPENT when lantern light or automobile headlamps touched them. Posters showed him black-coated and Bunyanesque, with sandy hair that touched clouds and a stance that spanned the South. One high-topped shoe sank into waves that curled like meringue off the coast of South Carolina. The other squashed East Texas, its toe cap taller than piney woods and oil derricks. Fingers of his right hand splayed under an open Bible. His left forefinger pointed at passersby. The eyes seemed to follow and the accusing finger to crook. Sinners could not escape them, or the words printed in P. T. Barnum type below the picture: WEVEL SNOPES WANTS YOU FOR GOD!

Now that other preachers whispered his failings, things were different.

Brother Wevel dropped his arms to his sides. His smile dimmed. Distantly, a fish hawk *screed*. One last paddle cracked on a fish skull. "Bottom of the barrel," he said to his manager, "ain't it?"

"Huckaby—" Gooch mourned—"school teaching." His voice guttered down like a snuffed candle. "What can you expect when a preacher goes soft on the Seventh?"

Before taking up managing Brother Wevel, Gooch had been a tent show operator, living a sweet, succulent life. He'd practically owned two dancing girls, a bearded lady, a large brown camel, a geek that ate raw chickens, a two-foot midget, and assorted grotesque mutants. He'd been a center ring performer who said to women *go* and they went, and *come* and they came.

Managing an evangelist had seemed a way to work a larger arena. But when the Lord answered Brother Wevel's prayer to end the drought of '27 by sending a rain that drowned out Mississippi, Arkansas, and Louisiana—and bounced Gooch off a girl he was humping on a flooded brush top like he did Paul of Tarsus off a little saddling jenny—Gooch took to muttering about sin. Each eye narrowed toward his nose. He got so sharp-faced he could pass for an ax and had to wear a hat night and day to prevent folks from slinging him head first into a chopping block. He guarded Brother Wevel from every sweet thing.

Oh, that man was a magnet for women!

A blonde in a flour sack dress strolled by, showing insect bitten legs. Brother Wevel gave her a rammish look and she flinched like a well-broke mule hearing the whispered intention of a whip.

Gooch muttered, "I seen that."

On a nearby porch a country girl in a blue dress lifted her eyes and opened their cornflower depths to say, *Run away with me, preacher man.*

"Don't look south," Gooch muttered. "Red light south."

Brother Wevel turned his face north with the stately grace of the Sprague. He did his best to hold hard, but a powerful tide pulled south. "Lord, he'p me!" he said.

Well, now!

At the sound of his voice the birds hushed their singing. A famished Bluetick hound lifted her muzzle from a puddle of green water to fix adoring yellow eyes upon him. Five gaudy cocks swirling around a dying hen like Memphis pimps breaking in a new girl forgot to breed. On the porch of the nearest store, a deaf and blind man eased down his chair from its back legs. His milky eyes turned toward Brother Wevel and his blind gaze asked, *Are you the one?*

Brother Wevel didn't heed God's smaller replies. He wanted a voice to speak from the burning bush or a ladder to poke down from the cobalt sky. He was thinking about that fine, blue-eyed girl. "I reckon you think I got to stay at the schoolhouse all the time, every day."

"That's right."

"You think temptation of the flesh would lead me to sin any time I came to town."

"Probably would. Yessir, probably would."

"I couldn't trust myself even to come in for a soda."

"Nope."

Brother Wevel snapped, "Hellfire. You don't give a man no slack at *all*."

As they walked out of downtown Huckaby toward the private school at which Brother Wevel was to interview for a job, the Bluetick hound drank her fill and slunk away. The dying red hen got uselessly mated. Birds trilled again. The blind man lost his inner vision. Rainbows disappeared from the sky, and fish stopped biting in the river. Brother

Wevel sung out without preamble, "The one that drowned his enemies and gave their women to his elect is the one called me. Old God."

Gooch's expression said, *Here we go again.*

"The last time I saw Old God he was about as big as a Coke bottle, and that same green."

"I didn't ask."

"The man is heavy. He weighs a ton. You commence to claw here when he's in you." Brother Wevel jabbed his breastbone. "When he comes out, he stands in air and stares. Just floats and stares. He's got little hard eyes with no wetness about them at all. He'll make you yell, 'Uncle! Calf-rope! Please, Suh!' mighty quick."

Gooch grumped, "What about Jesus? You don't ever talk about Jesus."

"I like Old God to leap among my enemies. I like him to afflict folks that need it. I like him to prepare me the jawbone of an ass, and put the iron in my arm to smite. I like for him to send me among Delilahs and Bathsheebas, and then redeem me."

"Listen! I asked about *Jesus.*"

Brother Wevel's face screwed into an expression of regret. "I never had the pleasure. Old God was the one called me, and I been as faithful as any dog."

The school where Brother Wevel had applied to be headmaster was a two-story building with a sliding board descending from an upstairs window. Not a sprig of grass marred the wavy patterns swept into the dirt yard. Whitewash gleamed on every tree trunk.

Brother Wevel led the way inside. He'd washed at the river and about him drifted black nap, the odor of Oxydol, and a fragile sanctity. At a sign that said SUPERINTENDENT, he knocked.

The office contained a filing cabinet, a rolltop desk, a church pew, and an oscillating fan. The fan jerked about like a sufferer in the throes of a seizure. The man behind the desk introduced himself as Dr. Owens, the school's proprietor.

Large blue eyes looked out of his rimless glasses. Yellow hair sprigged his skull. A mustache concealed his lips. Mustaches were useful for Mississippi delta physicians who had to tell folks they weren't going to die of typhoid, malaria, or yellow fever when they were.

"I'm Reverend Wevel Snopes, at your service," Wevel Snopes said. "This here is Alonzo Goochi, known in the trade as A. P. Gooch and Gooch the Eye-talian We've come about your advertisement for a school-teacher."

Dr. Owens looked from one man to the other. "You understand, don't you, that I can't take chances. I want a man of God as an example for these scholars. That's why I liked your application."

Gooch said, "He's blessed Brother Wevel with particular favor."

"What I intend to do is to prepare ten girls for Blue

Mountain College. When they graduate there they'll be pretty-much ladies. Five ladies could change Tunica County. Ten could change—why, the world!"

Brother Wevel's eyebrows lifted. "This is a girls' school?"

"Right, a prepratory school. We're producing the yeast of culture here."

"Let me read that ad again."

"You betcha." Dr. Owens handed over the *Appeal* folded to the classifieds. "Boys can't be changed after they're fourteen and have found their balls. Most are bound for hell. You know that your own self."

"This ad don't say girls," Gooch complained.

"Maybe they're little." Brother Wevel held his palm two feet above the oiled floor.

"No, I want fast results. Tunica County is waiting for the yeast."

"I expected boy scholars," Brother Wevel somewhat whined.

Dr. Owens leaned forward and gripped the edges of the desk top. "Consider the consequence of five ladies in Tunica County, Mississippi. Think, Brother Snopes!"

Brother Wevel circled the idea like a dog trying out a new bed, then shook his head. "I don't need this job."

Dr. Owens struck a match and lit a cigar. Rich smoke floated in the room. "I thought there was a Depression going on," he said through heady clouds. "I thought you had quit preaching and needed work."

"We don't need *this* job," Gooch declared.

"I'm playing forty a month in cash, not script. Mr. Gooch here can be janitor, at twenty." Dr. Owens leaned back and his belly swelled over a silver buckle. His face wore the expression of a gambler who's bought the pot.

Ten girls wandered into the assembly hall on opening day. Of the older students, Catherine was a wheaty blonde who blushed easily. Lucille rubbed her lips with an eraser to oral excess. Retha Mae drifted a scent of talc and laughed in a jolly way. As for Pearl—Brother Wevel was careful not to look again at Pearl. His gaze wanted to stick on her like she was a tar baby.

Outside, a mockingbird sang. Dirt daubers buzzed beneath the tall, white ceiling. Brother Wevel spread his hands and the girls' chatter hushed.

"Moses had to go to the Promised Land. Adam and Eve had to eat that apple. You believe that don't you, girls? It was God's will, wasn't it?" He watched until they nodded. Then Brother Wevel laughed and laughed. He whickered in his nose and slapped his leg, *pow*, and they jumped. The girls shrank in their seats and folded their shoulders like bats.

"Why, them are fables for the simple!" Brother Wevel said. He gulped down the sorrow this caused him. "I'd give a pretty if it was true. But a truth has to be true in every case. That story about Adam and Eve ain't. No, ma'am, it ain't."

The girls' eyes widened. Gooch shifted in his chair.

"The question is, did God mean for preachers to take the Bible for fact? You would have to believe this story if you believe God's, 'cause remember, a truth is always true."

Pearl watched Brother Wevel with the charmed expression of a doomed rabbit.

"Take this situation," he said conversationally. "Say a man gets a pair of hound pups, dog and gyp. He pours plenty of clabber and cornbread in their pan every evening. One evening this man sets out a plate of warm chitlins and tells the pups, 'Y'all don't taste this while my back is turned. Y'all eat the cornbread and clabber.'" Brother Wevel grinned and showed wide yellow teeth. "What do you think will happen if that bitch pup is a little bit forward?"

Gooch hitched his bulk out of his chair. He called, "Remember, these are children, Mr. Snopes."

"Wait! I'm getting to the best part. The fellow that owns the dogs has one son. You couldn't make that boy any better if you replaced any part on him. He don't act ugly any way. And that daddy of his makes up his mind to this. If the pups taste the chitlins, he's gonna whip them out of his yard and he's gonna make his son *die* 'cause they ate."

"That's crazy," Gooch muttered.

"It's sacrilegious," Lucille whispered softly enough to avoid impudence.

Brother Wevel licked his lips, cocked back his head, and sang in a clear baritone:

'Twas on the Isle of Capri that I met her
Beneath the shade of an old some-kind of tree.
She wore a plain gold ring on her finger
On the beau-ti-ful Isle of Capri.
Summer time was nearly over,
Blue Italian skies above.
I said, 'Lady I'm a rover.
Can you spare a sweet bit of love?'

He broke off singing. "Some of you girls done spared too much. Folks don't take kindly to that. Let a girl spare a sweet bit of love, and I tell you true. She ain't *nice* as far as public comment."

Pearl's eyes darted like pressure gauge needles. Retha Mae and Catherine lowered their blushing faces.

Brother Wevel looked up at the beaded ceiling where dirt daubers buzzed. A flap of hair hung over his brow. His goozle slid and his jaws worked as he savored the juice of holy words. Not a girl moved except a little one who raised her hand to be excused.

"Truth is where you find it," Brother Wevel said. "Sometimes you find it in the Bible. That Adam and Eve story says sometimes God is a bad daddy. He sets meat before us we can't pass up, then punishes us without no mercy if we eat. That song I tendered says there is a man ready to sweet talk every weak girl to perdition. That's the truth. Y'all ought to know it." He shook his head and the hair flap bounced over his eyes. "Men can't *stand* temptation! Keep yourselves pure for God and Doc Owens, who is giving you this fine education."

The girls smiled. Men's frailty was an old, old story to them. A rustle of noise returned to the room. Gooch told Brother Wevel that he'd brought the talk home, though after a worrisome beginning.

"I got to wear my bandana, Old Eye-talian," the preacher mourned. "I can't look at these big girls again."

He strapped a blue and white handkerchief around his brow. With his head tilted back, he could see to walk the corridors and to write on the blackboard. When he tucked his chin he couldn't see a thing.

Gooch asked, "Does it help?"

"Naw," Brother Wevel said. "I can still smell 'um and I can hear 'um rustle. When they breathe near me their breath makes me dizzy." He tilted his head to peep under the bandanna. "I think I'm a goner."

That very night Brother Wevel slipped off to town. He returned through a window at dawn, looking pale and depleted.

"Don't think you're fooling God and me," Gooch said, shaking his finger in the preacher's face. "You sinned."

"This one don't count. I repented."

"Yes it does. Old God counts every time your sparrow falls. You came to Huckaby with two strikes against you. Three, and you're out!" His right hand made the sweeping, thumb-up gesture of an umpire.

"Wrong, Old Eye-talian," Brother Wevel said, but he looked worried. Afterward he went to his knees, though they were bony and he preferred to spare them. Spit in his mouth turned gluey from prayer. His eyes flicked in sockets made dry by searches for a presence clear and green, the size of a Coke bottle. The voice he listened for was a delta voice, not some imposter's who chiseled words to edges and angles that wouldn't fit under the dome of a southern mouth.

For three days and nights he prayed. Then his face brightened, and he cocked his head to listen. "Uh-huh," he said. "Yes, Sir. I got the message. That's mighty fine!"

He made a test run to Huckaby on Saturday without falling into sin. Then he went to Prichard, Dundee, and Lula and looked at all their women. He bragged to Gooch, "At a funeral I hugged a widow in Christian love and didn't think about her body at all."

"That's good," Gooch said, "but was she ugly? Was she old?"

"Don't w-o-r-r-y about me. I may be a strike or so down, but the head coach has signaled *walk that man*."

"—Two. You're two strikes down," Gooch warned.

The next day Brother Wevel tacked a sign to a corridor wall, heedless of cracking plaster. GOOD ADVICE, the sign said. BRING YOUR TROUBLES TO ME. I'LL CARRY YOUR LOAD.

Gooch leaned on a broom. Straws curled against the oiled floor. "I know you've made a promise to God and want to do right," Gooch said. "I know you want to keep this job, but Wevel! Four of these girls are sixteen."

Brother Wevel smoothed the white placard as if it were a loved woman's flank. "Fifteen-year-olds are hard to pass up, too."

Gooch swept a circle around Brother Wevel's feet. He pushed plaster chips onto a piece of cardboard. He rubbed his lips and shook his head, but the words growled out anyway. "Give up this idea of advising schoolgirls. You're asking for trouble."

"Listen, Old Eye-talian, you act like because I slipped before, I'm condemned forever. I know I don't have any willpower. God knows I don't have any willpower."

"That's my point."

"One more slip and I'm out the Gate."

"Exactly."

Brother Wevel clapped Gooch on the back. "Don't you understand? I *can't* do anything wrong any more."

Gooch's gaze hung on Brother Wevel as heavy as a wet load of washing on a line.

"See, I put him under a management contract like you done me."

"You made a deal with God? You can't make a deal with God."

"Wrong, Old Eye-talian. God knows I'm not strong like Job. I can't stand boils and fleas and such. If he leaves me without help I'll slide to hell on the first woman's smile. He don't want that. I don't want that." Brother Wevel looked smug. "I promised not to fool around with women. I'll treat 'um like they're narrow pits. And God promised he won't let me sin bad enough to lose my place in glory."

"You got to be careful what you pray for."

"He don't want me in hell." Brother Wevel smiled a cunning smile. "I know what's the matter with you. You're jealous. You got the Call, ain't you?"

Gooch flushed.

"You got the Call, ain't that right?"

"Maybe. I'm not sure. It looks like I need God to make it clear. It looks like I need him to show his self."

"Fat chance, Old Eye-talian. You ain't among the elect."

Gooch limped away like a mongrel dog when somebody's yelled, "You, sir!" and picked up a rock.

A few hours later Pearl Chambers stopped Brother Wevel in the hall. She lowered her gaze and clutched her books as he walked by. "Brother Wevel, may I talk to you?" she said.

From under the edge of his bandanna Brother Wevel saw her pink, chewed lips. Firm breasts pressed against the edges of her books. Her eyes smudged with worry, making them sensual. "The way you say that is, '*Can* I talk to you?' But you better talk to your momma."

No one else was in the hall. School was over. Pearl followed as he walked away, stepping so quietly he did not hear.

"Hark!" Brother Wevel cried when she slipped into

his office. "Who's that?" He snatched off the bandanna.

She closed the door. "I just *have* to talk to you. I don't have anyone else."

He did a jig step between yellow walls. His gaze fluttered against the windows and door.

"What can I do?" Pearl clutched a handkerchief that fumed Evening in Paris. "Doc Owens wants me to marry him when I'm educated and good enough. He talked to my momma about it. That's why he started this school. Did you know that?"

"You're good enough."

"And my momma says do it," she wailed.

"Mommas know when a man's a good catch."

"But Brother Wevel, I love another! I couldn't give myself to Doc Owens feeling as I do."

"Like," Brother Wevel said.

"Sir?"

"'Like I do' is the way to say that." Pacing fast, he swung out of her gravitational pull. "Another time and I'd have showed you. I'd have showed you plenty. Now, all I can do is tell you how to make Doc Owens a good wife. See here, girl." He came near. "You remember playing make-believe when you were little?"

She nodded.

"Well, marriage is just make-believe. You make-believe the old codger you're with is a young feller you want."

"Is that all?"

He considered. "It helps to moan. Also, wiggle like

you're snuggling into a feather mattress." His orbit of the room took him closer to her. He shook with disequilibrium and plunged like a comet. "And hold on tight!"

Brother Wevel seized Pearl's waist and buried his face in the soap and sunshine smell of her yellow hair. She held a fuming handkerchief beside his ear. "Scratch," he said in a muffled voice. "Biting helps, too."

"Scratch?" She leaned back against his arms, breathing hard.

Brother Wevel's head popped up from her neck. "It don't take much to keep a man. If he's got good food and a willing woman, he won't stray." He thought a second, staring over her shoulder. "It don't have to be good food if its ample." He thought a while more. "If you can't remember to scratch, that don't truly matter."

"But, Brother Wevel, this other person—"

Brother Wevel disentangled his hands. He pulled down his frock coat. "I don't want to hear about 'this other person.' Doc Owens is a *doctor.*" He said the word reverently.

She sniffled. "I don't care if he is. He's old."

"Why—why—" Brother Wevel sputtered, staring into her eyes. "I see now. I told that Old Eye-talian to stay away from you. I told him particular."

She smiled. "You mean Mr. Gooch? It's *not* Mr. Gooch."

"Who then?" Brother Wevel locked his hands behind his back to keep them from temptation.

"It's you, Brother Wevel. Can't you tell by the way I shake when your hand touches mine?"

Brother Wevel recoiled. "Let's make believe you didn't say that. The Lord promised he won't let me sin too bad to lose my place in heaven. I'm not about to tempt him."

"But, Brother Wevel!" she cried.

"Go to your room. Get away from me."

Her mouth trembled. As she picked up her books her midi-blouse pulled tight over her breasts. As she turned, her belly flattened under the blue skirt.

"Girl, this is serious." He swept back a window shade. "You see that little cloud over there? The black one?"

She crossed the room to him. The scent of her compelled him to cling to the windowsill. She was close enough to smell, to hear rustle. "—If I was to lay hands on you a lightning bolt might strike me dead."

The pupils of her eyes widened to take him in. "Then you shouldn't do it."

He bristled like a scared dog as he cupped her face in his hands. "I wonder how far I could get if I was to hold your pretty face like this and look at it? That wouldn't be no sin, would it?" He glanced up at the ceiling. "And what if I was to kiss your mouth in purest brotherhood?" His fingers squeezed open her lips, exposing their tender insides.

When she could breathe again she said, "Oh, Weevil, this is heavenly."

"Wevel," he said, and added, "Would I be going too far?"

"No, you wouldn't."

"I ain't talking to you." He unbuttoned her blouse. "And what if I was to put my two hands on the fountains of man, and my mouth on Gilead from whence cometh my balm?"

"Gilead?" she said in a sleepy way.

His mouth unsnapped from her breast with a pop. His head pushed back against her cradling arms. "Was that thunder?"

"Thunder?"

"Naw," he answered himself. "That was T-model back-fire, or something like that."

He slid to his knees, nuzzling her belly. She swayed and said, "I've got to sit down, Reverend."

"Just ease it down onto that pew, girl." His voice was muffled. "Just put it on that nice, red cushion."

She sat on the bench. He pushed up her skirt. "What difference is it gonna make in a hundred years?"

"None," she murmured. She lifted her hips and snatched down her drawers in a practiced way.

"Besides which, it ain't my fault I don't have willpower. He never gave me any."

"Me either," she said. "Me either!"

"If a man really loves a woman, why is it wrong for him to love her with everything God gave him?"

"It's not wrong," Pearl said. "It can't be wrong."

Lightning crackled across the sky, brightening the room. Thunder rumbled.

"Okay," Brother Wevel grumped. "I got the message."

The Snopes Who Saved Huckaby

Pearl moaned and twisted under him.

"—and I got your message, too."

BANG! went a lightning bolt, striking a tree in the yard. Bark peeled. Steam arose from scalded cellulose. A sweet scent drifted into the room.

"Wait!" Brother Wevel said. He lifted his face from the bitten curve of her neck. "I'm stopping." He groped to help unbutton his trousers. "All I'm gonna do here is make a little contact. I can quit any time either one of you says to."

A static spark snapped between them. Pearl and Brother Wevel jumped apart. Pearl pulled her blouse over her breasts and tugged at her skirt. "That tingled. Maybe we'd better go to the storm cellar."

A cool, ozone smell filled the room. Hair arose electrically on Brother Wevel's nape. He jumped to his feet with his trousers dangling, his collar loose, and his tie slung over one shoulder. As he glared toward the window his erection wilted. "Now, you've done it!"

"Who are you talking to?"

Brother Wevel jerked a thumb toward the window. "Him."

"God? You mean God?" Pearl smiled. "I'd say you were talking to a cloud."

Thunder muttered.

Brother Wevel held up his palm to the window. "I'm stopping right now."

"Are you feeling all right? There are lots of wind

storms, and lightning storms, and tornadoes around here. Even floods."

"Not like this one." Brother Wevel's tongue had thickened. His words jumbled. "The voice you heard in that cloud is Old God's."

Pearl shifted positions and her blouse slipped. She looked down, grinned, and shifted more. She inched up her skirt. "Why don't you come over here with me? Then talk to God some more."

"Why?"

"'Cause, it makes me feel—real excited."

Brother Wevel felt his forehead. "That's not a fever I've got. It's just blood rushing."

"Come over here," she teased.

"No, ma'am! No, ma'am! I couldn't do that. It wouldn't be right. Temptation hath no power over the pure in heart. Were you to take me to a high place and offer me all below, I would still say 'no.'" He put a hand over his eyes but he peeked at her through the fingers.

She licked her lips and pouted. She put her hand between her legs.

Brother Wevel tucked his head and hobbled fast to the pew, his trousers around his ankles, his manhood rising. As he leaned over her he shouted to the window: "You remember, now. I ain't no use to you dead!"

ZAP! came the lightning, twinkling through the window, flickering like a firefly. A bolt no thicker than a pencil crossed the room and touched his brow. Brother Wevel's eyes glowed red. They whirled out of sight like cherries in a slot machine. He listed to one side and his mouth drew down into a crooked smile as he fell.

From Tunica County drummers carried a story about a girl in a finishing school caught with her drawers down and a preacher intruding upon her person. The preacher flared like a match when he connected, they declared. His hair fried. The experience left him sinless but an idiot.

Dissolute men, the kind who played Russian roulette with clap and syphilis in venturing every sin Memphis could contrive, booked passage downriver in order to risk their assemblies to incineration. When Boss Crump cleaned up Beale Street, call girls and streetwalkers moved south. Tourist courts and cafes opened in Huckaby to accommodate customers. The L&N established regular passenger car service. And the village became a town.

After Brother Wevel's frying, Gooch launched himself as a minister, fighting the sin of lust. He wears an ice cream suit, a crimson tie, and a gipsy ring to pound a leather Bible the size of a whole slab of bacon. The eyes above his smiling lips glisten with the fervor of a shill's as he booms the sermon which is making him famous: "How Many Strikes on *You?*"

Brother Wevel remains altogether unfocussed. His hands flail and his feet wander. The town is of two minds as to what to do about him.

Wags propose that the board of aldermen erect a statue to him as the man who saved Huckaby. They argue that in Enterprise, Alabama, there stands a gold-washed statue to the cotton boll weevil, which diversified the economy of that area.

The *Huckaby Hector* thunders, *If you commit this absurdity you must hang the statue in the sky with wings cupped. Fan its tail like a chicken hawk's when stooping. Put a predator look in the eye. Hook the beak. Spread the talons. Scatter pullets under it. And be prepared to explain to strangers.*

While the controversy rages Brother Wevel wanders the streets buzzing words nobody understands. Busybodies say he should be institutionalized. No one dares. Shadows leave their primary attachments to follow him. They flicker over large bare fields to shade him from the sun. His feet can't stumble. Inanimate objects that might trip him crawl out of his way and thump down like displaced dogs.

This year the snow geese changed their ancient migrations to stack in V's above the river. As Wevel Snopes hobbles the levee, shouting his inarticulate joy, they bend their necks and come down.

HALF ASS

It began as an ordinary Monday. Roger drank three cups of black coffee, pulled green Wellington boots over heavy socks, and walked from the kitchen to the barn to tend to the farm animals. Then all Roger Jones knew of reality shook and cracked.

For weeks, Penelope, the jenny, had turned her tail to him, flattened her tasseled ears, and ground her narrow hips in a Corsican dance of malice. Roger had rattled corn into her feed box and murmured comfort. She'd kicked heels past his spine that could have crippled him, and brayed terrible notes he could not understand.

"Shut up!" Roger had ordered. Penelope had lifted a whiskered muzzle, canted her jaws, shut her lashes, and brayed great *yawps* that exposed a muscled tongue the color of cheap salmon.

This day she limped to a corner of the stall, hung her head, and showed him a hipshot rump and ratty tail. All the spirit had gone out of her. Roger got out his farrier's box to dress the hoof she limped upon.

Penelope looked over her shoulder at him and hid her hooves in mud.

"Turn around," he ordered.

She glanced past her stall door, lifted her muzzle to watch a passing bird, and said she wished to go outside. It was hot where they stood. She nuanced her lower lip, saying *feed a snack*. She was a virtuoso of symbolic language.

Roger cupped one hand over Penelope's withers, ran his other down the raspy hair of her shoulder, knee, and cannon bone, and tapped her fetlock. "You're limping. Give me that hoof."

She didn't lift the hoof though nerves sprangled near the surface in the bony intricacy he'd tapped. She put her mind on other matters.

"Give me your hoof!"

She shifted her weight firmly upon it.

"Give me that hoof, Penelope!"

Leaning against his shoulder, the jenny uttered a relinquishing sigh and lifted the leg. Out of the mud a white human foot emerged with a kissing suck. It was tiny, about a four-quad, the color and texture of an unearthed slug. Roger recognized a four-quad when he saw one. His aunt had worn that shoe size and was vain of the distinction because her footwear had to be custom-made.

Roger stared at the ugly white thing at the end of the jenny's coronet. This was a practical joke. He grinned and pulled the toes. They weren't rubber. The texture was like flesh. He felt a buzz of anger. It *had* to be a joke. Smeltzer had done it, maybe. Roger dug a Case knife out of his

Levi's, flicked open the blade, and probed. The jenny flinched. Blood welled where the knife point entered skin.

Roger straightened his back. He was a logical man. There had to be an explanation. An ordinary hoof had hung there three weeks before, correctly hinged. The insides of his knees still showed yellow bruises from clamping the hoof to pare it. A hard jerk on the handles of Channellock nippers was required to clip Penelope's dense horn.

Abruptly, Roger's heart began to pound as if he'd just had fine sex. He dropped the foot and backed away, feeling queasy. His green rubber boots slipped in muck; his arms whirled in air; gray hair danced upon his head; his lips smiled in the grim way of an orchestra conductor who hears discord in his little world of harmony. The farrier's hammer slipped from his fingers as he fell to his knees. The knees made pucking sounds in the mud. *Why me?* he demanded of the universe.

He clawed into the stinking stuff on the floor of the stall, following each cannon bone, fetlock, and pastern. Three normal hooves remained to Penelope. He pinched up the human foot with his face averted, flared his nostrils, and held it out like a road-killed cat. Pink callouses rimmed the heel and ball of the foot, and the pads of the toes. Dirt tipped the nails in grimy little arcs. Green veins, which had varicosed before their time, forked under translucent skin. Animal bristles and human hairs mixed at the juncture where brute flesh and human flesh merged without transition. The human foot was a serviceable one, repulsive only because of its mislocation.

"Jesus!" Roger breathed. "What will the neighbors think?"

The neighbors wouldn't understand. Roger was an outsider, a liberal, who had moved to the Victorian house and eighty acres near Reelfoot Lake after the stock market crash of '87 to recover from ambition. In working with animals, he had found a cause.

Roger Jones discovered that he could read animals. It was astonishing that most human beings could not. With close attention, animal communication is easy to receive. Messages dart like the amoebas in tap water that leap into visibility only under a microscope.

At the simplest level animals sign. If Penelope rattled a bucket, that meant FEED ME! If Roger carried a collar, traces and hames, Penelope would stamp a hoof and turn her head as if a fly had stung. She'd utter an Italian sigh. Her shoulders were tender, *much* too tender, for skivvying wood, she'd say.

He received meaning out of silences, pauses between movement, projections of will, shifts of the eyes, tensing of muscles, and position changes. He did as he was asked: lit fires, poured food or water, opened and closed doors, went for walks, or gave affection.

He developed a theory to explain human ignorance of animal language. Domestic animals had mired down on their evolutionary journey not because they lacked opposable thumbs and an upright posture, but because their communications were feared and ignored. For human beings to exchange significant meaning with animals, to share a language, was to admit kinship and give up the superiority that justified taking hides and eating flesh and keeping slaves.

After Roger's animals learned that he responded, clouds of messages hummed at him. He *knew* what they were thinking. The dog "spoke," as did the cat, the jackass, one turkey, and the drake mallard. Soon, reception clogged his brain. He couldn't get any relief from it.

If he found a quiet spot to drink coffee, the pit bulldog stared at her water bowl. Her almond eyes glowed. Receptors inside his head chattered like a telegrapher's key declaring train collision. The bulldog wanted one quart of *cool* water, not less. *Wash the pan,* she'd say. *I don't like water in plastic bowls. Fill the pan full enough so that my collar doesn't bang the edge.* He'd put down his coffee cup and do as she asked.

"Now!" the animals insisted. "Do it now! Pat me. WON'T YOU PLEASE DO IT NOW? I LOVE you. Do it now. Food. Hunger. Food. Hunger. Pan. In pan. Put food in pan. NOW!"

Roger reeled like a pale, bleeding British heavyweight catching punches. There wasn't any joy in animal talk after the novelty passed. A child's speech can slide to reality by a shining path. Animal speech plods. He got numb from its pounding, and wished sometimes he could treat it as noise.

Half Ass

When Penelope grew a human foot, took that evolutionary step, it was speech in a syllabary beyond Roger's comprehension. Speech he could not ignore. Was God talking? Nature? Or, was this only the freakish product of monstrous genes?

When Roger had argued in his fervid way for talking to animals and treating them as fellow creatures, neighboring farmers had fallen silent, hidden their hands in their pockets, and looked at the horizon. He had bought with city money a farm they had expected to buy cheaply. He was a Yankee, contaminated by horrible liberal values. They would show him no mercy.

Roger jerked his head to peer around the barn lot, yard, and farm road, not expecting an accusing neighbor to pop from behind a tree or around his barn to charge him with something awful, something unthinkable, like a crime against nature or bestiality ... not willing it, certainly, but watching as a wild thing watches, ready for flight.

No one moved on the road or near the house. Not Smeltzer, the dealer who stopped by to pester him about selling livestock, not unemployed blacks who wanted work, not the mailman or meter reader. Not antique pickers who came to the farm and begged to look.

Roger compelled himself to breathe deeply. He took out a pocketknife and cleaned his nails as his grandfather had done to compose himself. He packed a pipe and smoked it, sending up a rum and maple smell. He thought calm thoughts and went through rituals of relaxation, but the problem shattered his every effort to achieve steadiness.

He squatted to examine the jenny's leg again. Everything looked normal from shoulder to fetlock. Then a circle of shed horn, part of the original hoof, ringed the pastern. It looked like a primitive bracelet or shred of dried placenta. An aberrant gene must have bided its time on a stalk of chromosome to flower this surprise. The hoof had shielded the baby foot until it was ready to declare itself. Jointed human toes had formed in secret. Horn had split to reveal a miracle too tender to walk upon.

Roger wondered if an unknown farm boy had tupped Penelope's dam. Or if the gene could have lain dormant for generations. Would anyone remember he had *bought* Penelope, and so couldn't be guilty of sexual turpitude? They'd think the worst of him, he knew. Wasn't he "hipped" on the subject of animals, a "nut" about fur coats? Hadn't a newspaper columnist called him Dr. Doolittle after he addressed the Rotary club?

Conversations from the past flashed through his mind, taking on dark implications. He'd preached animal rights at a ladies club meeting where women wearing furs had held onto polite smiles. He'd declared to his nearest neighbor, a sheepherder, "Aren't farm animals just other versions of ourselves?" Dark suspicion had flickered in the man's eyes. He'd folded his arms across his chest and thought awhile before answering. "Yeah, I *guess* I know what you mean," he'd said. "I sure *hope* I do."

Roger felt compelled to understand what had happened. He couldn't ask anyone, but he had a nineteenth century confidence in books. The card catalog at the university library revealed nothing. He thumbed through genetics journals. Nothing there. In the pharmacological museum he located Thurmand's *Genetic Anomalies,* Philadelphia: 1902.

Roger lifted the book to his face. The cover smelled hammy, like the inside of a dog's ear. Its edges folded secretly. A white octavo rectangle had been worn through the leather surface by the pressure of inside pages. The small rectangle seemed a boundary fencing a restricted body of knowledge. Roger opened the book again. Dust motes drifted. The author's name appeared in ornate script: Jason Thurmand. Philadelphia, 1902. Roger sneezed and whispered *excuse me.* No one was near enough to hear. He scanned to page eighty-six. Hair prickled on his neck. His left hand lifted to shield the page.

Pig People are squealy things, bobtailed, with the rounded hams of women. Boneless hands flap from their rolly sides. Farmers drown them in buckets.

Cow Boys are calved as twists of flesh and cartilage, jumbles of misassembly. A cow's liquid eye perches upon a man's cheek; a thigh is shot through with a flyswatter tail and a ruminant's teeth. For this reason, herders in the American West describe themselves as "drovers," not "cow boys."

Sheep People are all aborted. Ewes conceive hybrids more easily than do other domestic animals. Their slips look like pale shrimp. You may see them diaphanous and rainbow-colored upon spring pastures.

Goat Boys are hardy and precocious. They learn guttural English by six months, reach puberty at eleven, and then attempt rape of human females. All are darkly murdered.

Centaurs are the only human-animal cross assigned a biological phylum, described in history as well as mythology, possessing an art (playing the lyre), the ability to use weapons (the bow and arrow and the trident), hands with opposable thumbs, and a warlike nature. All are male. Mycenaean mares and ancient Greeks were significant producers. A modern centaur colt sired by a Caucasian male and out of a Thoroughbred mare is sealed in a drum marked CADAVER PARTS in the veterinary school of Kentucky. Its brain is anecdotally reported to be as heavy as Daniel Webster's.

Roger lay the book down. He wondered if fairytales contained truth. He wondered if monsters born today were hidden by conspiracy. The scientific establishment had refused to pursue lines of evidence opened by Velikovski ... Pauling ... Jensen. Maybe there were others.

Roger looked around for a professor or any authoritative person. He carried the book to the desk. The student sitting behind it glanced up. Roger's face heated. "Are you a pharmacy student?" he said. The boy nodded. Roger spoke in a joking way, looking to one side. "This can't be true, can it, what this old book says?"

The boy read the page "No sir. I'm afraid not." He grinned. "But isn't it a neat old book?"

Roger drove home, walked to the barn lot, leaned on a penta-treated fence post, and considered what to do. The jenny lifted her head to greet him.... He could not sell her for money. That was out of the question. She was still somewhat a friend. He *could* donate her to science if it could be done anonymously. The only anonymous donation he could imagine would be to tie her at night to a stout tree in a geneticist's yard and run away. Penelope would stamp her foot, bray his name, and point ears in his direction, though no one could read her accusations.

I'll murder her, he thought abruptly and without pity. *Dig a pit, sprinkle in caustic lye, cover her with discarded tires, and burn her*

The jenny tucked her ears and crouched on her hocks. She sprinted out of the barn lot on three hooves and zigzagged across the pasture, holding her aberration curled against her chest. A rusty wire fence barred further escape. She danced against barbed wire and opened her membranous, flame-colored nostrils to bray hideous accusations.

Roger edited his thoughts. *Not kill—put down.* Euphemisms were incomprehensible to her. He went inside the barn, rattled corn, dumped it into her trough, and called her name. She circled the pasture at a limp, watching with one big liquid eye from the side of her head. "Suit yourself. I don't care," Roger said. He dusted his hands and slogged away in green Wellies, stretch jeans, and Lands' End checkered shirt.

Penelope slipped across the pasture and hid behind the barn. When he heard corn grinding between her teeth, he turned. There was no need to hurry to close the stall door. She was a prisoner of greed as long as one grain remained in her trough.

A horn beeped at the farm gate. It seemed a clarion to Roger. He whirled. He hadn't shut Penelope's stall. At the end of the lane stood the livestock dealer's muck-spattered truck. Before he could get there Smeltzer's fat arms already leaned on the gate. The man showed the side of his neck in a vulnerable way, as if to say *bite here!* His vest bulged over a sweet little belly as if to say *I'm easy.* Hair lay like mowed straw above his strange red eyes and flared nostrils. His lips fitted like rolled putty. All his features crowded together, gaining intensity by nearness.

"Well!" Smeltzer said. "You going to open this up and

let me load that ass today?"

"Not today." Roger hurried to the gate to bar entry.

"Ain't you going to hear my offer?"

"Sorry."

Smeltzer eyes were the color of red-skinned peanuts. He rasped his chin with a palm. The rubbing surfaces swished like steel on a grindstone. He gazed over fields of wet grass and closed one red eye. "I might give cash." He breathed the word *cash* as reverently as Southern Presbyterian preachers schooled in homiletics do *Gawd*. "Could be I would. I been known to do such as 'at." The half-closed eyelid jumped like a released window shade flying up to rattle a spindle. "I would for 'at jenny if you wasn't outrageous fond of her. Know where I might could make me a piece of change. She'd be a kid's pet. Have a good home."

Smeltzer drummed fingers on the dented aluminum gate. He showed teeth like bundled yellow carrots inside the curls of his lips. Tufts of intimate hair poked from his nostrils.

"Sorry."

"The way you won't sell me nothing puts me in mind of my daddy and this bird dog pup he had. That thang set a bevy while it still wore milk teeth. Well, he was proud! Well, this fellow come along the road and wanted 'at thang. Well, you know what? My daddy sold it for twelve dollars. I like to of cried, I was so fond of it. Then my daddy gave me the best trading lesson I ever had. 'Son,' he said, 'the biggest gamble a man ever makes is to hold a puppy to make a bird dog, or a heifer to make a milk cow.'"

Roger forced a smile. "You'll have to excuse me. I've got work to do."

"You gonna keep 'at jenny when she could die on you tomorrow?"

"She's not for sale."

"She wouldn't be worth a penny dead. She'd cost you money. Yes sir, she would, just to get shut of the stink." He shook his head, "You're sure fond 'at thang! What'll you take for 'at pit dog?"

Roger walked away. Smeltzer hollered at Roger's back. "She bad? I know a man fights pit bulls, and all 'at." His voice rose a decibel. "Ducks? Folks say you got a flock of mallards ain't doing you any good."

"Get out of here," Roger muttered under his breath. "Get out!"

The next day Penelope limped out of her stall wearing one perfect human buttock—white, curved, and delicately dimpled. Roger frantically slapped his cap in her face and shooed her into the stall's darkness. He stood trembling with his back against the door, threw the latch, staggered to his house careless of mud uncleating onto the old carpets, chugged whiskey, and lit his first cigarette in six months. The fast hot smoke scalded his mouth.

When his heart didn't thump so unruly he cat-stepped back to the barn and peeped through a crack between boards. *Hot damn. It's real, all right.* He grinned, baring his teeth like a fox in a trap.

Penelope's ears hung in an inverted V. She didn't hold up her potbelly. Worry robbed her of all muscular pride.

Oh yes, oh yes! Roger chanted the meaningless sounds a man makes in unavoidable pain, as when a nail pushes through his boot sole and eases into flesh. Sweat trickled coolly down his sides. He visualized *National Inquirer* headlines shouting, HALF-ASS ASKS, "WHO'S MY DAD?" and close-up lenses of television cameras fixing on his sweat, enlarging beads of it to baseball size. Neighbors would shun him, thinking he should have killed the creature as degenerates always had, and spared them the opening of a door to the dark.

He got drunk that night, and rambled the farm with a whiskey bottle in his hand. Halfway between drunkenness and sobriety, a shining truth flickered through his mind. He backtracked it, pinioned it, and held on tight. He'd been wrong!

Men had known all through history exactly what they were doing to ignore animal talk and select beasts for stupidity ... to herd and remain in fences, gush milk, lay cloaca-splitting eggs, follow judas goats, lay on meat tissue, and walk docily to slaughter. Except for traitor dogs who policed sheep, betrayed game, guided the blind, bit intruders (the equivalent of fanging a god), or led other dogs in the slavery of dragging sleds, smart animals were destroyed. Even those that performed the little trick of regular escape were taken to slaughterhouses or "shelters."

Why had he thought that making animals more "human" was the right thing to do when the long history of human experience ran contrary? That fool Whitman had blathered, "I could go and live among large animals," and raved on about their "serenity." Roger *hated* animal gibber. It was the noise of idiots.

Animals are *bodies,* he yelled to the stars. They cry their wants and anguish from ten-watt minds, in nothing vocabularies. The waving tails and glowing eyes of dogs do not say, I love you. They say, GIVE FOOD! GIVE A PAT!

He'd kill the jenny. Roger staggered inside, crammed his pockets with red, waxy shells, loaded the shotgun, and crept to the barn. He peeked through a crack and shined in a light. He lifted the gun, snuggled his cheek to the stock, and touched the trigger. Penelope turned her head toward him, and the eye in the flashlight beam forced him to pause. It absorbed light rather than reflecting it back as a flash of green. It was a small, elongated human eye.

"*Shit!*" Roger yelled. Scatology filled his mind. He turned and his spine wash-boarded down the barn wall. He rubbed his nose with the back of his hands as he had done as a child, and raged at his weakness in not killing Penelope and burning her body to save the only life he truly loved, his own.

He thought about the large, inconvenient, smelly carcass a jackass would make. A hunter might discover the bones. The human ones might cause Roger to be charged with murder. It was all too late, anyway. The choice to destroy Penelope lay behind at some crossroads. He was a prisoner of her growing humanity. The only solution was for him to withdraw from the world.

Roger had the electric current cut off, switched his mailing address to general delivery, and canceled his newspaper. He fed the bulldog gunpowder and gave her lessons in meanness. He made posted signs from wood scraps and tacked them to trees, warning, PRIVATE PROPERTY. NO TRESPASSING. SURVIVORS WILL BE PROSECUTED.

Not daring to leave the farm to buy feed, he hung a collar and harness on Penelope's wretched frame, hitched the turning plow to trace chains, and plowed and sowed by moonlight. She groaned from aches in her mismatched hips and moved with a vulgar gait. Furrows wandered across fields like snake trails. They looped and circled, unrelated to sensible plowing. Roger couldn't stand to look at her. After the sprouting of her latest physical aberration he could barely meet her gaze. All of his kind words were just lies.

It was nine o'clock on a Saturday morning when Smeltzer came again. Roger had a fire going in the yard because the electric current had been disconnected. Two black wash pots of mush bubbled over yellow flames. So much humidity hung in the air the smoke could not climb and would not crawl. It lingered around the pots, stinging his eyes, as Roger stirred with a boat paddle.

The pit bull lifted her muzzle, emitted a tiny *woof,* and looked at Roger to say *someone is coming.* Through gray smoke, he saw Smeltzer cross the pasture. Roger put down the paddle, hating the necessity. Mush would thicken and burn if it wasn't stirred constantly. "Okay," Roger muttered to Smeltzer. "You son of a bitch, you asked for it. I tried to warn you."

Smeltzer walked bent forward, clutching his coat as if pushing against a strong wind. There was no wind. His red eyes squeezed tight. His perforated vinyl shoes, which aimed in different directions because of the set of his knees, volleyed up dust balls.

Vicki, the pit bull, wiggled her hard body and stared into Roger's face, asking for permission to greet. "Bite!" he commanded. She capered in a circle, head turned to one side, saying, *Him? That poor creature?*

Roger wanted to pull her ears and kick her. But neither would work with a pit bull. Only her feelings would be hurt.

Smeltzer was close. Roger felt trapped by the man's friendly expression.

"Hey, neighbor! Your gate's locked. Some chain is acrost your road. Nobody said they seen you. I come to see if you was all right." Smeltzer spoke in the hard jocular voice of a man taking an advantage. He pushed down a strand of barbed wire and cocked a leg to step into the yard.

Roger bent to the dog and pointed to Smeltzer. "Kiss!"

he whispered. "Kiss!" She raced across the yard, smiling a grotesque, glinty smile, stubbed tail wagging.

Smeltzer, who couldn't read dogs, saw her as horror and death. His mind was filled with television images and breed-prejudice. He screamed, ran to the pasture fence, and ripped his trousers from knee to ankle in getting over it.

He's only the first, Roger thought.

Soon, he wished outsiders *would* come. Then his torture would end. Day by day, the domestic animals converged on humanness. The pit bull refused to patrol the farm and became a terrible, sexless wife, demanding FOOD! COOL WATER! MAKE FIRE. I'M COLD. She sat her grotesque haunches on his best sofa and whined, and cried, and said a million times, *Love me. Pat me. Don't you care for me? Don't you?* With perfect articulation and the mind of an idiot, she was a monster of selfishness. He didn't have one uninterrupted thought. He couldn't stand to look at her crooked fangs poking from under one human lip, abide her sulks, listen to her endless demands.

The human knees the mallard wore on his short yellow legs weren't any good for kicking in water. He wanted to debate every issue with the certainty of ignorance and in a penetrating voice that could call down passersby from the sky.

The cat eliminated species from her venatic world. She hunted only for sport, sheathed her claws, and released prey. She watched nature programs on television, twitching her tail tip and narrowing her eyes. When the screen showed a bird she kneaded the rug to shreds.

Penelope couldn't bite corn off of a cob with her handsome human jaw. Roger was compelled to grind it for her. Ground corn caused flatulence, and she brayed from belly aches. He worked a whole day to stitch a leather shoe for her human foot, using an awl, waxed thread, pliers, and a large needle. He made a cape to hide her rump. She didn't like it, and tore it with spleenish temper.

His charges' lack of opposable thumbs and capacity to plan imprisoned Roger in duty. He exhausted himself with the troublesome present. Only by running away to Reelfoot Lake could he escape. He sat on the ground, touched it, and listened to wind over water. His senses opened like a wild creature's. He saw rocks at his feet and in the same vision, soaring hawks. He smelled pungent deer and foxes. He learned that the slide of air on large expanses of skin is marvelous. He relished the complexity of water, its slurping goodness, the reek of oaky leaves or special rot. When he returned to the gingerbread house the domestic clatter sounded awful.

The specially-abled animals, as Roger now thought of them, gathered at the house to protest his dalliance with the wild and his shirking of responsibility. They lacked the vocabulary to express it, but they knew he was distancing himself. They regarded him sadly, with the forlorn dignity of old friends of unacknowledged worth.

Penelope, with her poignant human ass and two silly feet, stood in the yard. Vicki, the pit bull, with a woman's red lips pouting in front of a mouthful of useless teeth, looked with doggy eyes from where she sat on an Adirondack chair. Mandrake, the duck, wearing his dreadful Marine haircut, crossed unsatisfactory human knees. He perched on the steps. They waited for one of their number to speak, but Roger knew what they wanted. *More.* They always wanted *more.*

"Go away, all of you," he said. "No petting! No demands!" And he went inside and shut the door.

DARK HEART

My brother looked upon me and said, "He has always had that mustache."

My ex-wife said, "You hate your mother."

Friends take jest for serious endeavor. My jokes fly like arrows bowed by an idiot with a slack string and strike hearts I would not wound.

People do not know me.

My ring name is Scholar, or was. I am a wrestler, or was. Last week my manager said after a match, "You are as bad an actor as I've ever seen. You are so phony-looking when you fall that if you truly died in the ring, people would boo. Take acting lessons. Get out of the business. Do *something*."

The guy I wrestled had scuffed my right ear in a head-lock that wasn't scripted. The side of my head puffed and stung. I fingered the top roll of my ear as I stood wrapped in a towel and tried to think of the name of the Bowery Boy whose ears turned down.

"Look at you," Amos said. "You are hopeless. You are bound for tank towns. Sit down, you."

Amos is my manager and trainer. His hands have skills such as aspirating an ear. The hands do not need Amos except as a platform to aim them. They work while he is looking away or his mind is in Poland.

I sat on the stool in the resigned way of a boy in a barber chair. Amos's hands moved like a cool wind. Alcohol washed across the sting, making me shiver, and splashed into a shaving bowl clamped between his plump belly and my neck.

"Sit still, you," Amos said.

"Are you going to cut it?"

Amos's hands open my ears with single-edged Gem blades from Wal-Mart when injuries are severe. They scrape ear cartilage with a dental gouge and insert a catheter connected to a blood-and-clot-sucking pump. Then they swab on carbolated Vaseline and mold a plaster shell to prevent swelling. You have a heavy ear when wearing a cast, but it does not change shape later.

When the cauliflower is very fresh, he uses a simpler method.

I would like to own Amos's wise hands. I turned my eyes to watch them mix plaster but turned away as they laid aside the pestle.

A hypodermic needle pushed into the ear, tugging a bit. Fluid from it jetted into the enamel basin. "Sit still, you," Amos said.

When he does such work he is fussy as a seamster cutting velvet. The edge of the bowl pressed dully into my neck. Amos's soft breath cooled the alcohol. A finger poked cotton into my ear channel. Two fingers gouged into a Vaseline jar and greased the ear. Hands molded a plaster shell onto the ear and nearby skull. "Get up," he said. "That wasn't bad."

"I can't quit the ring. It is my life, and I love you, Amos." This I said out of fear of change.

He held a bottle of liniment in his hand as he looked at my reflection in a mirror over the dressing table. He popped the cork of the bottle and sniffed it. His eyes were buckets of Warsaw tears—he is a sentimental man. "I know you hate me," he said. "Take off the plaster in ten days."

And so I went into the world. I left fatty backs, sweaty thighs, and serious pretensions. I departed bellows, grunts, and souls narrow as floor cracks.

Fifteen years my manager, he was, but betrayal does not hurt me.

The man with yellow curls and hollows in his face is not me. The man whose junior championship belt sags upon a slack waist, and who is attacked in bars by citizens without respect is not me.

No, friends, I am not even here. I am in Arkansas upon a thread of water, fishing. My guide has twisted a scarf of blue about his neck to match his eyes and blood. Otherwise, he has been dressed by Orvis. He says my flies are pedestrian and produces twenty caddises in a plastic case. He is an earnest scholar of the hatch.

No. I flick upon the glittery water a prosaic coachman. Its hackles stand awry from fishy kisses. It is old and made with magic.

Oh, bless you, Korean woman, who tied this Wal-Mart fly! Would that you could knit up my raveled body and I be cast at Ole Miss, or even Myrtle Beach, among women!

Line whistles. The coachman taps a rock, falls, and dimples water. It flutters disingenuously. A celebrity fish pops from the river with the sound of a plumber's friend sucking a commode.

"Ah-HAH!" I cry, setting the hook, as I was wont to cry in gouging an eye when I was a wrestler. I dance across rock and water as line screes upon the reel.

The guide's eyes bulge at the size of the fish. They appear to stand upon toothpicks as they would if ejected from the head by a crushing belly squeeze. Their nakedness and veined wetness are inviting. Something clicks within me. I seize the left eye by the root, yank it out, and hook it as you might a sturgeon egg if you were an ignorant fisherman.

What magic!

The guide howls in pain and indignation, a hand clamped over the hollow in his face. "How could you do this? I don't even know you!"

I say, "You and the world."

He cries, "You have blinded me!"

I reply, "Look inside and see truly."

Who sees truly? My wife wore a smile all of the time. It

was about the thickness of a hair. She said, "No one will ever get close enough to hurt me." But she warned me after we were married.

The sides of the magnificent fish shine pink as amateur-painted skies. There is mossy green and the tint of Andre champagne upon it. I fold the guide's hands around the fly rod. We have made a fair exchange. He sobs ungratefully.

"You can wear a black patch with matching elastic," I comfort him. "It will be dashing. Orvis will ask you to pose for the spring catalog. Women will be charmed. Ignorant fisherman with virgin equipment will demand your guide services."

He is crying and stumbling in the water. "You crazy bastard!" He clamps a handkerchief over his face.

I drop the eye, still hooked, into a wide-mouthed bottle which had contained roe. He snatches for it with slippery hands.

"You'd better attend to your fish," I caution him, as you would a child.

The trout has not been reduced to possession. Trout have fragile lips, and upon the lower ridge the battered coachman perches. The fish rolls, thrashing water to silvery foam. Its size menaces White River records.

The guide sinks upon a rock, staring morosely at the trout.

"Take the fish," I say kindly. "Accept your good fortune. For a lower price than any marriage or making love with strangers, your life has been changed. Nothing will ever be the same. And the cost was piddling. The eyes were duplicative, anyway."

"Don't unload such shit as that, you crazy bastard!" He leaps up and claws at his chest, dancing with anger. He pokes me with the spey blade of an authentic Swiss Army Knife he jerks from a lanyard on his fishing vest. The movement is ratlike so I shove him into the water ... It is hopeless for anyone to engage me when there is no script.

And there I leave him, sitting in water, clawing for a floating orange fly line, a better man than I found him.

I am glad to leave Nashville. Its rings were pooty. And Sewanee, where I looked upon Allen Tate's skully head and lived in melancholy upon the mountain, was not better. I speed westerly by back roads.... There is a Texan who wrestles with candor. Bonebreaker, he is called. The name is spoken with respect, as were the names Frank Gotch and Lou Thez.

Or, is it Arkansas we leave and a whisper of water and the cry of a loon? I do not know. There are two eyes in the roe bottle. I cannot remember how many there were before.

Ten fine homing pigeons purr in a crate in the bed of my pickup truck. In Nashville there were hills to cut the vision of soaring birds, and in the countryside rude boys with shotguns and traps interrupted messages. Texas will be better. It is the place to pursue pigeon excellence.

The heart of a pigeon does not so much beat in a mortal way as writhe and pulse like a watch crystal. A pigeon's mind is small but filled with intention. It wishes to eat, breed, and go home. If the bird is honest, going home dominates other desire.

Before leaving Nashville I cast a bird to the cote of a friend. The message asked: "What is my future in wrestling?"

He sent one of my birds in reply. It arrived late. It is a plebeian bird. I watched it coo and strut. It is not pure. It stopped to panhandle popcorn on the way.

The message in the capsule said: "You have worked for ten years to attain a reputation just under mediocrity. You are too honest to wrestle."

I did not kill the bird. I am not a barbarian. Its head sits upon its body at an interesting angle. Out of the air, a pigeon has the pudgy shape of a lump of clay.

The truck is a Ford eight-cylinder with long wheel base. It is for my new profession, public transportation. It will bed seven Mexican hitchhikers under tarp if you lay the little ones crossways. That way, they will not be underfoot, stinking and whining to use McDonald's rest rooms and calculating to knife me.

Along about Texarkana a funny-eyed Negro stands beside the highway, thumb cocked. I pick him up, and we stop at Shoney's for breakfast.

I am drinking coffee and tomato juice, watching people with let-out trousers and drooping bellies piling into the all-you-can-eat breakfast.

I hate fat.

"That kid there," I say. "If you poked him with a pin he'd bleed grease."

My companion, who is skinny, stares. "You ain't no praying mantis, honky!"

"You ain't been in my grip, nigger. Don't let your mouth overload you." I scoot to the side of the booth and jerk up my shirt so the belt can glitter. The medallion center is the size of a salad plate.

"What? Yo' belly?"

"The belt. The Southern Junior Championship belt. You'd think *praying mantis* did I put the squeeze on you."

The customer behind us struggles to his feet. When he does, his woman bangs her half of the booth to the floor like a deserted seesaw. Cloth stretches across the seat of his gray trousers. He rolls past like a perambulating hippo. "I'm just going to get one more biscuit," he calls over his shoulder. His neck is too fat to bend, so the words drift as public announcement.

Mohammed Y says to me, "Why don't you cut in front of that white man and cough into the gravy. Get the biscuits, too, 'cause he's had too many."

I watch and ponder.

"You ought to do it for your race."

"What's it done for me?" I say.

"You're going to be too late! He's already scooped the egg pan!"

"Why don't you do it?" I say.

Mohammed Y rolls his eyes. He is in niggery smugness. "'Cause I don't want to make him dis-grace his self by peeing all over the floor. If I *look* at a white man, he drop his eyes and beg me, beg me ... 'Don't hurt me, nigger. Don't cut me, nigger. Just let me pass home to Momma.'"

"You're bad," I say.

"I'm *real* bad," he says. "Sometimes I feel evil and drive slow in the middle of the road. Sometimes I go to the front of lines. They don't honk and they don't say. They eyes beg me, beg me, 'Don't hurt me, nigger. Just let me pass on.'"

"That's *road*, rhymes with toad ... not row-ed. I ain't impressed."

He commences twitching and jerking in an I'm-gonna-cut-you seizure. From somewhere I don't see, the hand over the table between us produces a yellow-handled knife. Mohammed Y's nails are thick, clean, and opalescent. The blade is folded. He stares as me for five seconds with one brown and one milky eye. "It would have took a team of stitchers to sew yo' ugly face together, honky," he says regretfully. "Now you watch this. You learn something, white boy!"

Mohammed Y slides out of the booth and joy-walks to the steam table. He pokes into this and that, banging aluminum lids. Then, he seems to feel a terrible sneeze coming on. He staggers, one hand rising to his mouth. The hand will be too late. You know it will be too late. His body snaps backward and forward. His head whips. "Ah-CHEW!"

The plastic sneeze guard over the food lifts and falls, clotted with stuff like whipped egg white. Mohammed Y wipes his mouth with his hand, looks into it, grinning stupidly, and reaches for the biscuits. They are brown-topped and succulent. Mohammed Y can't seem to make up his mind which one he wants. He fingers them all.

Oh, I like this man! I long for an America of lean beauty. Of women with hollows in their thighs. Of men with muscles like John Sycamore's. An America of ice and mountains.... My momma was a fat, mean woman. She had a sly, crooked smile that slid off her face. You couldn't see truth and beauty in her pooked-back eyes. I hate fat.

I have lost my wife, my job, my momma and my boy. This in reverse order of significance. Some of it I can't talk about. There is something going on in my head. When it gets too bad I say, who gives a melancholy shit? I'm not even here. I've gone away. I'm in Arkansas upon a thread of water fishing for a record trout. The next one I catch I'm not going to trade.

Twenty miles down the road I ask Mohammed Y about the mote in his eye. "The white flecks are nice," I say. "They give the eye a houndstooth effect. I am looking for an honest eye. Two honest eyes might be more than I can stand. Just one would do."

"I can't hep you," Mohammed Y says. "That eye you

think is good is mean. It's the brown one minds. That bluish one, I tell it look one way and it slides off on its own piece of business. These eyes is like having twin boys in a candy store, and no big sister to hold they hands."

I begin to brake the truck. My smile is hideous because I am trying to make it sincere and kindly.

He looks at the size of me. "It ain't no special eye," he whines. "Others have got better." He claws at the door. "I bet there is one better among them Mex we passed. In fact, I partic'ular'ly saw one."

"What Mex we passed?"

"You never noticed? They was hid aside the road."

"Damn it, I got to do better than that," I say.

I wheel about and find five of them skulking. A young, whitish woman with the outrageous look of a parrot crouches among them. She has an observable ass. I put her into the cab. The Mexicans protest in watery tones, pointing north, as I rope them under canvas.

Then I look about for my nigger. He is gone. No matter—they are plentiful.

The woman sits with her blouse open and the blowers humming upon her. She has ropes of blond hair and thin lips.

I wheel the truck about and the Mexicans begin to shout.

"People who play oboe," the woman says, "are crazy. The vibration of reeds in the domes of their mouths drives them to it." She nods with conviction.

"Ah," I say.

"People from Pennsylvania are crazy, too. It is because of the isolation of harsh winters and the inbreeding that has occurred. Their genes are locked on low-normal."

"I am struck by how you speak," I say. "You sound like my mind."

She grooms her yellow hair with stubby fingers, tucks her dusty feet, and observes me over a beaked nose. I observe her in return. Her eyes are the disappointing eyes of elephants.

She picks up a newspaper that lies upon the seat and commences to read. It is a *Clarion Ledger*.

"—President Reagan has called Chile a potential democracy." She adds, "And I am a potential woman."

"—An advertisement says the school district is accepting applications for the position of emotionally handicapped teacher." She adds, "You could qualify for that, or I could."

"—U.S. planes will have to wait until the late 1990s for a sure way to tell friendly planes from foes. Until then, they will risk shooting down friends." She adds, "Don't we all."

I cast upon her the glowing look of a man infatuated. Her words and the memory of her ass have affected me.

"They are wrong about Mississippi," she says. "Any state whose editors are so wise—who know the world is mad and print the stories that demonstrate it—cannot be last in all things."

Her thin lips arch under the beaky nose. She picks up my idle hand and begins to suck upon the fingers.

I wheel sharp for Mexico.

The Mexicans commence to whine and bang upon the cab. They do not want to go to Matamoros, they say. They want KAN-sas. Wheet! Trac-tors! They say KAN-sas as if I am stupid. Ha! They are the ones who boarded the wrong bus. I relieve them of ten dollars each for adults and three for little ones. It is a small price to pay for knowledge.

I have been discharging passengers right along. At two, it was my blood father, at 38 my wife. In '54 and '76 the old ones I loved went into death. I drove to Oklahoma to try to sense them, and rubbed my fingers across names and dates sandblasted into polished plaques on mismatched granite slabs. The earth had cracked into rectangles. I tried not to think about that. Sprigs of yellow grass and withered carnations in plastic vases decorated each grave. It didn't matter. The old ones were not there.

To my wife, good-bye and good riddance.

Ah, friends. Ride alone.

The parrot woman takes firm suction upon my thumb. I turn the truck into the entry gate of a nouveau ranch. It is one of those log entries with three skulls hanging, empty of bovine personality.

The love we make is not pretty. She engages me with passionate indifference. We slide in unguent. I am lonely and afraid she will give me a Texas disease. Fear makes me somewhat flimsy. My sputter in her is of no more consequence than a child's sparkler thrown into the night.

"Relieve me, you bitch," I scream.

I cross her throat with the edge of my forearm. It is the naked strangle hold.

"There is a photograph of me on a piano in Scranton," she snivels. "I am hugging a collie, and have braces. My parents play the oboe. They think I am the girl in the photograph, and want me to come home again."

"Don't relieve you, relieve me," I scream. It is a hollow scream. It is no joy to be ground at by a woman whose mind is visiting Pennsylvania. I open the truck door, muttering, "Read Wolfe, read Wolfe."

"Why are you doing this?" she asks, sprawling awkwardly upon her best feature.

"Because you have pig eyes, like an elephant. Hemingway and bloody-handed Roark were right. They stood within scent of beasts and heard the buzz of their flies. They noticed their eyes. They did not audit beasts with Roger Caras. I say unto you, America, use enough gun in the green hills of Africa. Bang away! There is no sin in it."

She picks up a dry skull to hurl at me, but it crumbles to powder and shards.

What magic!

"You will never be a dentist," I tell her. "You will always be a dental assistant and a terrible screw."

She watches me in a dazed condition. "But I'm not a dental—"

I drop the tailgate of the truck and uncoop a dapper bird with white-rimmed eyes and white wing tips. He looks like a minstrel man. He shakes himself in air and heads toward Nashville, carrying no message—a gesture in the dark that pleases me. Will he fly less well because his flight has no purpose? Do we?

I find Bonebreaker upon the range poking cows. He wears a derby, a gold embroidered vest, and an air of affability. He is tall and thin, with no fat and little muscle upon him.

He grins and shakes his head, taking in my size. "*Another* challenger. There just ain't no rest for top gun."

His voice is Texas, but off register, like a newspaper photograph that is blurry with superimposed images. The grin I took for friendly is not. A hard grimace lurks under it.

"I'm too honest to take a fall," I blurt. "And I am too good. Good wrestlers do not wish to risk themselves in my leg dives and heel pickups. They would pee upon themselves in my Boston crab. Yet, I am not popular with crowds. I lose without grace or pleasure. Children and old ladies hiss me. I cannot get a good match."

"Well, hell, pod'ner," Bonebreaker says. His accent has a slight eastern taint, but he grins in the way of cowboys, and his eyes are sky blue. "That must be awful, pod'ner. Still, you don't want to wrestle me." He strokes the neck of a potbellied horse. "This is White Horse, a champion

Quarter Horse. He helps me catch cows. Say 'Hello,' White Horse."

"Whew! Is he UGLY. And he is not pure. There has never been a white Quarter Horse that did not have trash in his bloodline. It is the wrong color for them."

Bonebreaker's smile freezes. Blue spots appear upon his cheeks. "You are too honest," he says.

"No, I am not. A man cannot be that. And I will tell you another true thing. I think you are the symbol of my death. I have been homing on you."

Bonebreaker shakes his head. "Boy ... boy. I'm just a kid from Pennsylvania who loves cows and the open range. I can't get any peace with you psychopaths following me about to prove you exist. I've worked my way to the farthest ranch in the farthest tip of the panhandle. There is no more godforsaken place than this, but still you come. You, personally, are so dumb you would not know a cymbal if it clanged in your ear. Your head has banged too many times against ring posts. And you are egocentric."

Bonebreaker sniffs. "You think you are the only wrestler that knows words?"

He has a hooked, runny nose. He stands in the saddle, looking into the distance. Leather creaks. "See yonder? Those are some of our cattle. We breed thousands on this place."

"That is sinful," I say, "and nasty besides."

The horse gives me a hateful look.

"He is volunteering to cut you with his hooves," Bonebreaker says. "You hurt his feelings by saying he is not pure, and now you have hurt mine. We will have to fight."

I put a cow chip on my shoulder and shout with boyish derision. "Knock that off. I dare you."

He steps down from the saddle. "Stay out of this, White Horse."

White Horse rears and clicks his hooves.

"White Horse! I mean it!"

Bonebreaker brushes aside the cow chip in a preliminary way.

I am wild with desire to grapple him. "I know you Texans depend upon fertilizer now that the price of oil is down," I say. "There is world demand. Probably you have produced enough on this ranch to supply all of Washington. Even all of the federal courts."

He holds up a small hand. "Okay, I will wrestle you. You do not need to keep on."

I go into open stance. He stands upright in French style. When we grapple I am astonished at his stringiness. Yet, I quickly break into a sweat, and he is not straining at all. He says in my ear with a dreamy look, "Our cattle are Santa Gertrudis. They descend from Monkey."

"I suppose a monkey will do anything if it will pick and eat fleas," I say.

We grapple across sparse grass, meeting takedowns with reverses and escapes. There is the awkwardness of bodies first meeting. Our holds are simple—leg dives, double arm drags, cross buttock holds, and headlocks.

"The name of the bull that founded the breed is Monkey. And what you see monkeys in zoos do is groom, not eat each other's fleas. You are terribly ignorant." His breath falls upon my face with a stench so powerful it has weight. I think stuff has rotted his teeth and loosened them in his gums until they are impacted with old steak and biscuits, and eggs and bacon. But there is pleasure in the wrestling. He is encouraging, as are all true masters. I am to go beyond technical competence, his touch says.

We move into sets as old lovers do, and then into the unpredictable. There are moves and responses without thought, too fast for thought. He smiles into my face as heat lightning flashes in the sky around us. Thunder rumbles distantly and rain streaks the sky.

He sniffs, turning his beak. "Rain?"

I strike him hip and thigh. Fred Blassie trained me. I have no mercy. His right heel is my lever as I throw my buttocks and legs hard against him. He falls, and I disable his right arm with the keyed arm-scissors. He is pinned.

Such a moan and clack of teeth!

He arises, shaking the arm. "Call me 'Breaker," he says. "You've earned it. My hat's off to you." He lifts the derby with the left hand and tugs down the embroidered vest.

"Another fall?" I say.

"No holds barred," he says.

I come at him full of joy. He backs away, shaking the numbness from the injured arm. "Your momma died," he says.

"Yes," I say.

Dark Heart

"She was dying, and didn't want to be delayed by you. Her eyes scummed like algaed ponds. You couldn't see into them. She wore a tight, secret, puckered smile that slid off her face. That was from the strokes.

"You'd say, 'Momma, how do you feel?'

"'Fine,' she'd say.

"You'd say, 'Momma, I'm sorry I lied when I was fourteen. I did steal that dollar in change you left on the kitchen table.'

"And she'd say, 'Fine.'

"And you'd say, 'Momma, when I was ugly about that man you were dating and drove him off with an ax handle, that was mean and jealous of me. It was awful.'

"And your momma said, 'Whist,' like she was shooing a fly. It was an impatient sound."

Bonebreaker's eyes are kind. "Son, you turned a shell every day. You never found your momma again, no matter where you looked."

I put a flying mare upon him and throw him hard. I say, "It sounds to me as if you have had me scouted. It sounds as if this is not the isolated place it appears to be. I've told the story of Momma and me a thousand times. Anybody could pick it up."

He gets up slowly, pushing from the ground. "What about this? Did you tell anyone about the boy—the son you lost?"

Tears film my eyes. Over his shoulder a huge sun burns in a yellow horizon. It melds into a gold-embroidered vest. He is upon me. I feebly lift my arms in defense. He takes me down in a winglock and easily clamps upon me the Boston crab.

"Calfrope!" I cry like a Texas baby. "I give up!"

My feet are under his armpits. I am upon my stomach. He lifts my legs, leans back with his shoulders, and sits. There is the little popping sound of my spine.

He gets up. "Well, I hate to break this up, but I have cows to attend to. Clarabell calls." He dusts his hands. "Nice to have met you. You are a good wrestler."

"—Was," I say. "You have broken my back with an illegal hold."

He stares down. "Tough shit. The name of the game was no holds barred. You have paid a fair price for knowledge, but I leave you better than I found you."

"Wait," I say. "My search is for an eye."

His boots are beside my head. The leather of them is rubbed, and the stitching is loose on the inside left. "You seem to have two," he says. "And I grow weary of appeals for organ donors."

"I mean an eye with which to see truly."

"Ahhh. Good luck to you, stranger." He walks away, and not impressively. His heels turn in. His legs trundle along, so thick they chafe. The rime of old sweat circles his shirt. He mounts the horse, and the saddle and girth creak for lack of oil.

"Wait," I say, with my mouth in the dirt. "At least release a homing pigeon if you are not going to call an ambulance. It will be no trouble. All you need is in the truck—paper, pencil, and capsule."

"Oh, all right." He goes there. "What is the message?"

"Help," I say.

"To anyone in particular?"

"The bird knows. I'm trying to make a connection. This is not just a gesture."

He prints carefully, one foot on the bumper, leaning over the hood. I am wondering whether the pencil is cutting through to scratch the paint.

"Anything else?"

"Yes. Say my head is being pawed."

"Quit that, White Horse!" he cries. "I told you this one was mine."

He mounts and rides away. That is the last I see of him.

After Bonebreaker, my luck turned bad. In Brownsville I caught my left fingers in the door of a freezer. In Victoria I went to a health clinic and found that the parrot woman had given me a memorable disease.

The only pigeon I didn't eat before I got to Mexico was hit by a prairie falcon fifty feet up. Gore exploded all over me and feathers drifted a long time.

I am running out of parts. The world has whittled me down. I am using the phone a lot to make long distance calls to hear people breathe. My ex-wife recognized my silence at Christmas. My son grabbed the phone and said, "Is that you, Dad?" and I didn't know what to say. Was it?

There are messages you can listen to like Dial-a-Prayer, and Time-and-Temperature, but that is not the same.

Friends, what does the Bible record of Lazarus after he was raised by the Christ?

Nothing. That is the answer.

Did his bones ever warm? Did his friends avoid grave conversation while watching him for fringe decay? Did his pecker work? Was he pursued by voyeurs of death and *Acta Diurna* reporters?

I wonder this. Could he die again, once raised by the Christ, or is he still suffering life?

I have taken up in Matamoros, where little boys still sweetly carol, "Fuck my sister?" There is humor in this. They know I haven't the price for love.

My useless legs were amputated when they blackened with gangrene. My arms are thick as thighs. I can walk on them, though usually I rocket about the city on a skateboard.

I travel the darkest streets. A murderer, backing away from me, shaking his head, said, "You want it too much." Taxi drivers will not hit me, though I dart between their cabs.

Mexicans have no social security or welfare. I wear a smile and the poor feed me. They listen when I tell of wrestling the mighty Bonebreaker, and though he broke my back, holding him to one fall.

Listen. There are two good arms left to me. I am close

to the ground and hard to get a purchase on. It would be a good draw. We could meet in Mexico City.

I am trying to make a connection. Pass it on.

I want a rematch.... Arm wrestle me, Bonebreaker! Meet me if you dare.

THE LAST FEMININE WOMAN
IN THE WORLD

The relationship I was in lapsed, which wouldn't have been awful except this was with Harlotta who smelled like sandalwood and who introduced me to color and truth. She was young and heavily brown, only about twenty-three, with wheat hair and sky eyes. She worked on her tan with no care for the sun's menace. When I could hobble to the car, I drove by the seventeen-dollar-a-night motel to see her lying on a gook chair at the pool. The soles of her feet were up to catch rays so she'd tan there, too. Sleepily she'd turn her head, lift her hand from where it dangled in water, and wave to me. Long lashes curled on her cheeks. She was brown just about any place you looked. A glimpse set my heart on edge.

I'd smoked my last cigarette. The last nooky I'd took was on Thanksgiving Day, 1989. My prostate was the size of black walnuts. I could just about make it from my bed to my chair. Whisky was no salvation. Chinese take-out cartons littered the room. My dog had taken to running off and could not abide me. He'd left fleas that crossed the floor in a wave to eat me and the deet. But none of this mattered. There are women, when they're gone, its like they're ripped out of your own ever-loving mother earth. I'd have licked her sweat.

Rollo, her new man, would have cut off my balls any day before breakfast, with a fork. It was not his size or general aura of evil that announced it, but Jimmy Carter eyes and icy smile. All of Rollo's angers were tiny and personal. I was at the nit-picking center of them.

We liked the same bar and sat at opposite sides, never meeting with a gaze or opinion. I came from the university cafeteria where I worked, stained in my whites, and a little smelly. It was like if Rollo and I ever looked at one another, somebody had to die. He told how he caught dengue fever on the docks in Mobile. Dengue fever is known as bonebreak fever for where it hurts most. His vessels burst and his blood flowed up on him and turned black below the skin. He thought about asking for a minority job preference. He had to give up the dope trade and live on little money. He used to light hundred-dollar bills with a Zippo to watch other men jump on the floor and beat out the ash with their hands. He sniffed cocaine in both nostrils simultaneously, and dusted a waste of it in his ears to hear the little crystals clink.

After the dengue he got very sore in his joints. His back went out on him. When he mourned, "My durn back has gone out again," I wanted to yell through the beer smell, *Where did it go? Where did it go?* But Rollo didn't need to worry about his lost back. I think he liked not having a back.

The thought of Rollo and Harlotta, the two of them together, put me down among angst and despair. There was an urgency about America in my gut. I sweated clammy stuff after a walk to the box to mail my protest letters to Congress. At night I woke up afraid a cancer had taken root in that place on my colon they sampled at Ochsner's Clinic. My cup was filling with horrors.

This Rollo was not good-looking. His first night in Parchman Prison they raped him twelve times and the next, twenty. Convicts passed his ass and mouth from cell to cell with no maybe. The bar got quiet from wall to wall when Rollo told it. He sobbed until snot ran into his mustache. People looked deep in their beers, and thought, *Why did he tell that?* Snot is so ugly a word I can barely say it, but crying is permitted any human creature. I am not a stoic. I regret that animals can't do more than bellow as they die. When I lost Harlotta my tears did flow. It happened worst at sundown when I sprawled in a gook chair in the front yard by myself. I was way down in vodka where the branches of trees got answers.

Harlotta! I went to her with no wiseness, like a whore with a French name. I said "I love you. I adore you!" right away. Women do not want to hear about "love" until they make you say it. I paid no attention to her sighs and little *no*s. I wrote yellow stickum notes to define our relationship in small contracts and posted them in visible places. My impossible strangeness spoiled it all. The hazardous wastes of my life leaked out no matter how I tried to be tight. Harlotta couldn't stand lies and held up little trapped dead ones under my nose.

She begged me to move out of her apartment so she could study junior college Spanish and be independent. But I wouldn't because she was the last genius of femininity. I wanted to take care of her, and make twenty babies with her, and pay their way through Ph.D.s. Strange men felt this, too. They would see her in the market among yogurt and strawberries and follow her home, wishing to give up anything of themselves to please her.

Giving to others was her true nature. She cherished children, foreign and domestic. She was happy. Then the media told her she was required to spraddle her mind around the world's larger problems.

Harlotta wanted to develop her mind, but I hate a human waste. I kept her in thrall. She made a mojo but it only caused me to dwell in absurdly lewd thoughts. She pored over a nine-dollar book on charms written to sell to New Orleans tourists and to people who cut their hair strangely and who wear T-shirts with dark legends. The charms were to drive me away. They had me chasing her at noon with my eyes bulged like a fertility doll's, thinking extremes of sex, and begging for it with no pride.

She was lovely! Even semiprecious to me. After she was gone I existed for a year in just the cleanliness she left behind. When her scent faded, I bought a bottle of Sandalwood and opened it and stood it on a table for the delusion. This Rollo Veritas of the phony name was less than me in all ways. Everybody said it.

After Harlotta took up with Rollo he moved her to Clear Creek to get her beyond my sight and road patrolling. His barn was full of dogs and wrecked and broken-down Studebakers. Seven of them. They were going to make him rich. Three earlier sons of his came out Sundays to scavenge parts and pull motors in the yard. There wasn't a tree in a hundred yards didn't have a motor hanging on chains. Harlotta unfolded her gook chair and took the sun in her blue bikini, examining the mysteries of books through dark glasses with her tiny mind. I watched her with a Sears, Roebuck telescope made for viewing distant stars.

When I edged close, those earlier sons sicked dogs on me. I wore my magical Reeboks and only the fastest hounds could catch me. When they bayed me I'd sit in a tree, chunk sticks, and laugh at their hopeless rancor.

Wishing for Harlotta, I lost a little sanity. I moved to subsidized housing, and forgot to zip my trousers or lift my feet. My tie tucked under my belt. I became this stubble-faced guy with geezer memory who pored over old magazines with pictures of women as they used to be. I wheezed history. "On October 24, 1929, the stock market crashed," I'd say. Men in my bar would pound their fists on the bar top, splattering the suds. "Why not the hour, geezer? Do you know the hour? Tell me the hour." And I would tell them. Then I'd add, "It was World War II that took women out of the home!" I'd weep a little. They knew where that line went, and turned away.

Then Rollo moved Harlotta into a motel with a cracked swimming pool, a cheap monthly rate, and high crime. It had a water bed in every room and exhibited X-rated movies. The clerk dealt money through a locked grill surrounded by bulletproof glass. Rollo claimed he had to "get away from the niggers at Clear Creek and their dogs." What happened was, the churches of blacks out there had got up petitions against him.

At night I drank wine or Sterling beer at a splayed kitchen table in the subsidized housing and plotted. Rollo came out of my fantasies like chopped liver. I played poker for pennies and nickels with blacks and cheated. But I didn't go back to the bar I liked. I was afraid my hate would seep out and Rollo would smell it.

When I did meet him it was by accident.

I had driven to a Dumpster near Sardis to dump empty Gallo bottles and explore some different trash. The crowd around it was surly from generational hunger. They were not violent, but they snarled and demanded tribute. There wasn't any high class trash at all. All the salvageables, which courtesy required be stacked outside the bin, had been carted away. The stuff inside had been picked over. I found catfish heads and sun-dried worms. And eighteen Coors cans on the murky bottom.

With a screech of tires, a car wheeled in a half-circle on

the macadam. I surfaced, turtled my head into the air, and clutched my aluminum cans.

A Studebaker convertible screeched toward the Dumpster on cracked whitewalls. It stopped, bounced, and swirled dust. Six of us garbage spelunkers stared.

Rollo jumped over a spot-painted door. I crawled over the Dumpster side. "You been pestering my woman," he said, and moved on me.

My lips flickered many placating smiles. Then I screamed, "Stand back! I've got a gun." This was a hopeless lie. I wore striped trunks and sneakers and some coffee stains and fish guts. Every bulge on me was identifiable.

Rollo showed his teeth like the gunmen in Italian oaters, but he needed dental care. The crowd grinned horribly, with pieces of food in their teeth. They had uncovered a crate of old turnips. They hoped Rollo would kill me. Then they would check my mouth for gold and take my cans.

But, no. My fine body squatted on its bandy legs. In a graceful move its muscles had saved since peerless youth, it grabbed Rollo's armpit and wrist and slung him somewhere.

I dusted my hands and looked around for admiration. But no men and boys squatted on their hunkers chewing onion tops and wilted lettuce. They'd cleared out, because here came Rollo from wherever I had slung him, wearing dangerous eyes. I snatched a curtain rod out of the trash and danced away, an aged picador with no hope. My feet stumbled over a globe that showed deceased countries in vivid colors. Rollo caught me and broke my teeth.

A fat man arrived in a pickup to throw away a string of fish beyond the edible. They'd dried in half-circles, with pearl eyes, and no rainbows. The fat man laughed, with his hands on his hips. I thought he looked like B.B. King. "These honkies fight with they *hands!*" he said, and threw me a tire iron.

I whanged Rollo's neck. A fine vibration tingled up my arm. "Shit!" the black man yelled. "You overdone it, baby!" He jumped into his truck and spun out.

But I thought he was wrong. Rollo's pulse fluttered under my fingers. His eyes looked only stunned. I trussed him with draw cord, and left him as salvageable.

I drove with terrible speed to Harlotta's motel and pounded the door of her room. It opened. Expectation made my heart leap. But Harlotta had come away from femininity like Columbus from Spain, and peered into the gloom ahead for a new land not on her charts. Reading glasses hung on a nose that once had held sun speckles. A frown creased her brow. The first finger of her right hand hung ink-stained and deformed from shoving under printed lines. Her dazed eyes showed that her mind had reached sepia but was not going to make technicolor.

She wore a pointed hat like old Mercury's on the dime, or a Frenchman's tricorn, and a bikini top too small. The trousers she wore bulged with indulged legs. But her physical disaster didn't matter to me at all. My heart pounded an ovation. Harlotta glanced at me without interest. An eyebrow arched above her glasses. "Hello, Robert," she said. "How are you doing these days? Where's Rollo?"

I wanted to suck in wafts of her scent, bite her neck, and hear Barry Manilow music. I wanted her lying on her back on a white piano with her former legs in the air, screaming despair at her loss of me. I merited hate for stealing her apartment. I couldn't fire up anything like intensity in her. I couldn't save her. She gave me a stranger's smile and peeked into a book of soft-core philosophy. She couldn't wait for me to leave so that she could fill her mind with correct attitudes and self-help.

The woman had wasted her genius. She had made her greatness just a drab thing.

After seeing Harlotta I sat in my yard in a gook chair, puffed cigarettes from between the roots of my fingers, and drank a cooler of beer and some vodka. This time the tree shapes didn't give answers.

Congress had quit answering my letters. Secret service agents interviewed me quarterly to ask what I meant when I wrote to the president. Newspapers would not grant me op-ed space. If I wrote a hundred letters to Congress to squash a bad bill like a road kill, it just resurrected the next session with a newer, better name. This was not insane maundering. I was shaky from lack of love and food, was all. Smelling Harlotta had brought down a mournful host of memories that went straight to my heart and head.

At 2:00 A.M. I staggered to my feet, remembering something I had forgot.

Rollo.

He'd waited. The pockets of his trousers poked out like little white tongues in the dark. Some religious old black had folded his hands and laid pennies on his eyes. His eye whites flashed too much without them.

For a minute I was desperate about what to do for him. I screamed, "Arrest me, you blithering idiots!" But just drunks who concentrated on walking straight and dope-heads who saw only the green wandered the dark.

All of him wouldn't fit into my trunk. Some spilled out as I wired the lid. Lights winked out all over my housing project as I unloaded him. I dragged Rollo inside and told him how sorry I was about everything. I've got some Creek in me and propitiation is in my bones. The big knife *scree-scrawed* on the Arkansas stone as I talked. Fine white paper with one waxy side spread on the counter-tops. Blue-stickered tape hung ready. The cold registered ten degrees in the commercial freezer the university gave me when its compressor failed. I put on my whites to commence.

The next morning I drove to the Yocona dump. It had been a hungry night. A crowd there rooted for the edible.

Women clawed through greasy paper towels and licked pork-and-bean cans. Two kids sucked chicken bones. A man with a lined face and gentle eyes demanded, "What you got?"

What I had was some black and Indian and maybe Greek. What I had was racial memory of the belly-gnaw, and doing time in commodity lines. What I had was rescue.

The leader of the pack lifted his nose to sniff the white packages that became visible when I threw up my car trunk lid. He wore shoes with hard heels and mean cleats. A black man standing nearby wore a discarded football helmet and waved a golf iron. Behind the men, women clutched kitchen knives they had probed the garbage with.

"Meat!" I yelled.

They came toward me in an avalanche of unwashed bodies, rumbling and sighing. I jumped away in terror. But the strongest man fell, cursing and grabbing his ankle. Leaping over his tumbling body came women, swinging knives.

That night Rollo did a far, far better thing than he had ever done. Barbecue grills smoldered and zipped sparks in the dark. Gray smoke crawled the ground, heavy with a mutton odor. The meat tasted some sweet, too, but hungry bellies filled on it.

I hate a human waste. I truly do.

That's why I returned to the motel, asked Harlotta to

my place, and quick-froze her. I did it for the future generations so that they could see a true woman. At least, a transitional one. I was gentle so that she did not suffer any fear or pain.

Now she's an artifact entire, like a woolly mammoth with its mouth full of grass. Her head tilts. She was looking up at a man. You can tell that from her posture. Though large, she's quite pure for the feminine. Her lips curve in a smile. The hands open and lift in appeal. They are wonderful, except for a doomed, aspiring, slant-tipped forefinger she pushed under printed lines.

THE INCREDIBLE
LITTLE LOUISIANA
CHICKEN KILLER

In the middle of one night in August, 1986, through old man William's bedroom window, poured the melancholy squawk of a hen in the embrace of her assassin. Other chickens talked at once over each other's voices. Wings throbbed and fat bodies thudded against walls and whanged into stretched wire. The fallen plopped to earth with the ripe crack of split melons.

A cacophony of *puck, puck, pucking* soared from the hen house.

"Chick'n killer!" Lela hissed from her side of the mattress. She poked his ribs.

Old man William sat up too fast. His chifforobe, rocker, and bureau assumed looming forms. There wasn't time for his spirit to rush home from its wandering and settle. Until it did, he stared around his room with a pitiful sense of geography.

His shotgun stood against the wall within reach, but he couldn't remember where. A new, unfamiliar thing thumped in his chest. The old man poked his bare feet into black rubber boots beside the bed, feeling their damp, reassuring chafe. He fumbled along the wall until his hand wrapped the cool, solid barrels of the gun. Something inside his chest flopped like a fish announcing itself inside the metal skin of a boat. The feeling caused him to pause and listen. He sat on the bed with the gun across his lap, sucking air.

Lela tucked her face to her knees under the quilt. She was a young, fleshy woman, and made a large bump under there. She said, "Don't go, William," in a muffled voice.

"Hesh."

"Something might be tolling you."

"Hesh."

"Don't go, William. You had a sign. I'll go." She didn't move to go.

He shook off the eerie feeling, pulled on his trousers, took up his shotgun and flashlight, and walked into the dark. The hen's cries of "Murder! Murder! Your poor hen is dying!" and the clucking of other birds yelling "Yes, she is! Yes, she is!" raised a clamor out of proportion to their significance. They misperceived their importance. He kept chickens because he needed egg money to pay the mortgage on his pine plantation, not because he liked the nervous things.

He tiptoed along a path lit by a clean, hard-edged beam of light. Three new batteries fitted the flashlight in his left hand. They gave it an arrogant beam. He'd taken that precaution. His right hand gripped a .12 gauge shotgun by the narrow wood behind the trigger guard. He told himself to remember the loose front trigger fired with just a touch of pressure. The gun chambered waxy, No. 4 shells. The old man didn't know how significant a varmint he'd find in the dark.

He did know that someone wished him evil. That message had been delivered seven days earlier. He'd been standing on the porch, hands in pockets, looking at the sun. It made only a short high arc over his house. Tree crowns allowed circles of light to dapple the porch for less than an hour. Pines pushed around his house with the impertinence of tamed wild-things. They had no modesty. Dried rosin spilled white down the old ones' bellies. Their cups couldn't contain all the trickle. They looked obscene.

Old man William lifted his head to sniff a new odor in the forest. The usual scent was wet and clean. He smelled now the rot and salt of the Gulf. That fecund odor this far north puzzled him.

When he looked down at the dead zinnias in the flower bed, at first he didn't recognize the menace in the contraption of feathers and chicken blood and beads and chunks of red corncob lying there. He didn't appreciate its significance. Oh, he knew what it was, recognized it the way a man might recognize death or the face of a relative he's never before met. But there was an indefiniteness about it. It didn't have anything special to do with *him*. It didn't speak his name. "Lela," he called.

"What," she hollered.

"Hasten!" *It ain't got nothing to do with me. What's Lela done to make somebody mad?* He fretted without urgency.

Lela stepped to the door. She walked lightly, for a fine woman. Without turning his head he could picture the smile her mouth and eyes made.

A moth flittered in the zinnias, releasing trembling dust motes. He looked through their glitter at the object on the ground and felt melancholy and didn't know why.

Then old man William turned to Lela, feeling pity. She was scared of every little thing. "Come see, baby," he said.

"You got a *snake?*" Her voice ran fast. She curled her hands and shook them from the wrist, like they were wet and needed drying. She tapped her knees, like she had to go. Anybody could read every one of this woman's feelings from the distance of the road.

"Naw," he said. "Somebody conjure you, Lela ... a mojo there against the house." He felt a chill premonition of her not lying warm against him in the bed. A feeling of loss started in his belly.

"Knock it back!" she said.

"Why'd you go and make somebody mad?" he said, aggrieved.

"Knock it back!" She came with the broom and slashed in the zinnia stems. They crackled and puffed dust. She pushed the thing away. "Git away! Git away!"

It didn't look scary out of ambush, lying in the light. Old man William regarded the thing. Two big wrinkles framed his mouth the way they did when he studied. They worked up and down, making elastic quotation marks in the flesh, speaking his puzzlement.

"That thing don't frighten you?"

She turned to him with her eyes wide. Her voice ran soprano and full of innocence. "Nobody mad at me, William."

The parentheses around old man William's mouth flexed. Then he grunted like a shoat does when a little .22 bullet carries a surprise message nicking between its eyes, the message that says, *You're meat! Just meat!* That fast, the mojo in the flower bed took on his name.

Only a week later, something was after his chickens.

On his way to the pen through the dark, old man William turned his body from side to side. The flashlight sliced an arc through the blackness. He shined it up the worn, safe track to the house. Its beam probed ahead to the chicken pen and inside.

The eyes of mismatched hens glistened as they cocked their heads to the light. They squawked and fluttered. Their yellow feet crabbed along white-splashed perches. The beam lowered to the ground. It settled on the body of a huge Buff Orpington. She was the one Amazonian blonde in a flock of scrawny Bantams and Leghorns. "Aww!" old man William mourned. "Aww," the way a stockman will for the loss of any creature, fine and female.

Something had mauled her. Down matted the chitinous

surface of her outer feathers. A bare and chewed neck protruded like the shaft of an arrow, aiming the triangle of her head. Under the dented yellow hook of her beak her narrow tongue hung indecently revealed. He'd never seen a chicken's tongue except when he'd worked one day as a slaughterer, ice-picking birds through their beaks.

His flashlight picked up a creamy, floating feather. It settled in a bright interstice of wire. Others drifted with every shuffling step old man William took. The air smelled of dander and dust. He probed the chicken's suffering eye with light. Within its center he saw life.

He eased into the shed. Small, nervous chickens drummed up windstorms. A black hen crashed into the wall with dizzying force and scrabbled down it, legs whirling. "Shoo, shoo," old man William cooed. He tested every corner of the pen with the hard, fresh beam. Only hay and blackness showed inside the hollows of the five-gallon ink drums he'd placed on their sides for nests. The tops of the drums lay flat in the litter, just where he'd dropped them. An aluminum feeder filled with mash offered no hiding place. The two glass waterers showed only greenish liquid and floating chaff inside their smeared domes. A hook tightly fastened the door through which he let the chickens out to range, and through which a killer might have entered.

He examined the wire enclosure, foot by foot, and then the tin roof. He was a steady thinker, and would not be rushed. He focused his mind like an old scratched lens.

How did this wild thing get in? He didn't know. It was a mystery that might be better solved in daylight.

Old man William brushed out a spot in the litter and laid the shotgun down. The Orpington hen was too thick-bodied to hold in one hand. He tucked the flashlight into his left armpit before lifting her. Her legs bicycled slowly, and her wet neck dipped in weariness. Her feathers felt sticky hot, and her heart fluttered against his fingers.

"Will-yum." Lela's cry came from the house.

"It got away!" old man William yelled.

"Come to the house!" she yelled back.

He didn't answer. He bent his head to the side the better to examine the hen. "Shoo, chicken, shoo," he said.

The big wrinkles bowed up and down in his cheeks. If a weasel had dug inside, the pen should be littered with sprawled bodies with throats torn, or heads eaten. A fox would have pounced a reachable bird and deftly toted it away.

He probed the hen with knowing fingers. A sweaty pillow-scent arose from her, a scent he remembered from hot summer nights. Bubbly wetness matted her neck. Claw marks scratched her sides. She had been gnawed by an ambitious little predator with incompetent teeth. "What in the world?" old man William exclaimed. Something was very wrong.

A circle of a lantern light approached along the path. Lela's voice called a little anxiously from it. "William—"

"Here," old man William said.

The Incredible Little Louisiana Chicken Killer

She carried the lantern they kept for power outages. It spread a glow over her wrapper and feet. The upward cast of light struck along her cheek bones and lit the delta color of her skin. Her eyes were unreadable in black sockets, but fear stiffened her knees.

"A snake gonna git you," old man William teased.

"I got a lantern." She stopped outside the henhouse and held it high. "What it was?"

He turned the flashlight on the hen.

"She dead?"

"Naw."

"I'll take her to the house."

Old man William pursed his lips. He'd had it in mind to fasten the hen in a coop and care for her there. He didn't like animals inside. They made messes and noise. Too much attention spoiled them. Lela babied everything.

"I'll put papers on the floor," she answered as if reading his thoughts. She lifted the lantern. It cast a wide net. "You look *good* for that thing?"

"It got away."

"You look again!"

"Lela, you are the scardest woman—" He shined the beam of the flashlight onto the ground. He flicked it across the ceiling. He put one hand on his knee to ease the discomfort of stooping and pointed a beam into a nest drum. "Uh," he grunted, and bent his head close. He stared a long time.

A strange lump lay in the back of the second drum. It could be an old dirty rag. Old man William reached a cautious hand into the opening. Then he saw such a flick as would come from the eye of a varmint surprised by light. His hand jerked and his heart kicked violently in his chest. He picked up a lid from the ground and slammed it onto the drum, but the lid failed to fit. He lifted the drum and lid together, and shook free the obstructing twigs and sawdust.

A wild thing inside ran end to end, squalling and bumping.

He turned for help, but Lela had set down the lantern. It looked as if it sat on a shiny plate. She leaned against a shed post, with her upper body and head in the dark. Not a word did she say. Her breath rattled and keened with the sound of boards going through a planing mill.

Old man William held the drum on his hip. The thing inside was weak. Its bangs hadn't any authority. He studied how he could get it into a coop without help. He didn't want to shoot through the drum in the henhouse, and scare the chickens out of a week's laying. He didn't want to dump it outside and chance a shot in the dark as it ran. "Hesh," he said to Lela. "I can't focus my mind with you breathing so loud."

He got to his feet holding the drum against his waist. One hand held the top, one the flashlight. "Bring the shotgun," he said to Lela. "That's all you got to do."

In the dark, holding the drum with one hand and the coop lid with the other, he dumped the predator. Without a free hand to aim the flashlight, it was hard for him to make out the thing that spilled squeaking and scrabbling into the coop. Old man William carried the wooden cage to the back porch the better to see what he'd caught.

It was a little-bitty white man. Under a forty-watt bulb, it was plain he was a chicken killer. Yellow feathers stuck to his shirt and pants. One hung in the front of his sparse, reddish-gray hair. Blood rimmed his nails. They needed paring. His shirttail hung out in an careless way, not just from exertion but because he didn't tidy himself once he'd caught his breath. Clearly, he didn't care what kind of impression he made. He was either a hardened thief, or a drunkard reduced to raiding henhouses. Rheumy eyes and burst capillaries in his cheeks hinted that. When old man William poked him with a stick, he yelped and blathered in a foreign tongue. It was not Spanish.

Lela stood outside the screen door. "What it is, a 'coon?"

"It a man."

"Say what?"

"It a man."

"Say what?"

"It a *man*."

She eased inside the porch and examined the catch from a distance. Her eyes circled and her lips parted. She came closer, staring at the little man with an expression of joy.

The little man tried to hold in his belly and make himself significant, but his skull was sprigged incompetently. His cheeks and chin bristled with neglect. His lips wore the trembly, humble smile of someone lost in the wrong part of a city, asking directions of large strangers. That took away any fright he might have caused.

Lela turned to old man William. "Ain't he *cunning!*"

He studied her. The lines around his mouth tightened and slackened. "I reckon you'll want to keep it. If you do, I'll tell you this. It got to pay its way."

"Will-yum! A little man like that can't work! You think he can drive a tractor? You think he can fish?"

"That thing got to work. I ain't taking on no more mouths to feed."

They wondered about the little man's origin. Old man William held that it was an illegal immigrant. It had sneaked into New Orleans on a ship, like the Norwegian rats and Argentine fire ants had. There were Pygmies across the water. Immigration had never allowed a black one to enter the country. Maybe it wouldn't allow white Pygmies in, either.

Lela said that, whatever it was, it was a poor starving creature nobody loved. Even if it was an illegal alien, she was going to feed it. "It's just a *baby* thing," she said.

The little man looked pertly from one mouth to another as they talked. He spoke gutturally, pointing to each of them, then to himself. William and Lela watched without understanding. He articulated with large lip movements, the way adults speak to children or foreigners. He tried various delivery speeds, as if he believed that speaking with rapidity or slowness would narrow the blurry band between languages. He seemed to think that differing tongues could be fine-tuned and called in like radio stations. Then he marched to the center of the coop. Wooden bars the thickness of dowels surrounded him. He pantomimed a titanic struggle. The tale he told was beyond their experience.

"You reckon he's talking about a *chicken?* . . . about killing a *chicken?*" William asked.

"Ain't that cute," Lela said.

The little man sat down on the dirty coop floor. He seemed discouraged and held his face in his hands.

"It don't seem real smart to me," old man William said. "It ain't said one word a man can understand."

The next day, because the big hen's heart still beat unsteadily, William cut off her head with an ax. He could kill, if a creature needed it. They ate the hen baked. The little man had a ravenous appetite for baked hen and dressing, gravy, and tomatoes. It didn't prefer raw chicken at all.

The shattered corncob, bits of feather, and broken beads that had seemed a threat disappeared from the yard. They didn't notice when it happened. The charm had become a rejected, powerless thing. Perhaps an animal carried it away because of the blood scent. Old man William and Lela felt they were floating on a tide of fortune that had begun with the capture of the little white man.

Lela wanted to name it, fatten it, mother it, teach it to talk. Old man William wanted to put it to profit without having the authorities take it away. Wonder about what to do caused them to consult the wise woman who lived in the sunlight on top of the hill by the highway. The sign in her yard said, GOOD ADVICE $5.

Their catch was not an alien. It was a weak devil, she assured them. It hadn't done enough bad in life to acquire stature. It was doomed to piddling errands. It didn't have the power, even, to blight a tomato patch, but it could turn a bucket of milk sour. Maybe that. She held it down for examination like a weanling puppy, ignoring its yowls. It had awful dietary habits, she said. Bleeding gums and weak teeth showed that. Its distended belly pointed to minimal kidney function. "Too much alcohol, I'd guess," she said. She saw jaundice in the skin. "Very bad, very bad." Its arm muscles were the size of macaronis. "No exercise," she said. No doubt it was infected with sexual disease and moral slippage. "How else could such a measly thing become a devil?" she asked. They stared at each other, having no answer.

Its health was so bad it could die any day—maybe turn into a puff of smoke. She made an exploding motion with her hands. *Poof!* Then a bigger devil might come, or more of them. "Ha," she said. "How would you like that? It could be very bad." She offered five hundred dollars for it.

They refused. She turned in the doorway as she left. "It speaks only Polish," she said spitefully. "You'll never understand a word." They did not believe her; she was trying to drive down its value.

Old man William knew his fortune was made. All he had to do was attract tourists to see the creature without attracting caseworkers who would remove it to a foster home, or law officers who would charge them with bondage, or immigration agents. He posted a sign beside the highway. Unwilling to claim the amazing truth that the little man was a devil, he painted the sign to say, SEE THE LITTLE MAN.

"We goin' call it the little man," William told Lela. Then he went to the barn and pounded a cold chisel on old silver quarters and half-dollars to make silver chips, in case of need.

All that summer people came. In one day three vehicles rolled in from Pascagoula and Gulfport—a dusty Monte Carlo, fender-banged from headlong careening, and two Chevrolet Silverados with high-dollar mud flaps and bed guards.

Old man William let in folks with pushy ways about them any time of day. Why he tried especially to please the mean-eyed people, he didn't know. He'd poke the little man with a pencil if it hid under its covers. "There!" he'd say when it yelped. "See!"

Children jeered, danced around the cage, poked out their tongues, wiggled their fingers beside their ears, and littered its cage with thrown popcorn, bread, and tomato pieces from sandwiches. They commanded it, "Eat! Eat, you dummy!" while Lela fumed.

People who were timid and liberals who overrespected him, old man William treated icily. He stood on the porch with hands in his pockets, rocking on his slanted heels, squinting with his webbed eyes, wearing a curl to his lips. He behaved as if he were a guard at Graceland. "Naw, it ain't convenient for you to come in. Naw, I don't want no extra tip. The little man got to have rest."

When Lela pointed out how he was behaving, William didn't know why. He puzzled about it. "It's just my worser nature coming out," he said. "Since we got into this business, I'm about all gone before my day cranks up."

In some ways the devil was a disappointment, and having visitors only trouble. It covered its eyes with a sheet, cowered in a corner, and did nothing interesting. It made no effort to be hospitable. Its bad manners fretted old man William. He hopped from foot to foot, and poked harder with the pencil.

One day when the little man was sleeping and received a jab in the side, it sat upright and glared. It grabbed the pencil shaft and pulled. Growls rumbled through its rotted teeth. Sparse hair tumbled across its brow. It sat on its rump, dragging hard. Old man William pretended to struggle. When he released his grasp, the little man sprawled. It jumped to its feet and struck the pose of a swordsman.

William grinned. "Us going to have a fight." He poked another pencil between the bars. The little man's body flattened. Its arm and weapon elongated into one keen line. Graphite pricked the web of William's hand.

He howled. Everyone laughed. After that, a sword fight became part of the show, though the little man wasn't performing. It glared fiercely, pronounced tiny mean words, shook its rubicund jowls, brushed back its hair in exasperation—and when William poked it with a pencil, fought to kill.

Even with this addition, the little man disappointed some visitors because, except for size, it wasn't significantly different from other folk.

"It's mostly a gyp," a woman in a cornflower blue dress told William. "I mean, driving this far to see no more'n this. My own Uncle Charlie was that small until he was thirteen. He had a bad case of worms." She popped her gum.

"It must have been *real* bad," William said.

Others pointed out that there were fresher, more interesting attractions. Two fishermen in Pascagoula were kidnapped by aliens and taken for a ride in a spacecraft. You could watch the men drink beer for nothing.

The Cross of the New Apostle in Memphis was worth seeing, too. A bearded man from somewhere off carried a cross of Jesus to Memphis, Tennessee. There he laid his burden down. No one saw how or when he went away. The sheriff found a Christian cross unattended, weighing fifty-two pounds, and made of railroad ties. In his office, the creosoted wood of that cross sprouted shoots. Yes sir, green shoots.

"Wait!" a lanky visitor said, leaning against Lela's polished kitchen stove, scratching the enamel with his belt studs while he picked his teeth with a match. This man's scalp grew to within two inches of his brows. It looked as if everything slid toward his eyes. It gave them a dusty intensity. "Wait! I got one to top that." On a refrigerator in Baton Rouge, he said, a portrait of the Mother of God appears at dusk Her cheeks on the refrigerator turn wet. You can wipe a handkerchief in her tears and touch your body with them. One man had his hernia seal. It had been big as a Florida orange. A woman possessing a short leg that required her to limp had it lengthened just right. Like it was measured.

"That ain't nothing! Nothing!" Old man William scoffed.

"William—" Lela warned.

"All that can be explained. This here is true." He pointed to the chicken coop on the back porch, and to the lump under the dishtowel in it. "This here is a *devil*!"

The gaunt woman with eyes the color of the cornflowers in her dress, and strands of white hair, mostly caught by a brown plastic clip, said: "Okay, mister. We haven't said nothing bad about your devil, even if he is puny. Why'd you go make fun of that man's miracle?"

The man chewing a match took it out and hung an unlit cigarette between his lips. He jiggled the cigarette as he spoke. "You reckon your devil would light my *far*?"

None of these visitors dropped more than a dime into the hat.

With the tourist season over, William lacked $1,297.47 of being able to pay taxes, interest, and immediate debts. He reasoned that by charging a higher admission he might still collect enough money. His next cardboard sign said, SEE THE LITTLE MAN, $5.

Rain fell upon the cardboard. It bulged with moisture and toppled. When he replaced that sign with one of composition board, someone tore it down.

William and Lela sat at the kitchen table and considered what to do. Lela, in her busy way, made a pot of coffee. Then she drank all of it, firing herself up until the skin ticked by her left eye and her hands hopped in her lap.

"William, we got to let that child out of the cage. We got to treat that child kindly," she said.

William knew she felt passionately about kindness—came near to hating a person who wasn't kind. "That thing is a devil," he reminded her.

"I don't care! It's little and weak, and it's mine. It's the only child I'm ever going to have." She glared at him.

William thought how best to proceed. He looked wisest when he was least sure. It seemed to him that teaching the devil to talk or turning it loose in the house would be foolish. They argued for days.

Before their argument was settled the creature began speaking an earsplitting version of Cajun, something it stole from a tourist or a fraudulent Louisiana cook on the radio. It jabber-jabber-jabbered all day. It got so troublesome in its talk Lela stopped coaching it when old man William was away. "Wha' dis?" it would cry, pointing to an object, "Wha' dis?"

Lela thought it would drive her crazy.

"Lela!" the creature yelled first thing in the morning, its bulby nose pressed between cage bars, and its beady eyes shining. "Gi' de coffee, woman. Why you so late a'bed for? You goin' cook chicken today? You goin' to make de bis-cuits?"

While William fed the stock, as she bent over the stove, it would swagger to the bars of its cage and survey her flanks and bosom with its hot eyes. "My, my! You a fine looking woman, Lela! What you stay wit' a old man for? Why you do dat? You oughta be wit' a young fella. Treat you right!"

Its awful chatter went on and on. When she'd had a canary, Lela could at least drape a cloth over its cage.

Nothing silenced the little man but its fear of William.

"Help! Help! Murder!" It would scream in its shrill, harsh voice if he approached wearing a scowl. "Lela, come quick! This son, he is dying."

Differences between William and Lela had never had a place in their bed. After their first argument, she had turned onto her side and taken him into her arms. "We not going to let the sun go down on our anger," she had said. But once the little man began to remind her daily about William's age, and to "chat" about everything he did, she moved to the mattress edge and turned her back. The middle of the bed lay like a cold river between them. William couldn't find entry to her warmth, and every little thing about her irritated him because he was so lonely for her.

The skin around William's left eye learned a twitchy dance. A gray ridge circled his lips. He looked older. But Lela doted on the little man like a good woman does a bad child, even though she declared, "This baby wearing me *out*."

One morning in December, after one of their nightly fights, William returned from the chicken house in the 6:00 A.M. gloom and stopped at the kitchen door. The pearly glow of the soft white globe that usually warmed the room was absent. Shadows crouched in the corners. No smell of biscuits filled the air. Bacon didn't sizzle in the black skillet. Coffee blended rich with chicory didn't perk and bubble to whet his appetite.

The table was set for one. Something white and gritty congealed in a bowl. Cold grits.

He sat at the table, rested his head on his hand, and lifted the spoon beside the bowl. It was a big cooking spoon, larger than a tablespoon. "Lela," he yelled. "You git in here!"

Silence. Calculated silence. Then dragging steps moved up the hall. She stood in the door, hands on hips. He forced a smile. "I can't eat these cold grits with no spoon like this. Where your mind, baby?"

"That the right size to fit your mouth," she said. Then she whirled and sashayed out of the house without a wrap.

William heard the truck motor crank and the slide of wheels. He leaned his brow into the pocket of his hand.

On the back porch, feet scurried. The little man leaned against the end of its coop. From there it could see into the kitchen. "What da matter you, William? What da matter? You got no *man* about you?" it said in its piercing voice.

William shifted in his chair and groaned.

"Dat woman talk, talk, talk. Wouldn' no woman talk-talk, me. No, sir, me! Golly, no." It struck a pose of bravado and banged its yellow pencil on the cage floor. "I whip her *ass*, me!"

Old man William thought about cutting a switch about as thick as his little finger and blistering Lela's butt. His anger fed on anger. *Oh, my, that would feel good.* Then, he turned in his chair and stared at the little man. The pupils of his eyes narrowed in their filmy setting. "Tell me some-thing," he said. "You a devil? You really a devil, ain't you? You a curse on me, ain't you?"

The little man laughed. "By gar, William, you one funny fellow. You call me dat and your own woman don' fix you no breakfast. She get in yo' truck and drive away." It grimaced and laid a finger along its bloodshot nose. "Who know where a young woman wit' old husban' go? Maybe she go to church to pray he live a long time?" It rocked over its belly and laughed.

"Uh-huh!" Old man William said, "You done said too much."

He walked into the bedroom, tugged open the top chifforobe drawer, and selected two red shotgun shells. Early light beamed steadily through the back window. He sat at a table by it, picked open the crimped ends of the shells with a pocketknife, and threw away wads, shot, and cup. He worked delicately. Beyond the shot lay the white membrane of an over-powder wad. Beyond that, pro-pellant. Beyond that, at the end of a brass channel, the percussion cap. He didn't probe beyond the shot con-tainer.

From a brown paper sack he poured the metal chips he had chiseled from old half-dollars and quarters. He packed the metal into the empty red cylinders, refolded the crimps, and sealed them with duct tape. He shook each reload by his ear. They scarcely rattled.

He went back to the porch and picked up the crate. It

hung on his hip, sending the little man sliding. In his free hand he held the shotgun.

"What you doin', William?" the little man screeched, clinging to the bars. "You crazy?"

"Shut your mouth," William said.

The wise woman lived with three Catahoula curs in a sunny house on the hill near the highway. She wasn't a fortune-teller, but a woman of uncommon common sense.

The dogs stood and stretched as William carried the crate through their yard. The big male lifted his head to sniff. William's long walk had filled his boot soles with information.

"What's that devil done today!" the wise woman exclaimed when William stepped into her kitchen with the crate. She smiled fondly, standing with her hands on her hips. "I declare! He's a grim looking something." She reached two fingers suddenly through the grating and pinched its waist.

It wailed, "Le' go me! Help! Lela!"

"I got to do something with this little man," William said. "You still want to buy it?"

She threw up her hands. "Lord, no. I got too much to do now to keep it out of mischief."

He worked his jaws. "What am I going to do with it then?"

"Do with it?" she exclaimed impatiently. "Do with it whatever you want. It's your devil."

William carried the crate into the deep woods and opened the latch. The little man cowered. It wouldn't run when it had the chance.

He dumped it onto rust-colored pine needles. It just crouched there, looking at opportunity with hopeless eyes. The thing seemed to have a defeated nature. "I want Lela," it whimpered.

William picked up the shotgun. "Git!" he said. "You sir, git! I got this gun loaded with silver."

The little man got to his feet and backed two steps. "You say silver? In dat gun? By gar, William, you one bad fellow." It held open its soft palms.

William jerked the gun. "Git."

The little man talked fast. "You t'ink this over good, William? A man sleep cold wit' a fine young woman beside him in de bed, it bad on him, William. It *bad* on him. This your son and Lela's son. She don't forgive you, never."

The gun swung up and socketed into a familiar cup in William's shoulder. "Git or stay," the old man said. "It don't matter." But his heart pounded awfully. The humanity of the thing weakened his resolve. *I'll just run it off,* he thought.

Abruptly, the little man turned and ran. Swifter than a scuttling fox it ran, twisting past the thick boles of trees, its reddish-gray hair shining peppery in the light, its belly poked ahead, its elbows churning. On it ran, without a backward glance. Its tread did not shift one needle on the forest floor.

Ah! William thought, looking at the undisturbed ground. *You really are a devil.* He touched the gun's shaky trigger. A shell exploded its silver load. Its *blam* echoed against the hills.

Only the pattern edge struck the little man. Just fifteen or twenty shot perforated it. A large cluster of shot sliced off a tree limb, and peppered into a trunk, exposing cinnamon underbark. But the little man leaped into the air with a horrible hiss. William dropped the shotgun. Before his eyes the little man shrank like a released balloon. It blathered around in erratic zips inches off the ground, making flatulence. Its face shriveled and turned inward on its nose. Its feet kicked absurdly, exposing cardboard-soled shoes. Its body flattened to the thickness of well-pounded schnitzel.

Old man William grabbed up the shotgun and scurried behind a thick tree. The thing zipped over the forest floor ungovernably, spurting froth from its holes. He didn't want any of it on him. He braced the shaking gun against the tree to follow the whizzing.

Then William sensed a presence. He heard panting. His heart flopped within him. Hair erected on his neck, and his mouth stretched in an unreleased cry. *That's it,* he thought. *My old heart done kicked off.* He whirled to see a dog. *Only a dog …*

It was a pallid dog with one glass eye and a diffident step. The male Catahoula cur had trailed him. Its tail clamped between its back legs, and the bristly end of it wiggled under its belly. A thick red tongue flopped to its chest. Saliva dripped. The white and black hairs along its back bristled in timidity. Its brown eye and its glass eye stared like a pair of begging strangers into William's face. Both eyes wanted permission to bite.

Old man William said huskily. "Sic him, boy! Git that devil."

The dog sprinted past him, bowing and unbuckling its knotty back. Clots of wet pine needles kicked up from the forest floor. Its ears flopped back to show pink linings. A bawl of notes floated up and spread under the canopy of trees, making wild music.

In three turns the dog overtook the flying remnant of the little man. Snap went its jaws. It made a wispy crunch.

"Let go!" William yelled. He felt awful. But the dog stood spraddle-legged, gulping. A lump slid down its throat. Its pale eye and its brown eye flashed to William. Its tail wiggled for approval.

William felt the sense of loss one feels in giving up a familiar infirmity. He went home and told Lela what had happened. As he confessed, she looked to one side. The softness came back into her face. She was silent when he was through. Then she said, "That wasn't no real baby I had. I wanted a baby so bad I made our little man one."

"That's right," William said.

"We won't have no more trouble around here."

"That's right," William said.

"You have killed your devil, and you goin' be a sweet man to me."

"I will do that," William said.

That very night something raided the chicken house. It was an incompetent little varmint in a terrible rage, who mauled the largest hen and masticated her head. Then an entire succession of plagues descended. Fire ants poured from hot mounds to bite chickens. Pine borers wandered in dazed and lost trails through the cambium of turpentine trees, hurting them to death. Frenzied armadillos tunneled the land until it was a shell and a hollow trap to walk upon. A murder of crows dotted the browning trees. They made ugly comment and peered down at abrupt angles.

Old man William lost his deliberation. "What's happening?" he yelled at Lela. She didn't know, and withdrew behind a watchful gaze.

William made his way to the house in sunlight. The wise woman who lived there wasn't surprised to see him. She had pooky lips that could fold into a terrible look of disgust, and they were already congealed in it when he arrived. She pointed to a drawn chair, and a hot cup of tea steaming on the table.

She shook a finger. "I warned you about losing your devil. Don't say I didn't. This could be very bad. Very bad, indeed."

The Incredible Little Louisiana Chicken Killer

When he returned home, old man William stood on his front porch and looked up at the sick pines. In the kitchen Lela grumbled about fixing a late breakfast. He'd had to tighten-down on her. Nothing he did seemed to please her. He chewed on a hateful idea; he had made a mistake in marrying this woman. Now that his heart had quit hopping in his chest, he might live a long time.

He went into the kitchen and sat down to a breakfast of ham and two eggs and biscuits and savory coffee. Lela waited table. When she was neglectful, he grumbled, "Gimme some biscuits, woman," and she did. Oval flaky ones, lightly browned, smoking and buttery. He ate three and patted his belly but felt no pleasure.

And not then, nor later when Lela ran away with a trucker, and termites ate the house beams, and fire ants polished the bones of his last chickens, and pine borers cut the cambium of his tall green trees and made them skeletons with bare limbs to rake the sky—nor in his penny-bound old age when there was nothing else to do but listen to the unending murmur of his heart—could old man William think of an enemy who might have thrown a mojo against his house.

HOW WEVEL WENT

A. P. Gooch tapped the tight-nailed coffin with his center knuckle. It sounded a resonant *pung,* as if the soul of Brother Wevel Snopes, which had stirred thousands in the year of '30, sought voice in humble oak.

For four days after his death, burial of the body of the evangelist had been delayed by territorial disputes among local churches.

On the fifth day this mourner of prominence arrived in Tippah County. He drove a spoke-wheeled Ford truck, heavily loaded and canvas-covered. He came straight to the farmhouse, walked in without knocking, and stood among the old women sitting with the body.

"He don't hardly stink," A. P. Gooch said. His voice throbbed like a reed organ playing "Nearer My God to Thee." He sniffed mightily, a sniff that practically sucked the poor daisies from their vase, lifted the rag rug from the floor, and ripped the ladies' hair from combs and pins.

The ladies took notice.

Before them stood a dark man with curly hair, an overhanging belly, a white shirt frumpy with sweat, and a somber tie dangling futilely from a bull neck.

He paced circles around the coffin and its sawhorses. Despite the dark suit, solemnity rested only lightly upon him.

Gooch whirled on the women, pointing a forefinger. He grew before their eyes like a center-ring performer hearing a fanfare, as if a spotlight had picked him up resplendent in a white suit, as if snares had rolled and cymbals clashed, as if he were crying "PRE-SENTING!" to a circus crowd. "—Fact is, this body don't *stink* at all! What do you make of that?" he said.

"Why," Miss Rose said vaguely, looking a little to one side of the man, "I don't know what to make of it." Miss Rose smelled of talcum powder, and some of it beaded in the folds of her neck.

He turned to the other body watcher. "What do you make of it?"

Miss Verna's eyes flickered from side to side, stitching the air. She was built thin and spoke conspiratorially. "It's not natural!" she hissed. "Sometimes, after just two days, I have to have sweet shrub in my hanky or carry a bodock apple stuffed with cloves. Sometimes it gets so bad—"

"—Uh-huh, uh-huh," Gooch said. He lifted one end of the coffin from a sawhorse. His eyebrows arched and his lips pouched. A smile spread from eyebrows to nose to lips, like sunlight touching mountaintops. His hands slapped together with a *smack*. The ladies bounced in their rickety chairs.

"Y'all tell the preacher, and the banker, and anybody

else handy that the Reverend A. P. Gooch, the LIGHTER-THAN-AIR EVANGELIST, has arrived."

They opened their mouths in round O's of delight. "You're Reverend Gooch?"

He bowed over his belly.

"—the one that arrives like an angel from on high?" Miss Rose asked.

"—the one that takes folks that accept Christ for a ride in heaven?" Miss Verna whispered.

"The very same." He extended a foreleg and folded over it like a circus horse. "I call it the Foretaste of Glory Ride. And I am called by God Almighty, the one True God, the God of Elijah and Brother Wevel Snopes, to come here today to this humble home and speak to you body watchers."

They gasped at the honor of the thing.

Then the front door banged, rattling glass and letting in a wave of heat like a house dog waiting his chance. Gooch swung heavily. The ladies cocked their heads and put on expectant smiles.

A bold woman wearing rubber boots, a man's shirt, and a torn skirt stalked into the room. The hard lines around her mouth relaxed when she saw Gooch. "Gooch! You've come! I was milking when I heard the truck. Oh, my, it's good to see you." She locked her eyes on his. "Can we talk in private?"

"Why certainly, Mary Belle! Y'all excuse us, ladies. This girl and I haven't seen each other since we went about as followers of Brother Wevel." He beamed upon Mary Belle. "I'll bet she hasn't forgotten the blessings we shared."

"—or, the wonder," Mary Belle said.

"The wonder?" Miss Verna echoed.

"Jesus." Then Gooch added in a voice that disassociated him from blasphemy: "I was praying when I said that."

"Maybe you could help me throw down hay. We could talk while we work," Mary Belle said.

"Oh … well … I've given up barn work since I took up the Call. It don't seem right."

Mary Belle pouted. When she did that Gooch stared at her lips as if he wanted to bite them.

"We haven't had a man here all day," Mary Belle said. She sighed. "Not in years, for that matter. If you don't help with the stock, Miss Verna and Miss Rose will have to."

Miss Verna and Miss Rose flashed Gooch sacrificial looks.

"Oh, no! Don't worry about us," Miss Verna said in a whisper. "I'll be glad to do anything I can." She coughed into her handkerchief.

"Sister has never been strong," Miss Rose said. "Let me." She struggled to extricate her hips from the chair arms.

"Cows are good at waiting," Gooch offered. "There's weeds in the lot they can eat."

"They make the milk sour," Miss Verna said.

Miss Rose flounced her ruffles.

"Oh, well. I reckon I could help, but we got to do this

real fast," Gooch warned Mary Belle. "We won't be no time at all," Gooch said to the ladies. "Y'all call if you need us. Just yell."

In the barn, Gooch slowly climbed to the loft. "You sure this trip is about hay? Usually it ain't when women invite me to their barns." Gooch's voice climbed to falsetto. "'Oh Mr. Gooch, could you stop by my barn and show the wonder?' That's what lotsa women say. It gets hard for a man to keep his mind on the Word."

Mary Belle kicked off the black rubber boots. She unbuttoned her blouse. Her breasts poked out pointy faces like fox cubs from a den. "Would you, Mr. Gooch? Would you show a poor, lonely girl the wonder?"

"That ain't fair!" Gooch covered his eyes and edged toward the stairs. He paused there and sneaked a peek. "If thine eye offend thee, cast it away," he keened. "That's what the Bible says do."

"Would you let me see the wonder one more time, Gooch? I've remembered it all these years." Mary Belle settled on the hay.

"I hadn't taken up preaching then. That was different. I was a different man before the Call."

She slid the rough cloth of the brown skirt up her thighs.

Gooch bounded over two bales of hay. "Hot damn! I know this ain't for old times sake. I know this is gonna cost me. But I don't care how cold a woman's heart is, if it don't cool off her thang!"

When Gooch stopped heaving on Mary Belle, his weight settled. She couldn't breathe for all the somber inactivity upon her. "It's plain—to see—why girls—want to get *you*—in a barn!" she said.

He rolled off her. "Don't give me none of that woman talk, Missy. You don't have to soften me up more'n you already have. What's on your mind?"

Mary Belle twisted a locket of hair dangling beside her hard mouth. "It seems like I've got myself into a terrible fix. That's why I sent you the telegram. You know how dumb I am."

"You're in a family way."

"Heavens, no. After what happened in Huckaby, Wevel couldn't."

A pinpoint of anxiety appeared in Gooch's black eyes and widened until it absorbed the pupils. "You ain't—"

"I'm not what?"

"You ain't got the clap, have you?" He looked at the wonder in horror, seized it back of the head, and shook it like a terrier does a big rat. "I got to soak this boy in Co-Cola right now!"

"Me with the clap? You're kidding. The men around here, most of them, are scared to death of me."

"A man can't take no chance about clap. Them that do carry rubber tubes in their coat pockets to run up theirselves so's they can pee." He got briskly to his feet. "You got a Co-Cola at the house, or do we have to go to the store?"

She shook her head.

He jerked up his trousers. "You got a nickel? I figure you ought to pay the nickel."

She looked at him incredulously. "Why?"

"It was your treat. I never had no interest in it."

"Listen to me!" she yelled. "Put that thing down and listen to me! This is real important. Wevel can't be buried by anybody after this Foretaste of Glory ride you're giving his body but Mr. Overby. He's the undertaker in Booneville. You got to help me."

"You ever had burning when you peed? The yellow drips?"

"I'm sure I haven't. The reason Mr. Overby has got to bury him is ... the reason is that him and me, we already collected on Wevel's burial insurance. Mr. Overby said he knew a way to make some money, and I said do it."

"You what?"

"We needed the money."

"What for?"

"You know those signs on barn roofs that say, 'See Rock City?' Well, I did. When we had collected more money, we were gonna run away to Memphis. I always wanted to spit in that big river whenever I wanted to."

"Uh-huh."

"So, Mr. Overby turned Wevel in as dead and buried. He *was* dead after that stroke, as far as all the use he was to me ... The burial policy paid two hundred dollars."

"That much? Lordy!"

How Wevel Went

"After we spent the money, Wevel ups and dies. Then this preacher, Alcock Baines, and the mayor come out and tell me I'm not a relative and don't have any say about this burial. All Mr. Overby says to me, in a mournful way, is, 'Not *again*.'" She turned up her palms. "If they let somebody other than Mr. Overby do the burying, why *he* will claim on a lost policy, and Mr. Overby and me, we'll—"

Gooch nodded. "I see your predicament."

"—why, we'll go to Parchman Prison!"

Gooch inspected the wonder from each side. "Yes ma'am," he said, "you surely will. Insurance detectives will cold-nose that trail straight to you." Gooch stood, jerked his butt, and the wonder slid out of sight into trousers that gaped like tent flaps.

He dusted hay from his black suit. "You reckon the ladies will think this is from feeding the cows? I got a reputation to protect."

"Let me help." Mary Belle went down the ladder, dodged a bawling cow, dipped her handkerchief into a water bucket, and climbed back. She got to her knees and wiped Gooch's suit where he couldn't see because of the belly.

"Quit that nuzzling. I'm in grief and remorse."

She looked up and widened her eyes. "What will become of me?" She wrung her hands twice and wailed without enthusiasm. It seemed a minimal display, unworthy of Southern Womanhood.

He patted her shoulder. "Don't you worry, Missy."

"What can you do?"

Gooch grinned. "Brother Wevel Snopes is departing in *style,* like the horse woman in pink-spangled panties behind eight bow-necked steeds ... like the lady trapeze artists with their white legs wrapped around elephants' heads, and them big thangs gaiting like saddle ponies, while the sousaphone goes *ooom-pa! ooom-pa!*"

"I don't get it," Mary Belle said.

"You ain't supposed to. Leave everything to me. You and what's his name that stole the policy got nothing to worry about except me getting the clap."

"You haven't asked about pay. Mr. Overby and me, we don't have a *dollar* left. We can't pay you until he collects on more insureds, or thinks of another way to make money."

"You know money don't matter. You remember when I managed Brother Wevel how I handled requests for rain-making and healing. Everybody got the same treatment."

She grew intent. "I remember. Don't treat me like you did them without money. Please don't."

"Why, Child! My only goal is to help sufferers on the road."

When Gooch appeared before the Tippah County Ministerial Association, eye-catching in jodhpurs, purple scarf, and aviator helmet, some were persuaded by his very presence. Others were captivated by the audacity of his plan and the purpose to which they could put it. To levitate Brother Wevel before burial? To have him soar bodily into the heavens and symbolize the ascent of Elijah? To demonstrate the triumph of the life of the spirit over sin? What revivals might follow such a demonstration! Church roofs might be repaired, mortgages be lifted, and manses and parsonages be made habitable.

There were other advantages, Alcock Baines pointed out. Unseemly conflict over which church should conduct the service for the one-time evangelist would be ended if all had an equal chance at love offerings at the fairgrounds. Territorial disputes about which cemetery he should be buried in would be resolved if the body soared out of the county.

And the price the Reverend Gooch asked seemed reasonable. A fee of forty percent of the love offering would mean that all would profit. The cost of Brother Wevel's burial elsewhere would come out of Gooch's percentage.

"But what will happen at the end?" asked the doubters. "What will folks think when he comes down somewhere and is buried like an ordinary corpse?"

Gooch stood and shouted, "Be concerned for the Spirit, Brothers! Be concerned for the Spirit! It's best if you don't know the county of final resting place and can't say. It's best if in your revivals the people of Tippah County remember only the body of this good man rising—" he paused, rolled up his goaty eyes, and lifted his palms, elevating an invisible tray "—rising to meet God."

The morning of Brother Wevel's ascension the sun glistened like a tin dipper in a blue enamel basin. Sudsy clouds foamed across the north. Farmers looked up and frowned, puzzled by the mix of weather signs, and packed tarps under the seats, along with greasy paper bags of meat sandwiches and Mason jars of spring water.

Wagons and Model-T's crept narrow roads until they arrived at the double concourse of Highway 15. There, drivers pulled up in astonishment at the traffic. Jerking lines, gee-hawing teams, or honking horns, they bucked into the flow, to be swept like flotsam on a great river to their destination.

The fairgrounds sprawled in undisciplined vigor to the south of town, beyond the dime-colored tracks of L&N, past even the loose-boarded houses of Negroes and the acrid tannery. The funeral platform stood on a weedy square of ten acres, fenced by rusty wire. A carnival air prevailed, with barkers crying wares, crowds eddying, and trade dogs yapping from hitches on the perimeter fences.

Prick-eared curs with curled tails stared rigidly into the ground, tracking the underground goings of field mice and other subverters. Hounds that could do a job of work at a den tree lolled like public drunks and stared from red-hawed eyes. Some scratched their armpits. Others licked their balls, or popped ragged ears in shoeshine rhythms.

Evangelists harangued the crowds. Each stood in the center of a loose, half-circle warming up for the main event. They began slowly, greeting people in brotherhood, pressing their flesh, then raising voices to include newcomers. Without intention, they shifted into high, shouting to multitudes. One was a Crier, whose voice beat staccato against the hard-of-heart. His hair dangled in wet curls. Sweat stood on his pallid face. His voice croaked in fatigue. The eyes of those about him locked on his mouth, anticipating and savoring familiar words before they emerged. They swayed in the reciprocating rhythms of lovers.

"—And I uh say to you. I uh say to you. I uh say to you. God saves! Only God saves! And oh my friend. And oh my friend. If you are not washed. Not washed in the blood. Not washed in the blood of the Lamb. That grave is deep. Oh, that grave is deep."

From a corner of the grounds came the shout of a Whooper. A black crowd circled him in admiration. Loutish whites, twigs in their mouths, leers on their faces, stood on the fringe.

In the center of the circle a mannequin lunged from a Negro preacher's arms. It seemed not so much held by him as coming out of him, out of his chest and heart. The thing's short arms flailed ineffectually. Its fingers were stubby afterthoughts. All the detail of the mannequin focused on the head. The carved features suggested it was a high yellow, maybe an octoroon, but the face shone with oil and lamp black. Its blue eyes fixed the audience with a baleful stare. Painted red lines branched from the pupils, not for decoration, but like roads on a map, indicating something important—that it had cried, maybe, or was weary unto death. The jaw line jutted with the delicate and stubborn flare of a plow point. A rubber tongue flicked in its hinged mouth, spraying foam and dribbling its chin with suds. A voice like a fox's bark issued from the dark round hole in the dummy's throat. This was the celebrated Brother George.

The ventriloquist who held Brother George was smiling and kind, not his type at all. His gray hair beaded in a dense collection. The smile on his lips hung deferentially. His natural body posture was obsequious. He crouched forward with his old coat flared, and from it came this fiery thing—this reverse centaur, in which a beast issued from the body of a man. It leapt out of his coat, out of his chest it seemed, full of hate. Poor Uncle Tom could barely contain it.

Sometimes when Brother George got out of control and said brash things that would get an uppity Negro shown his place, white folks chuckled while Uncle Tom struggled to gag the mannequin with a bandanna.

This day Brother George whooped.

"And la-ter they tell me ... they tell me his mind went back."

"Oh, yes," Uncle Tom chorused humbly.

"His mind went back to the words Je-sus had said."

"What's that?"

"Before the cock crow ..."

"Uh-huh!"

"Be-fore the cock crows twice ..."

"Oh, oh."

"Thou shalt *deny* me thrice …"

"Oh, no."

"And they tell me …"

"Sweet Jesus."

"That early Friday morning, he had a cross on his shoulder …"

The crowd clapped in syncopation. A voice from it shouted, "He had a cross on his shoulder, going up that hill!"

Uncle Tom said, "Oh, oh," in a mourning way.

"—and they tell me," Brother George yelled.

"What do they tell?" Uncle Tom inquired.

"—that he had your and my sins on his shoulder."

"Oh, yes! Yes, he did! Praise God."

"—and they knocked him *down* on his knees."

The audience mourned.

"And they tell me … he got up from his knees." Brother George's body jerked and Uncle Tom struggled to hold him.

"Bring it on home now!" an old man yelled.

Brother George's voice raced, his arms flailed: "And he kept going up that hill …"

"Bring it home!"

"And he died! Didn't he die?"

"Oh, yes."

"He died for you and me.… *Whoeee! Eeeeee—Oooooo—Ahhhhh—Ummmm!*" The voice of Brother George soared like a leaf in an updraft. The black audience swayed, caught in the passion of a Whooper.

Gooch paused in his hammering to listen, and shook his head in admiration. "Why, if he was a white man he could make a hundred dollars a Sunday," he said to no one in particular.

The fairgrounds had become a four-ring circus with Gooch in center ring. His was the featured act. Above mooring stakes Gooch drove into the hard ground with the flat side of an ax, wobbling against itself like a fat woman's belly, hung the largest balloon ever seen in Mississippi. Its top half shone the frosty color of icy nether regions. The words OTTO FLOTTO CIRCUS showed through the paint. Dry cracks rivuleted the surface. Around its middle gold ropes twitched and jerked with each breeze. Its bottom was as gray and loose as an elephant's ass. It tapered to a yawning orifice, dilated for inflation by hot air from a fire pit.

Gooch sized up the crowd. Nearby, an albino Negro wearing a derby, a blue suit coat and brown trousers cried, "Hot tamales!" A woman with a wry neck and blue eyes flat as paint against her doll's face folded clever paper hats from pages of the *Southern Sentinel* to sell to children for a penny.

Abruptly, Gooch's smile stiffened. His fat neck turtled into his collar as a gaunt man with the rumpled, dangerous look of a migratory hawk closed from his left.

Through the lapels of the man's coat stabbed two pins. One said, TRY GOD! The other displayed the American flag in blue and red and white enamel. He carried a pamphlet folded so that the headline showed. It said, THE POPE IS A TYRANT.

A circle of boys standing close to the balloon-man scattered.

"Momma and I were close," the man said without preamble. "She was in excellent health until she passed over, and I feel like she would be glad to come back."

"Uh-huh," Gooch said.

"I got her in the icehouse." The man rolled the pamphlet and tapped it. "My wife had a dream. In it there was this real fat man with a flying machine. Momma Presson was in that flying machine. She was in that flying machine wearing a white scarf, a flying hat and a sweet smile. She called down to me, 'Don't worry, son. I'm on my way to meet God.'"

"Uh-huh." Gooch edged away.

"I've only got half a stomach," the man confided. "I drink a Co-Cola and pour a Stanback down my throat to digest ever' bite I eat. It's hell when I eat fried stuff." The man's lids seemed to roll from the bottoms. His goozle popped up and down as it valved stomach gas. "I want you to take Momma with you. I done the best for her I could. I give her the flat-out Gospel service. I told her, 'Git up. Come on. Git up! Rise up and live in the name of

Jesus.' But she wouldn't." He looked around darkly, his hand tightening on the pamphlet. "She never did *nothing* I asked her to."

"That right?" Gooch said.

"That's why you got to take her with you."

"Well, it ain't up to me. This trip is for Brother Wevel. If the ministerial association wants another trip, why that's all right with me. All somebody has to do is get the money to bring the balloon back here, and make me a suitable love offering."

"How much?"

"Fifty dollars for the fare, and fifty dollars in the plate."

"You can't take two?"

"Naw."

"Listen. I got Momma down the road in the icehouse. We can get back real fast."

"This ain't a flying machine. A flying machine has got wings and a propeller." Gooch nodded over his shoulder where the balloon shook its tassels. "It don't fit your dream. I ain't the right fat man."

The man's neck and head and layered black hair swung as a unit from the shoulders. His hooded eyes swallowed Gooch and all the landscape. "It was you all right," he muttered.

Abruptly, a cornet smeared a fanfare. A blond boy in a red band uniform with gold piping stood on the catafalque near the coffin. He leaned back, tucked his butt like he was engaging in obscenity, and issued a wavery high C. It sent chills up and down many a spine. The crowd cheered. The man with Gooch shuddered as if that note pierced him deep.

Gooch stepped back. "I got to get ready. The main sermon is about to begin."

"You sure you won't take Momma Presson," the man said, "even though God said you would?"

Gooch skittered away and adjusted a net of yellow sisal that enfolded the coffin. It was to cradle the coffin under the basket. He traced six yellow hawsers that stretched from the net to eyebolts on the red and blue gondola. "Stand clear," he ordered.

The crowd rushed close, thickening at the catafalque, but ministers moved unimpeded through the press of people. Above them the balloon stood erect but infirm, like a half-stimulated penis.

Gooch shoveled charcoal into the pit beside the platform. "Y'all stand back! Y'all stand clear. We don't want nobody falling into the fiery pit!"

Six ministers ascended the platform and lined themselves behind the coffin, heads this way and that, like crows on a limb. Miss Emma Kurtner struck up her portable reed organ. Her haunches shifted as she gusted chords. A choir of eighteen women lifted their faces and spread their legs to warble the opening stanza of "Come Let Us Join Our Friends Above."

Come let us join our friends a-bove, who have
ob-tained the prize. And on the ea-gle
wings of love, to joys ce-les-tial rise.

The Reverend Alcock Baines lifted palsied hands and cried, "Je-sus is King!" Talk ceased. Heads bowed, showing their polls, as if a great flock of sheep humbly awaited herding into green pastures.

Alcock Baines stretched tall. His white beard unreeled in the wind. The long-fingered hands of which he was vain trembled with age, but his voice boomed undiminished. "Lord God, you raised up your son Wevel Snopes to high places, and when he proved unworthy cast him among swine ..." "—Among swine!" Gooch whirled and said to Mr. Presson, because he was handy, "That's gonna cost them fifty dollars more. Me and Horace and Mary Belle had our faults, but this is too much. This is too much."

"Momma could ride over the side," Presson said in a reasonable way. "You could hang her on a rope, and tie her dress decent. Nobody could see up her, and the smell would be below you."

The man took a limp leather Bible from his coat pocket. He licked the cover. "Did you ever taste the Bible? Really get it into your mouth? It's salty." He tore out a red-lettered page and put it between his lips like lettuce. The print was cheap and it bled. He chewed it rubrically and gulped it down. "I'm a Jesus-filled man. I thrive on the Word. I don't *never* have to take a Stanback when I'm filled with the Word."

Gooch froze as if the ground had shook. He looked at the ax he'd dropped.

The man picked it up and held it with negligent familiarity.

Somewhere a scattered bevy of bobwhites called their names like drunken conventioneers introducing themselves. Time seemed suspended.

Then Alcock Baines spoke. His voice reached into the private space in which Gooch and Presson stood.

"God knows what he is about. He clothes the lilies of the field in beauty. He fills the mouths of the simple with wisdom. Oh, you say to me, *that* man? That addled, lightning-struck old preacher? And I say unto you, Wevel Snopes was special in God's sight."

Mr. Presson twirled the ax. His wrists pivoted where his hands double-gripped the hickory handle. He was quiet, his bituminous eyes expressionless.

"Here now, Nemesis!" Gooch flinched back. "I knowed you was my Nemesis!"

The man swung the ax toward a hawser and stake, giving it a practiced twist before it struck. As in slow motion, Gooch saw air split ahead of the shining, metal edge. Wood cracked. A severed rope undulated on the ground like newly cut hog nuts. The attached end flipped below the gondola.

"What's a Nem-sis?" the man asked. The ax stretched from his reflexively bent body, nearly touching the ground behind. A belly-tuft showed through his puckered shirt above a worn silver buckle. "Huh!" he grunted, targeting a hawser that touched the ground, slicing and half bury-ing it.

Whack! Whack! Whack! The ax worked now almost of its own volition. Twirling above Presson's head. Dis-closing its wicked glint. Whispering down.

Brave men dodged in and out of its orbit as skillfully as children entering and leaving a jump rope. None could reach Mr. Presson, even with the benefit of instructions shouted by women and preachers.

An anchoring stake split away and the balloon lurched up. Two remaining hawsers rumbled across the platform, snatched tight against the coffin weight, and folded the balloon on its side. Gooch leaped for a shroud line, his face a blur, his mouth open in a scream lost in crowd noise. The coffin dragged across the catafalque, knocked loose two boards from the fencing, and scattered preach-ers left and right. Then it swayed into the air, a twisting pendulum.

"Y'all grab the tie ropes!" Gooch yelled. "Y'all stop this thing!"

"That catapult has throwed our preachers," somebody screamed back.

Lean, country boys leaped for cut lines and coffin netting, gripping with hands and knees. They banged through board fencing and kneeling Christians, flinging this way and that, falling away.

A gust caught the silvery balloon, pushed it into the nearly horizontal position of a commode tank bulb, and aimed it at the crowd. People dodged and howled, running to escape bludgeoning by the dangling coffin. It banged the ground each twenty feet, popping yellow netting with the flat sound of .22 shorts exploding.

Gooch got an arm and a leg over the gondola lip. His black-clad ass protruded like a large gall on a small stem. Presson ran underneath with a seeking ax. A young preacher galloped behind Presson. His legs flew every which-away, and his string tie blew back like the reins of a runaway horse. His skull gleamed through an amateur haircut where earnest shears had nicked deep. He cupped a hand and yelled, "Mr. Gooch! We aren't ready for the ascension, Reverend Baines bid me say! The love offering isn't taken yet."

Gooch's face turned red. He clung by one hand and one leg and shook a fist. "Tell him *don't give me none of that!* Tell him, read the fine print of the contract."

The wind steadied. The balloon straightened and swept to the east, dragging the coffin fifty feet above the ground like a stick on a kite tail.

A man running just below suddenly dug in his heels. People jammed behind. Voices called warning.

Gooch twisted his neck to see the balloon drifting toward a windbreak of tall Lombardy poplars. Their spiky tops dipped and erected in invitation. Brother Wevel's coffin closed on them at treetop level. With a crackle it plunged into greenery. Gooch covered his face.

There was a gasp, then a hiss of released breath from a hundred throats as the coffin emerged on the other side, dangling from one rope. It was in the clear and the balloon in an updraft. People cheered. Gooch strung out a banner advertising THE LIGHTER THAN AIR EVANGELIST, and an American flag.

The balloon ascended vertically, with Brother Wevel's coffin dangling below the gondola, oscillating slowly. The sun broke from behind clouds. The yellow pine of the coffin gleamed. Preachers lifted their hands in exhortation. People dropped to their knees and prayed. Deacons and stewards rushed to pass out collection plates in that hallowed moment.

When the praying was done, snare drums rattled, the bandmaster lifted his baton, and the Ripley High School band struck up "Stars and Stripes Forever."

It began vigorously. People clapped time to the music, watching the balloon. But Gooch seemed agitated. From a distance they saw him haul in the flag, reverse it, and fly it upside down. He leaned over the gondola edge and pointed down. He stretched wide his arms and semaphored letters a Boy Scout in the crowd identified as S.O.S.

"What's happening?" people said to each other.

The music faltered, diminishing to a ragged sextet, then to a ninth grade clarinet wheezing *deedle deedle dum ta dum ta dum dum.*

Little ropes around the middle of the balloon jerked voluptuously. The gondola jumped twenty feet into the air as the one remaining hawser popped without sound. Before their horrified eyes, Brother Wevel's coffin plunged like bird squirt. People below had time to count, "*One second, two seconds, three seconds, four seconds ...*" to hear Gooch's plaintive cry, "No-o-o-o," long after they had seen his mouth stretch and his features contort to utter it. They had time to shrink from, or to run to, the spot where the coffin would hit.

It struck with the *phlug* of a bullet entering water. Hinges burst, wood split, and content burst through the container and ripped on splintered pine.

People seeing the red of shredded velvet cried out. The tender of stomach, and some who had eaten hot pork sandwiches with lots of ketchup, retched.

"I knew they never should have done it," Miss Rose shouted in contralto. She fanned herself uncontrollably.

Presson dropped the ax. "That poor boy is squashed like a ripe persimmon." He grabbed a nearby woman's arm. "I'm sure glad Momma Presson never made the trip. I've got her safe at the icehouse."

Old Hollis Upchurch pushed through the crowd, his cane clearing a way like Moses' rod. He glared with milky eyes, poked through rubbish, then shot his hands high, showing ragged cuffs. "He ain't here! Brother Wevel is gone to Glory."

He *was* gone. Men tossed through broken boards. Woodmen who could track a rabbit across ice found no flesh, no hair. But there were signs, the woodmen said.

"Relics," the preachers corrected.

Brother George and Uncle Tom watched from the front row as white ministers recovered, and held in the air for the silent crowd to see, two black shoes, one white Arrow shirt, a blood-red tie, one dirty linen suit, casket cloth, nails, strap hinges, and a rick of kindling wood.

"Where'd he go? Where'd he go?" squeaked Brother George. "It's a trick."

"Be quiet, fool," Uncle Tom said, shaking him like a clogged ketchup bottle.

Brother George grabbed Uncle Tom's neck and clung tight. He pointed to the balloon in the sky. "Don't be taken in. That man removed the body. It never was in the coffin. This is all a trick!"

Uncle Tom brushed Brother George aside, his eyes dreamy and deep as if he heard distant music other people only wished they could hear. "Be quiet, fool. You've seen the hand of God."

When A. P. Gooch got his balloon on the ground, he came into town sweaty and mad. "Where's the body?" he demanded. Nobody knew or would admit it if they did.

Baptist ministers and others of simple faith insisted that

Brother Wevel had been levitated out of his shoes and through the box in which he had been nailed. Like Elijah, he had ascended into heaven.

"God is not mocked," Alcock Baines said. "We did wrong in imitating a miracle. Now, God has shown us a real one."

"Just call Brother Wevel *Houdini,* then!" Gooch exclaimed, hands on hips. "Whyn't you do that? It would make more sense. No, there's a trick here. I just don't see through it yet, or why."

There was also a sinister theory ... that Brother Wevel's body had been sold by a person or persons unknown to the medical school in Oxford, and drifted there in a tank of formaldehyde, with accusing eyes, and long hair and nails that continued to grow after death. Out of massive foreboding, none of the Southern medical students would dissect it as a cadaver. Something horrible happened to a Yankee student who made one cut. He contracted leprosy and his hand fell off.

The third theory was, and this was advanced by an Episcopalian, that certain obsessive fundamentalists had stolen the body to convince the faithful of God's power. He could not explain when body thieves had access to the coffin, which had been sat up with night and day, or how the thieves could predict that it would fall to earth, an event necessary to the drama.

Those favoring a police investigation included the Presbyterian minister and the county attorney—who saw in it the possibility of a wire service story and a trial that might ease his way to higher office.

During the emotional upheaval of the revival which followed, twenty-six souls were saved and twenty-four infants conceived, most by married ladies. Funds were raised to support a missionary to heathen China, and to tin-roof any number of leaky parsonages.

Gooch, having done no provable wrong, survived investigation by the county attorney. He stayed on at the old farmhouse, drank whiskey out of Mason jars, and reflected deeply.

One morning he climbed out of bed, put on his preaching suit and a ministerial expression, wrapped himself in a quilt that remembered in its fibers the scent of Mary Belle, and sailed away on the winds of morning.

Farm boys had seen by night the fire pit that heated the air to fill the balloon. Four came, and stood transfixed at dawn as the silvery structure ascended into crystalline air, silently, elegantly, flickering its shadow across fields in a race with the sun.

Gooch poked his head over the gondola edge and looked down. "Glory to me when I sail on the wings, having done the work of the Lord," he called. "Y'all remember, the workman is worthy." He took a swallow of whiskey. "Tell 'um put that in their pipes."

"Sir?" the boys said, and then in ragged chorus shouted, *"Sir?"* But he did not speak again.

Miss Mary Belle and Mr. Overby disappeared from Ripley at about the same time that Gooch's truck did, although no one saw Gooch and Mary Belle together, or the truck when it left the county. This indicated a night departure, or during Sunday service.

Charlie Coltharp remembered filling the truck with gas for Mary Belle a week before Brother Wevel's house was found empty and all her things gone. He remembered because she paid with a twenty-dollar bill, and he had not seen a bill that large in a year.

ACKNOWLEDGMENTS

My thanks to Barry Hannah and Evans Harrington—encouragers, critics, and friends.

For editorial assistance and advice, my thanks to executive editor JoAnne Prichard and production editor Anne Stascavage of the University Press of Mississippi, and to Robin Hendrickson.

My gratitude to the judges of several literary competitions. Allan Gurganus chose "The Snopes Who Saved Huckaby" co-winner of the Pirate's Alley William Faulkner Prize for Fiction. The anonymous judges of the Hackney Literary Competition also awarded this story a prize. Ernest J. Gaines selected a manuscript that included "The Snopes Who Saved Huckaby" and "How Wevel Went" winner of the Deep South Writing Conference Competition. Gordon Weaver chose "Dark Heart" winner of the Kansas Arts Council/*KQ* Award. George Garrett, guest fiction editor of *The Texas Review*, included "My Father's Voice, Lifting" in his edition; Jim Clark gave special recognition to "The Last Feminine Woman in the World" and "The Incredible Little Louisiana Chicken

Killer" in awards issues of *The Greensboro Review*. Charles East, and others, chose a manuscript incorporating most of the stories in *Body Parts* as a finalist for the Flannery O'Connor Award.

Finally, I acknowledge my indebtedness to William Faulkner, proprietor of the surname Snopes, for the use of it, and to José Ortega y Gasset, whose *Meditations on Hunting* gave structure to my thinking about the animal-human bond.

JH